Illuminati Hunter

Copyright © 2012 Ethan Harrison
All rights reserved.
ISBN 978-1-78222-355-9
Edition II 2014

The rights of Ethan Harrison to be identified as the author of this work have been asserted by him in accordance with the Copyright, Designs and Patents Act of 1988.

All rights reserved; no part of this publication may be reproduced, stored in a retrieval system, or transmitted in any form or by any means, electronic, mechanical, photocopying, recording or otherwise without the prior written consent of the publisher or a licence permitting copying in the UK issued by the Copyright Licensing Agency Ltd.
www.cla.co.uk

Book design, layout and production management by
Into Print

www.intoprint.net

+44 (0)1604 832149

Printed and bound in UK and USA by Lightning Source

Foreword

After this brief introduction the following text, apart from the addition of the footnotes and their hyper-links, is an exact reprint of a book that I found in a junk shop in London during the summer of 2012. Originally published in 1913 by Necromancer, a small English publishing house that has since vanished, it seems to have only had a limited release as after much extensive searching, I have not been able to find another copy anywhere.

There are several reasons I decided to republish the book. Mainly because it is a fantastic adventure story written in a surprisingly modern way that I feel the contemporary reader will appreciate but also because when I checked the story's details on the internet to my astonishment many of them, however outlandish, were borne out by existing records or so close that it was hard to believe they could all be coincidence; hence the addition of the footnotes so that you can see for yourself.

If the extraordinary account in the book is true it would throw a completely new light onto what is already a remarkable period of Bavarian and World history that I'm sure you'll find fascinating especially if you have a laptop at your disposal and use the web site addresses listed in the appendix.

I hope you will enjoy researching the background of this adventure as much as I did and of course be thrilled by the truly amazing story itself. *E.T. Harrison. 2013*

ILLUMINATI HUNTER

Adam Weishaupt and the Eye of Horus

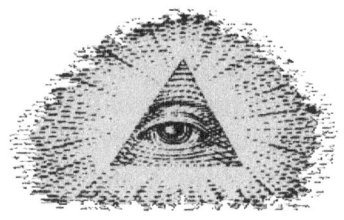

By Sebastian P. Drechsler

Published in Great Britain by Necromancer Press 1913.

Introduction

This volume is formed from a collection of memoirs discovered in 1898 at the University of Munich in Bavaria. Sebastian Pierre Drechsler was a student and eventually lecturer at Ingolstadt University between 1783 – 1800, before the faculty was closed down. He later went on to become Professor and then Director of History at Munich University until he retired in 1833. It is understood that the original memoirs were dictated by the scholar on his deathbed (circa 1852) and that he had not wanted them to come to the public's attention for 'some time' after he died so as not to besmirch his fine reputation achieved after many years working within academe. He was on record to have made claim that they would be valuable 'To those in the future who are already illuminated, or are ready to come into the light.' It should be noted that the transcript was dictated to an Englishman, a court stenographer by trade, who was not fluent in the Bavarian tongue but the far-sighted Professor had understood that his scribe's natural dialect was fast becoming the international language of the world and so by means of this translation would secure the text's widest readership when it eventually saw the light of day. This detail and the fact that it is a vocal record would explain the sound effects, British measurements, occasional vernacular and the constant personal observations of a humorous nature.

A. Jones Editor Necromancer Press 1913.

To my darling Francesca

I will never forget you.

I, Sebastian Drechsler, finding myself of sound mind but failing body, in the year of our Lord 1852, at the grand old age of eighty seven, do finally commit these words to paper and solemnly swear that though much of the following text may at times sound unbelievable, it is, in fact, a true and accurate account of the extraordinary adventures in which I played my part as a young man in my homeland of Bavaria many, many years ago. Also, I truly hope that if the text has survived as long as I have intended before coming to the public's attention then the incredible tale you are about to read no longer contains a very necessary warning for the world. But if that is the case then may God Almighty have mercy on your souls.

It was a ghastly night. The wind roared and the rain lashed about in the black trees creaking outside my window. In my bed, I thrashed from side to side anxiously listening to the storm until at last I fell into a deep, deep sleep...

I had a terrible dream. In this fearful vision I was climbing up a mountain of moaning, writhing bodies. Far below me lay an eternal blackness and I knew it was the abyss. In the distance, way above me, radiating from the top of the enormous pyramid of flesh, shone the brightest light I had ever seen. So bright that I felt it burn my very soul, so bright that I knew it was also the abyss. As I climbed I could feel the faces of the people beneath me, their ears, their lips, their teeth, all of them imagined through my finger tips for I dared not look in case I caught one of the desperate stares. Under my feet I could feel their shoulders, their knees and their grasping hands clinging at my naked body. But I kicked hard to break their grip and struggled on even though I knew it would be the end, the end of everything, I still climbed upwards towards the light clambering over the seething wall of people as they cried out their awful calls.

I awoke with a gasp, covered in a cold sweat and filled with a dreadful sense of foreboding. It was at that moment, sitting up in my bed shivering with fear, that I first decided I would visit Professor Van Halestrom. I was sure that I had overheard one of my fellow students saying that the eccentric scholar had the skill to read dreams. That was how it all began for me. It was because of the dream. As I pulled my nightshirt about me and tried to go back to sleep it would have been impossible for me to imagine the incredible adventures fate now held in store. Indeed, had I known the extraordinary series of events that first real meeting with the Professor was to set in motion and the effect it was to have on my future and the future of the entire world, I might never have decided to see Van Halestrom at all. For back then I was merely a student at the University of Ingolstadt immersed in the study of history, philosophy, canon law and chasing women. A simple freshman from a small village; recently arrived in a big town and trying to make the same acclimatisation with his thoughts as to his new location in life. No mean task for a man who had received as strict an upbringing as mine and had picked up his father's stifling self-consciousness – a trait which I was more than ready to shake off so that I could find out what was out there in this new world and discover within me a new self. Ah, but I digress. This tale is of such great importance that it must be told properly. So I will begin ...

Illuminati Hunter

Chapter 1

Innocent Beginnings

Although my nightmare had put me in a frightful state of mind I was in much better shape as soon as I had begun my walk to Ingolstadt University on that warm May morning of 1784. The streets of the beautiful, ancient city were already bustling with throngs of traders, artisans and townspeople going about their daily business. The summer smells of the thriving town mixed pleasantly with those wafting from the river Danube filling the air with a scent that thrilled the senses. Another thing which thrilled the senses about this marvellous place to which I had moved, but eight months ago, from the tiny and distant village of Tuffengarten was that there seemed to be beautiful girls around every other corner and back in Tuffengarten there were no pretty girls at all. Believe me, I'd looked.

I smiled hopefully but with little effect at another lovely young maiden as I crossed the street and passed through the university gates. Back then, of course, I had no idea why my lack of success persisted with members of the fairer sex. I knew I wasn't a bad looking chap. Although, unfortunately it was still only my mother who would say so, I was actually quite a handsome man. Six foot tall, well built with thick brown hair and a generous face which sported a proud chin and a set of noble features. Maybe it was a bit too proud and noble for the girls, or so I thought. Of course, in reality, I was a spoilt brat and a total idiot, especially when it came to women, and so spent most of my time with my head stuck solidly up my Bavarian arse. Though the inexperience of youth kept me blissfully unaware of these crucial facts. So, in my innocence, and bad dreams aside, I had every reason to have a spring in my step that day because one thing I knew for certain - this was the time to be alive for a twenty-one-year-old man with a thirst for the amazing theories and discoveries of this wondrous age of learning.

For the Great Enlightenment was everywhere. The thoughts of men like Rousseau, Newton, Voltaire and Copernicus were sweeping away the old ideas of the past and resigning their hocus pocus to the rubbish bin of history. Yes, this was the time to be young and open-minded. And the best place to be all these things was Ingolstadt University with one of the finest reputations in all of Europe, which meant the world. I was indeed very lucky and very proud to be attending this austere institution, although perhaps not always trying as hard at my studies as any proper student should.

I entered the university through the grand old doors and stepped into the darkness of the central hallway. After establishing with the campus clerk that Professor Van Halestrom was giving his morning lecture and that I may watch from the gallery, I made my way to the appropriate hall and quietly let myself in. The hall was packed with attentive students as his lectures were always very popular and I squeezed myself amongst the crowd at the back. I had met the intriguing scholar at the university chess club when he had congratulated me on my victory over one of the other masters and we had talked of chess and gone on to discuss military campaigns and great battles of the past. I found him personable, learned and very humorous at the same time, which was in complete contrast to all the teachers I had met before. Looking around I saw undergraduates from other courses who obviously felt they could learn something from the renowned academic, even though their particular subjects were unrelated. They were probably right. At fifty-five, the eagle-eyed and animated Professor Van Halestrom was at his peak then and famous for delivering thoroughly illuminating lectures encompassing many themes and that morning was no exception.

"And that is why, Gentlemen, the inherent problems of a debt-ridden monetary system make it anathema to civilised society. This system will always produce aggregated capital over much too wide a range which in turn produces an undesirably large gap between the haves and have-nots. As we have already learnt this will lead to a problematic rise in crime, illness, child mortality, spread of disease, general suffering and all the associated unnecessary political upheaval that they bring in their wake. This particular form of capitalism can be shown as a cone. The majority of the people living on the bottom whilst a very few occupy the pinnacle at the top. It is my opinion that the shape which should be aspired to, when creating a system of trade and equity, is, in fact, the sphere which produces no spike, no high, no low but is the most harmonious of shapes within Greek geometry." He energetically sketched on a large blackboard as he talked, "It is the shape that matter or energy most readily assumes, suggesting that there is equilibrium within the system. It is also, and I believe this is no coincidence, the most common of natural forms in the universe and also the mirror of our own and naturally balanced world."

He finished a cleverly detailed drawing of the earth before turning to his audience and putting his finger tips together with a grin. A short pause was followed by warm applause from all around the lecture hall at which Van Halestrom raised a hand continuing, "Thank you. Thank you. Although I am flattered, your praise will not stop me from being extremely unhappy with you if you do not finish Adam Smith's 'Wealth of Nations' and write a four thousand word essay on it by next week. I would also urge anyone who is not a student of this class to read this volume as it is very instructive and also outlines the rather ominous global economic realities of our future."

With this Van Halestrom collected his things and made his way out of the hall. I left along with the other students who gossiped excitedly about what they had heard and made my way round to the Professor's rooms where he was enjoying a cup of tea and a smoke of his pipe. *[1]

He welcomed me with his typical aplomb, "Ah, Herr Drechsler. Good to see you. Would you like some tea? It's Darjeeling, a particularly pleasant flavour, I think you'll agree."

I greeted him and sat down. After briefly discussing chess and how I was doing in my studies he asked what the purpose of my visit was and I told him of my dream from the previous night. Upon hearing

---

[1] There is no record of a Professor Van Halestrom working at the University of Ingolstadt at this time but staff records are sketchy at the best so this is no surprise. Although no solid information exists to back up this theory, for which you will have to forgive me as it is one of the most speculative in the footnotes, it is my belief that such was the Professor's part in local history in some way it has led to it being the inspiration for Bram Stoker's famous character Professor Abraham von Helsing in his 1897 novel ***Dracula***. This point is given credence by the fact that before penning his masterpiece Stoker had spent several years studying European folklore which I believe may have recorded some of Van Halestrom's exploits. If this seems unlikely then I merely suggest you read on.

my description, to my astonishment he calmly said, "I have recently had the same one."

Flabbergasted, I asked him, "But ... what does it mean, sir?"

Speaking with scholarly authority he declared, "It is capitalism, my friend, the greatest conspiracy of them all. A vile trap, in which you will be condemned to climb forever over the rest of humanity to reach your own pitiful end and the powerful light you saw at the top, was the eye of Horus, The Illuminated One, Lucifer himself."

Well, of course, all I could do was sit in my chair dumbfounded so much so that I thought I might be back in my horrendous nightmare. As my mind tried to make sense out of these seemingly bizarre statements the Professor surprised me once more. Whilst pouring another cup he asked, "Would you consider yourself a good horseman, my lad?"

I was still too busy thinking of 'Lucifer himself,' to properly reply and let out a protracted, "Err…"

Regardless of my confusion he carried on, "Only, I heard some of my students saying that you were very accomplished in the saddle."

He looked me up and down as though evaluating my capacities for something that I was uncomfortably aware I knew nothing about. Whilst puckering his lips on his pipe he added, "I may have a task for you, a small matter of little consequence. Can you use a gun?"

This was another jump in the proceedings and finally I found my tongue.

"If the matter is of such little consequence, sir, why should I need a gun?"

"I understand your father is a gunsmith. So I would presume you would be familiar, to a certain degree, with fire-arms."

He lit his pipe with an ingenious system of flints contained in a miniature hand-held box before nodding at me knowingly. Feeling a little off guard anyway these remarks of a more personal nature unsettled me further.

It was true that I was a dab hand with a horse and I was known for doing tricks on my horse Petrova in the local stable yard. Also, as a member of the university shooting club, it was common knowledge that I could use a gun and that my father was a gunsmith but that the Professor knew all of this was a surprise to me. I felt a little trapped and replied politely but firmly, "It is true that I can ride, sir, and that I have, to a certain degree, some familiarity with fire-arms but what that has to do with anything at the university is entirely beyond me. I am a simple freshman, Herr Professor, as you know from our brief meetings at the chess club and around the faculty. I am but twenty-one years old and know nothing about the indecencies of city life. How I could be of use to you in this matter, however small, is something I cannot even begin to imagine."

This was not entirely true. I had, in fact, enjoyed a number of secretive adventures back in Tuffengarten, mostly running away from angry farmers and tavern landlords. The Professor seemed to sense this. "Oh, don't do yourself down, Sebastian. You have an excellent mind for one thing. Remember I've seen you beat Herr Kandinsky and, back in his day, he was a chess champion. You're here at the university, for another, which means you're prepared to learn. You've a ready wit which is always handy and you have a fast horse which I'd bet a whole month's wages on to win against a thoroughbred." He puffed on his pipe concluding with a flick of his eyebrows, "And a month's wages at the university is quite a lot."

With this he looked unnervingly right into my eyes then came away with a broad smile, suggesting, "You also look as though you fancy a bit of adventure. It's a good look. I've seen it before; sometimes in the mirror, sometimes in my students, but always on the face of a man with a desire to live a life that's his own. So what do you say? Will you run a small errand for me and collect a letter from a messenger out on the road to Stuttgart?"

I didn't know what to make of the man at all as he sat there sucking his pipe and blowing out two evenly matched rings of smoke. My parents had warned me of the dangers of accepting offers from strange men in the city and with all the staring into my eyes I was feeling as uncomfortable as I had since arriving in Ingolstadt the previous September. I had thought he was an eccentric intellectual before this moment but now I felt a tiny shudder go up my spine and remembered him boldly declaring, 'Lucifer himself.'

This thought produced my answer, "I'm afraid I must refuse, sir. I hope you don't mind but I promised my parents ..."

"I fully understand, my lad. But if you change your mind there's fifty thalers in it for you which I'm sure you will find useful. Now if you'll forgive me I have another lecture to prepare."

"Of ... course, Herr Professor," I stumbled. His abrupt dismissal had brought on another wave of anxiety in me. I found myself standing up very quickly and performing a very low and overly-earnest bow then clicking my heels as I'd seen my father do when taking leave of someone he believed socially superior. I immediately regretted it and caught his eye. He smiled and, almost laughing, said, "Good luck, my friend. See you at the chess club."

I left his rooms and walked up the corridor thinking of everything that had transpired. If I was so interested in discovering my new self why had I not jumped at the Professor's exciting offer faster than a rat blown up a drain pipe with a pair of blacksmith's bellows? I cursed my self-consciousness blaming it on my father's influence. Whatever the Professor had said about my dream it was, after all, only a dream and he was merely an unconventional old gentleman. As a man of reason I should not be scared of either. So caught up in my thoughts was I that I nearly walked into another student coming towards me before exiting the dim building into bright spring sunshine.

Maybe it was the rays of sunlight that snapped me from my ruminations but I suddenly remembered Jan, my old friend from school. I was meant to meet him at ten o'clock at the coaching inn. I had been so consumed by the dream and other matters that I had totally forgotten. At that moment the bells of St Maria's church rang out over the roof tops. I counted the chimes fearing the worst; eight, nine, ten, Oh dear, eleven times. I was late, very late indeed.

Chapter 2

Old Friends

When I reached the coaching inn some ten minutes later I instantly spotted Jan standing outside. There were a couple of reasons I saw my old friend so easily. First, his unruly mane of bright red hair clashed so violently with his vulgar purple clothes that they could have been seen by a blind man. Second because for some strange reason Jan Kohler, unlike myself, was found most attractive by members of the opposite sex and although the scoundrel had only just arrived in town he was already in the company of two pretty young ladies.

It wasn't his looks that attracted women to him. He would be the first to admit that he was no oil-painting and perhaps no watercolour either. Neither was his figure so alluring because, although he was as tall as me, Jan was, well to put it bluntly, he was fat. No, the secret of his attraction did not lie in his physique or his features. It was immediately obvious to anyone who met him that he was very, very funny and that was the reason that the ladies liked him. And that's why I liked him too.

"Jan Kohler, you old rascal, how are you?" I cried and as quick as a flash he replied, "As happy as a Chinaman who has found a huge dog in his kitchen and twice as good for seeing you. You're late!"

We embraced and as we pulled away he laughed, "You, Sebastian Drechsler will never change so I am not surprised to see that, as usual, you have not."

"You too are as I remember. Your face is pulling exactly the same stupid expression as it was five months ago when I last saw it at Christmas."

"And yours, Seb, is as simple as it ever was. Not ugly, of course, but still simple. Tell me; has that face felt the fair hand of a woman in the throes of a passionate embrace or has it remained simple?"

I squirmed with embarrassment in front of his new coquettish friends who were now giggling at me. He butted in, enjoying his enduring advantage with the ladies, "Well, my old friend just help yourself to one of mine. This is Astrid and this is Katrina." He bowed at the tittering girls as he introduced them and continued, "Now you must take me somewhere where I can eat. I was on that stagecoach for six hours and here at this coaching inn for another and in that time I have found that neither serves a good breakfast."

Jan was certainly my best childhood friend though, to be truthful, there were no others who qualified as candidates. We had only fought properly once when we were very young. This was a fight he had won using his superior weight to hold me down. After that the pair of us had become good friends; riding, swimming, shooting with guns borrowed from my father's workshop, talking about girls at great length although enjoying their pleasures to a lesser extent and always he more successfully than me. This was something I had always been a little jealous of and he knew it. Jan had not been able to afford to come to university and, as we had discussed, was maybe not of the right temperament anyway. In truth his Latin and Greek were worse than a monkey's and no way near the required standard for further education. He had said he thought 'the pursuit of academia trivial' although I secretly suspected that he was envious of my academic talents.

So, in a way, our jealousies balanced out. His uncle had found him a position at the local money-changers in Ingolstadt and I had promised to look after him for a short time until his room was vacated. Anyway, I always wanted to see him and I could do with a laugh: Funny old beggar that he was.

I led Jan and the ladies to the nearest place where we could get something proper to eat, and at Fassbender's on Milchstrasse we did just that for the next four hours. Jan had certainly not lost his ability for great humour and we laughed so much that the whole afternoon passed without me thinking once of the Professor or my troubling dream. Later we moved to a bierkeller in the centre of town where the student fraternities spent much of their time and the jokes and drinks flowed steadily as we laughed and reminisced into the night.

It must have been ten o'clock when, returning after a much needed visit to the privy and feeling quite the worse for wear, I could not find either the girls or Jan at the table where I had left them. Slowly gawping around the room I finally spotted my party gathered in front of a well-to-do but nervous looking couple sitting at another table. I focused my bleary eyes to see my old school chum holding up his handkerchief in one hand and a beer mug in the other whilst drunkenly announcing, "Ladies and, Gentleman," he pointed a swaying finger at the man sitting at the table adding, "That's you, sir," before slurring on, "For your pleasure and most hearty entertainment I shall turn these two everyday objects into a piece of meat." He wrapped the handkerchief tightly round the mug and gripped it between his thighs then reached down and picked up the hand of the man's pretty friend placing it under the mug. He smiled before proudly boasting, "Behold. Have you ever seen such magic? What a Frankfurter!"

There was a pause as everyone looked at the phallic arrangement in Jan's groin then at the triumphant smile on his face before the girls' initial tittering turned into a mighty howl. Surprisingly, the young woman, still resolutely holding the phallus aloft, slowly joined in with the laughter but for her poor companion this was the last straw. He stood up and slapped Jan round the face with a glove, of all things. Unfortunately this made the girls even worse and this final humiliation was too much for the insulted man. Seething with anger he grabbed Jan by the ear and dragged him through the tavern and into the street where honour could be satisfied. Seeing that the gentleman was carrying a sword, I ran after them to try and prevent any unnecessary bloodshed.

Falling out of the door into the street I found Jan swaying around in front of the angry duellist who was thankfully having some difficulty freeing his blade from its scabbard. Jan, like a fool, was oblivious to any impending danger and carried on drunkenly repeating, "It's a Frankfurter! A Frankfurter! Get it? And, of course, when I say Frankfurter I mean cock!"

The incensed gentleman only grew angrier at Jan's crude japery and struggled in vain to free his sword. By now a small crowd including his female companion and the girls had come outside to see the fight. Though what actually transpired was hardly a fight. In fact, it was one of the most pathetic brawls I have ever seen. For when the man eventually lost his patience trying to unleash the sword he raised it anyway presumably to bludgeon some manners into Jan. Finally taking exception to this Jan grabbed up at the weapon and the pair of them proceeded to wrestle about for its possession. The struggle came to an end when Jan let go but such was the duellist's eagerness to get the sword back he went pitching backwards through the window of a china shop in the narrow lane.

Although the fight itself was pathetic enough to embarrass the patrons of a kindergarten, the crash was loud enough to have been heard at the town gates. For it was not only the window that broke but two shelves of chamber pots as well and the carnage drew a deep gasp from the audience and even a few fearful screams from the ladies.

The destruction was sufficient to render me sober and even Jan became momentarily lucid as he witnessed the wreckage. The two of us exchanged worried glances as the last piece of glass fell to the floor before running to the aid of the hapless fellow who was miraculously unhurt. Dragging him from the splinters of wood and shattered glass we could hear the shouts and whistles of the town's night watchmen already approaching fast. Suffice to say within a minute we were both arrested and another thirty after that locked in jail.

Our fortunes continued to wane when we found out that the idiot with the sword was the son of a local councillor and so, unsurprisingly, we were charged with affray and spent the night in the local clink. The jailer told us that the authorities held a dim view of the antics of drunken students and though Jan argued relentlessly that he was not a student we were told the fine would more than ten thalers each. Languishing in our cold damp cell that night listening to the sound of Jan's snoring and the rats scurrying around in the darkness I had already decided what I would do come the morning and freedom.

Chapter 3

Under the Doctor's Knife

"It wasn't my fault, I tell you," complained Jan for the umpteenth time as we shuffled away from the town jail in the chill of the early morning.

"But then, in a much truer sense, yes it was." I could not lie. It was.

"How can I be blamed for another man's lack of good humour?"

"Maybe you could have guessed he was not going to find your joke amusing in the first place."

"But it was an excellent joke. A Frankfurter! Get it? A Frankfurter!"

"Yes, yes! I get it. Now could you please stop repeating it at the top of your voice - it's making my head ache even more."

"You've changed since you've become a la-di-da student, Seb. Back in Tuffengarten you'd still be laughing at that in a week's time."

Maybe he was right. Perhaps I did feel as though I had more responsibility on my shoulders here in Ingolstadt. I knew I felt a burden of duty to my parents not to let them down and to flourish in my studies before graduating, hopefully. Since my enrolment the previous September I had not committed a single transgression and although I was a little behind in my work, maybe more, I had not come to the attention of my superiors at the university. This indiscretion would change all that. The city council were in constant contact with the faculty's administration so I knew that this incident would definitely be reported.

We reached my lodgings and, after entering as quietly as possible, sneaked up to my room as it was still very early in the morning and I did not wish to wake my nosy landlady Fraulein Warburg. Unfortunately, my huge guffawing friend made too much noise going up the creaking stairs and she came to her door in the hallway calling up from below, "Is that you, Herr Drechsler? I know it is as you did not come back last night. You should not come in at this hour because you will wake my other guests and you still owe me two month's rent."

Jan sniggered, "She'll wake the whole street if she doesn't shut up. Never mind the house."

I told him to shush and we eventually found my door at the top of the stairs as her voice faded behind us. I let Jan have my own bed, washed and shaved, had a small breakfast of cakes and cold coffee, collected my books and made my way to the university to attend my morning class.

The weather had changed and a grey, drizzling mist hung over the city. On my way through the narrow streets I reviewed my accounts. Although no lengthy calculations were necessary, my financial situation was obvious. I had been swindled a little in the first few months after my arrival in Ingolstadt, as all freshmen are. So I was told, although mainly by the ones who did the swindling. Also, the books I had bought for my studies had been more expensive than I had planned. Combined with my habits of a little drink, purely for social purposes of course, and the feeding and stabling of Petrova and, indeed, myself, I had already been feeling the pinch. This last small problem of one smashed window, five broken chamber pots, two counts of affray and the subsequent fifteen thalers fine had pushed me over the edge. Now I was broke. I had been reluctant to inform my parents of my money problems not having wanted to worry them as they were prone to do, especially my mother. My father would have merely said I should have been able to purchase my necessities for a fraction of their actual price as he would have, no doubt, been able to do 'back in his day.'

I had already decided that I would agree to help Professor Van Halestrom. Not only would his intriguing offer give me the opportunity to explore my new self, the money would be essential if I was to keep up with the deluge of debts with which I was faced. So keen was I to resolve my financial woes that I had planned to see the Professor before my first lecture which was three hours of canon law but I realised would not have enough time. I cursed Jan's pranks and also my selection of subjects.

Law was the least favourite of these. But as I was certainly no genius or wealthy young man, I had had to come to the university under the patronage of our local lord Count Von Friedrich. This philanthropic aristocrat, having no offspring of his own, took it upon himself to sponsor the education of a few of the more promising young men of Tuffengarten and fortunately the latest of these was me. Although this arrangement meant there was an added sense of responsibility for me, knowing that my parents would feel greatly humiliated back in the village if I were to let them down. It also meant that I had to study a mixture of topics that were pre-selected so as to 'make it easier to obtain proper employment when entering the modern environment of work,' or so I'd been told. After I had graduated and found suitable employment I would be expected to reimburse the Count's estate.

This was fair enough but canon law? I didn't enjoy it for several reasons. Mainly because it was incalculably boring and immeasurably complicated but also to me lawyers, whether they worked for the church or not, seemed like professional liars; clever charlatans who would say literally anything, although very correctly and persuasively, to get what they wanted and this was simply immoral. Another reason was my teacher, Herr Adam Weishaupt. Although incredibly intelligent - amazingly for a head of faculty still only in his early thirties - he was also cold, aloof and possessed a strangely menacing air about him. Indeed, such was his icy character that it had been responsible for earning him the nickname of 'The Doctor' amongst the fraternity, as he always managed to make his students feel like they were about to go under the surgeon's knife. Also, late students were his pet hate. So on hearing the bell of St Maria's ring quarter to eight I pulled up my collar, put my head down and marched a little faster through the drizzle that was now turning into rain. *[2]

I made it just in time and found a seat at the top of the lecture hall not wanting to draw attention to myself from the fearsome Weishaupt. At exactly eight o'clock, dressed in his black gown, the

---

[2] Adam Johann Weishaupt. This immensely intriguing character was certainly lecturing at the University of Ingolstadt in 1784. Although S. Drechsler refers to him as 'The Doctor' he was, in fact, Professor of Canon Law and the first non Jesuit to hold this position at the faculty in over 90 years. It is one view that the young academic's education by the Jesuit priesthood, which would have probably been extremely harsh, was the reason he adopted his revolutionary anti-Christian philosophy. At the time the story is written he is known to have denounced his Catholicism and adopted the doctrines of the Hermetics, Manicheans and those that revolved around astrology, medicine, magic and the mysteries of ancient Egypt taking special interest in the pyramids at Giza.

stern tutor appeared and took his place behind the lectern watching the rain-soaked stragglers come in with a disapproving frown.

After the last had taken his place he began, "Good morning, Gentle...." Only to be interrupted by one more latecomer, Herr Grubber, a portly chap with a look of constant surprise on his face. He nodded at the Doctor apologetically mumbling, "Sorry, sir, I ..."

Weishaupt coolly intoned, "Tell me, Herr Grubber do you think that the ancient civilisations of the past could have ever achieved the glorious triumphs which still resonate throughout our world today if their citizens had perpetually turned up late for everything?"

Grubber looked even more shocked than usual and answered, "I was run into by a horse in the square near..."

"It was not a question, Herr Grubber!" snapped the lecturer, "It was a rhetorical statement of empirical fact. Now sit down. You will report to me afterwards. Let this be a lesson to all of you. Bad time keeping will not be tolerated in this class. Now everyone open your book at page one-hundred and seventy-five and we shall finally begin."

It was a good job lippy Jan wasn't there or we would have been expelled before the good Doctor could shout 'Habeas Corpus!' I put my head into my book as did the rest of the class and the lesson began.

Perhaps it was the previous night's drinking and incarcerations or just plain boredom but I awoke with a start on my seat at the back of the hall and tried to compose myself. Fortunately my slumber had not been spotted by Weishaupt and as I looked around I saw two of my fellow students were also dozing. It was dark at the back of the hall and I'm sure the Doctor's eyesight was not good enough to see those of us who were in the shadows. He was still delivering his lecture and I forced myself to concentrate thinking that I should at least try to take in something if only for the sake of my parents and, of course to stay awake.

Weishaupt rumbled on, "In this classic case of canon law the orders in the constitution clearly define our legally binding claimant to the rendering and inscription of new legislature be that disposed to a country of colonies, rightful heir or royal sovereign i.e. king or queen."

He paused as if pondering his notes before lifting his eyes above his spectacles and meditatively continuing, "Actually this may be a moot point as one can envisage a time in the future where society will organise itself properly and we shall see the abolishment of the aristocracy, property, social authority, nationality and the return of the human race to a happy state: A single family without artificial needs or useless sciences: Every father being a priest and a magistrate. These priests would not teach a religion that most of you would be familiar but more a God of Nature."

The Doctor's concentration was broken by the clerk ringing the bell in the hallway marking the morning recess but he re-focused irritably seeing the haste with which his class showed in leaving. He shouted out above the din of the departing students, "Herr Grubber. I trust you have not forgotten our meeting?" and gestured to the foot of the lectern. The dejected pupil slowly made his way to the bottom of the stairs from where he was escorted out by Weishaupt. Keeping at a safe distance I followed the pair and saw the Doctor open the door of his private chambers and usher Grubber inside. When I passed I briefly caught Weishaupt's eye before the door closed with a bang and I heard him growling at the unlucky Grubber while I hurried off to see Van Halestrom.

I knocked at the Professor's door and he bade enter and greeting me with his usual smile. Before I could speak he started, "I'm so glad you have decided to accept my offer. Actually, I was expecting you a little earlier. Perhaps something happened last night that prevented you from coming sooner?"

I stood frozen in the doorway like an old man crossing the street who's realised he's about to be run over by a stagecoach. I stumbled, "But ... how did you know I would come?"

"It was in your eyes, my lad. And the eyes have it."

Chapter 4

Mystery under the Serpen's Caput

I left the university with fifty thalers in my pocket, a gun in my belt, a map inside my coat, an ingenious star clock and instructions for my labour with times, directions, distances, et cetera all specified to the very last detail. The Professor had told me that there would be no need to take the gun this time but that I should keep it because it might be of use in the future. I had wondered about this but imagined that the older man was over-reacting to the possibility of highwaymen out on the country roads. Anyway, I was pretty confident of my riding skills; in fact I had never been beaten on my beautiful mare Petrova, a superb gift from my generous parents.

I had history classes through the afternoon so it was close to six o'clock when I returned home to report the excellent news of my recent solvency to the no-doubt still sleeping Jan Kohler.

I was right. The slumbering giant was still in my bed but awake enough to moan at me from where he lay, "Where have you been? I need some coffee and some idiot has left the pot on the wrong side of the room."

"If you get up now, I will buy you a huge jug of coffee and the largest meal on the menu from the finest café in town."

"Have you sold your head? No, wait. You would not get two thalers for that piece of mutton."

"No fool. I have found employment from within the university which could lead to more work in the future and very well paid work as well."

"That's the student crowd for you. Always sticking together and keeping the good jobs for themselves. Like cats licking each other's arses."

"That's ridiculous, you idiot. Professor Van Halestrom is a friend of mine and I would still be his friend had I met him outside the confines of the university. Anyway, this work has nothing to do with anything academic. It's more like the sort of thing that we used to get up to back in Tuffengarten; horses and riding and being secret."

"What is it then? What do you have to do?"

"All I have to do is pick up a letter and deliver it to my master without it being opened."

"Sounds simple enough, what's the pay like?"

"Fifty thalers a letter."

"I'll be up in less than a minute. Then you can keep your promise to buy me the most expensive dish on the menu."

He jumped out of bed in a flurry of sheets and pillows, throwing his clothes on and calling out, "I don't know why, but expensive, for some reason, has always been my favourite type of everything."

We went for a huge meal at Café Teure Küche on Friedrichshofen, the most expensive spot in town, and enjoyed every extravagance on the menu. Jan had me in hysterics and wooed the pretty waitresses with his larks and excellent humour. After this indulgence I paid off our fine and some rent, vowed to keep my expenditure down and waited to start my first job which was not to be completed for three days yet. So I concentrated on my studies and even the erratic Jan calmed down as he prepared to begin work himself at the money-changers.

Presently the day of my task arrived. I remember it like it was yesterday; bringing Petrova out of the stables on to the lane behind my lodgings her shoes clacking down the uneven cobbles. The warm night air wafting aromas of honeysuckle and willow from the banks of the Danube filling my senses with recollections of summer nights spent as a boy. Gazing up into the heavens I thanked my good fortune. It was the clearest of nights and a huge waxing moon hung in the dark-blue mantle above. Such was the brightness of the glittering constellations I could have easily found my way from the stars alone. The bright pin pricks of light from the Serpen's Caput were clearly visible striking down to the horizon in the west. After checking to see that I had everything I needed one final time, I mounted Petrova, and set off for the road to Stuttgart and my intriguing rendezvous.

The first part of the journey was as uneventful as any I have ever made. I only saw a handful of people on the road as I travelled to the meeting point which was at the turning to Katzenstein castle, laying half a league south of the village of Kosigen. It was there I was to meet my mysterious colleague to whom I was to say nothing other than the code word 'Minerva,' and hear from them only the reply, 'Goddess of war.' Whereupon I was to be passed the envelope and return to Ingolstadt; bringing it to Professor Van Halestrom the next day. Easy money; I reckoned and continued to make good speed through the countryside which was so magically bathed in moonlight that night as to make a man think he were in a dream. As my thoughts drifted to the beauty of the landscape I recalled Weishaupt's words, 'God of Nature' and they resonated through me as I rode along. Some three and a half hours later I spotted Katzenstein castle. I was much impressed with its sturdy but graceful architecture and spent a wistful moment admiring its silhouette set against the night sky. *[3]

I could afford to rest for a while. I was ahead of time. I knew this because of the star clock Van Halestrom had lent me from which I took a reading every half hour during the journey. The Professor had told me that he would perform minor but painful surgery on me if I lost it because it had once belonged to Copernicus, the famous Polish astronomer. Having only known the Professor for a while I was sceptical about this but it was irrelevant who had owned it before; it was very useful on that starry night.

After setting the outer dial of the device to the correct date, the time could be ascertained by reading off the central yoke when a spy hole on the mechanism's edge was lined up to the planet Venus and another mark aligned on the horizon. The last reading had indicated half past eleven, half an hour to go and only couple of miles left to travel. I slowed Petrova to a walk and kept my eyes open for the meeting place. It had always been my plan to turn up early believing it was better to be safe than sorry. Also, I presumed that the other rider would arrive exactly on time as he would have made the journey before. I suspected this because the Professor had told me that the same messengers were used as much as possible as it ensured the safety of the letters. So after finding the fork in the road, I waited where I could see the junction but remain hidden under the canopy of leaves of a large maple tree which covered me in shadow.

At exactly the prescribed moment, the rider appeared on a

---

[3] Katzenstein Castle. This impressive fort, originally constructed in the middle-ages, is situated thirty five miles west of Ingolstadt on the road to Stuttgart and is shown on the map at the beginning of the book. It probably still looks much the same as when S. Drechsler saw it and can be viewed on the internet if you wish to verify the authenticity of the author's account. Bavaria is home to hundreds of similar castles.

powerful chestnut mare. He cantered up to the road before expertly bringing the horse to a halt on the junction's axis. From my hiding place I watched him wheel about for a moment before setting off at a trot. This seemed to unsettle the horseman who had, perhaps, expected his regular ally to be on the road. I quickly reached him and pulled Petrova up so her nose was a length from the head of the other mare. My accomplice was wearing a black three-cornered hat, a dark cloak and, round his face, a black neckerchief. I felt immediately vulnerable having not thought of concealing my identity. Was this a mistake? Had the Professor forgotten to mention that I should disguise myself? 'Stupid old bird,' I cursed. But somehow that didn't ring true. It was then that the secretive rider spoke.

"You're new."

I was startled. Not only had this idiot broken our sworn rule; i.e. to say nothing apart from the codeword but it was a woman idiot. Also I could detect a French accent - never a good sign. 'Well that's no surprise,' I thought, 'she's probably never done this type of thing before. But then how could she have known I was new?' I argued with myself for a moment before whispering, "Minerva," in case it was a trap to test my fallibility.

Impudently she replied, "Oh yes, that. Very well, if it pleases you, '*Goddess of war*.'"

Damn this wench's insolence. Someone should take her over their knee and give her a good spanking. I made up my mind right there and then to report her disobedience to Professor Van Halestrom. I would recommend that her services be terminated forthwith and that a substitute, preferably male, be found to replace her. I was annoyed that she could see my disapproval but I could not see her reaction and damn it - I was certain that she was laughing at me from behind her neckerchief. Confounded, I stuck my hand out expecting the handover to occur as pre-arranged, that was to say promptly and without fuss but to my further annoyance she mockingly asked, "Aren't you going to say please first?"

This was too much and I lost my temper. Damn the rules!

I hissed under my breath, "You have spoken to me three times now, which I know you know is forbidden."

"You don't have to whisper, sunshine," she scorned, "We're in a forest, on a lonely track, in the middle of the countryside, at twelve o'clock at night, which narrows down the chances of meeting a stranger and makes using a password a bit stupid. Password for this, password for that, they all think they're so important. I've got other things to remember apart from a hundred different passwords, thank you very much."

Her horse stirred slightly and she settled it with a tug on the reins before carrying on - after a fashion, "Very well. Here you are then."

From inside her cloak she produced a large, white envelope with a heavy, red seal on its back and passed it over. I eased Petrova forward a couple of steps and took the envelope, placing it in my satchel. Closer now to the impertinent young woman I could see she had the most exotic eyes. Much to my surprise one of them winked at me before she called, "Take care, Herr Jungkinda. There are a lot of other people out there who don't obey the rules."

With this, she lifted the head of her horse, skilfully spun it round and made off in a shower of dust from the road. I watched her disappear back down the lane and for some reason stayed there for a minute staring after her. I collected myself, checked the letter was in the satchel and made off myself. Riding at a steady canter all the way home I stopped only twice, once for water and again for a moment at the top of a hill to rest my mount. Arriving home around four o'clock, I placed Petrova in the stables, gave her a bucket of oats and returned to my lodgings, sleeping only a few hours before rising and preparing myself for my classes. When I awoke the room was empty as Jan had already gone to his job at the money-changers in town.

That morning, as soon as my first lecture was over, I was proudly standing outside the Professor's office door. After checking the letter's position amongst the papers in my satchel I composed myself, knocked smartly and, expecting my eagerness to come as a surprise, was most disgruntled to hear, "Come in, Sebastian."

Chapter 5

Fine Work if You Can Get It

I entered Van Halestrom's room to find him sitting behind his desk stirring a pot of tea. He beamed through the small cloud of steam, "That went well, did it not? Although you had a problem with our friend with the hat. You know - the girl with the beautiful eyes."

I was starting to wonder if sending mail to this man had any purpose whatsoever, as he would no doubt always know what was written in the letter before he had opened it.

I joked, "Wouldn't it be simpler for the messages to be sent to you via some type of telepathic link?"

"Yes. And cheaper too but I have not quite developed that skill to the extent where it renders written correspondence obsolete."

He chuckled to himself but such was his offhandedness I really could not tell whether he was serious or not. I sat down and passed him the envelope. He exchanged it for a cup of tea remarking, "You'll like this one, East Indian," and rotated the letter in his hand. After a twitch of his nose he turned it towards me and asked, "Recognise the seal?" I shook my head having never seen the crest before. It showed a spear crossed with an axe and, pointing downwards in the middle, an arrow. As I looked closer I noticed that on the end of the spear was a Phrygian cap and, around the axe, a bundle of sticks or fasces.

"These symbols have been used by several organisations over the course of many centuries but in the end it always means the same thing - Revolution. In this particular case ..." he flipped the letter over and inspecting the large glob of wax on the back, "...it's a revolution planned by the Bavarian Illuminati."

"The Illuminati!" I exclaimed. Of course I had heard rumours of such an order but thought tales of its secret control of heads of government and the aristocracy were hypothetical at best and downright fanciful at worst - the type of ludicrous thinking typical of students who drop out of university and end up in the opium dens round the docks in Frankfurt. But before I could say anything the Professor's incredible gift for mind reading beat me to it and he calmly pointed out, "Before you try and tell me it's the type of ludicrous thinking typical of students who drop out of university and end up in the opium dens round the docks in Frankfurt, I can prove, without a shadow of a doubt, that there is indeed a sinister organisation which seeks to gain secret control of the heads of government and the aristocracy." He paused, smiling inscrutably before finishing, "Hardly hypothetical theories and downright fanciful tales now, eh, Herr Drechsler?" *[4]

It wasn't the last time Van Halestrom would respond in such a startling way and although he did it many times I never actually did get used to it. I tried to bring myself round. Although I understood the outlandish claim my young mind was having a problem accommodating a conspiracy of such proportions.

"Surely, sir, these are merely imaginary forces dreamt up by fearful delusionists to explain anything strange that occurs in the corridors of power but after the proper officials have been set to work getting to the truth of it an explanation soon comes to light."

"And everybody lived happily ever after. It sounds as though you are the one with the fanciful notions. Could it be rationally expected that dark forces would not try to control those in places of power, and that those people would never be corrupt if their actions remained unscrutinised in the shadows? It is a good thing you don't see the evil that can lurk in the hearts of men, my lad. It means you project your own moral principles on those around you and especially those above. It is part of the way we are conditioned to think. It does you proud young Drechsler. Remember that. It also means you are at the first level and ready to enter the next."

I pondered this wondering what he might mean until curiosity got the better of me and I asked, "And what is the next level, sir?"

---

[4] Bavarian Illuminati. This infamous secret society was founded on May 1st 1776. From a modest beginning of five members, after much administrative, financial and organisational help from other 'free thinking' collaborators, its ranks had swollen to as many as two thousand by 1784. Membership included many well-connected and influential figures such as; Johann Wolfgang von Goethe, Johann Gottfried Herdér and the Dukes of Gotha and Weimar. So much has been written about the order by hundreds of notable historians and their less reliable counterparts that it is hard to deny any other quasi-political organisation, apart from the Freemasons, has been responsible for such speculative hysteria, intriguing legends and conspiratorial myths that still continue to this day.

"To understand that the first level is simply not the case."

This thought halted my mental faculties. I was not expecting it at all as it seemed to contradict the initial understanding. He sensed my confusion and added, "There are many things that you might know of the true ways of the world, my lad, but for me to tell them all to you now would leave us both with beards long enough to hide the table in. Although tell them to you I will, as time passes. It is information that will bring you great understanding but also great moral problems. It will be up to you to solve these as well as you can. Perhaps it would be best to remember that nothing is *ever* what it seems. This will make it easier for you to understand precisely what you need to know."

This was such an esoteric speech it asked ten times as many questions as it answered. I felt my forehead crease. My mind naturally wanted to start reading from the top of a very long list of questions but Van Halestrom spotted this and raised a finger. "As I said there is simply not enough time now. So we must make that for another day, soon. You have excelled, Sebastian. I will be in touch. Good day, my friend."

I finished my tea and stood to shake the Professor's hand, permitting myself a slightly less exaggerated bow which he seemed to appreciate, and I left his rooms.

Over the following weeks I was to perform many similar errands for the Professor. Meeting the same cocky, masked lady at the fork in the road near Katzenstein Castle then returning the messages to Van Halestrom the following day. Sometimes I was asked to take the letters to a small farmhouse twenty miles to the east of Ingolstadt where I would hand it over to a kindly old lady called Frau Hoffmeister. "One of our agents," the Professor had informed me.

It seemed strange that this nice old lady could be an 'agent' of ours but what did I know? Anyway she wasn't the female ally who most intrigued me. For, I quickly found myself developing a deep fascination for the saucy rider in black. Her unladylike demeanour only worsened as our meetings continued and I was soon smitten with her irreverence and mystique. I had to check myself on a few occasions realising that I was falling for a women I had never seen and of whom my parents definitely would not approve. Still what did I care? No one would ever know of her or my failure to win her heart which I was convinced, was bound to happen as soon she discovered my true feelings for her. For she was aloof, confident and worldly while I was naïve, nervous and immature; and she probably thought me a boy. But although we had the strangest of relationships it was still a relationship, however fleeting and absurd, and I knew I would miss it painfully were it to end.

At our next encounter I was made aware that our task might be more dangerous than I had first thought. She arrived ten minutes late and seemed uncharacteristically flustered. Glancing over her shoulder a couple of times she mocked me from behind her neckerchief.

"Better looking and more punctual than your predecessor, Jungkinda, still no man can have everything - or so it would seem."

Sensing her uneasiness, as she passed me the envelope I asked a question that had been much on my mind.

"What happened to the one who worked before me?"

"Ah, his face was not as simple as yours. I think he is doing something less profitable now."

With this she kicked the flanks of her horse and flew off with much greater haste than usual, shouting, "Take care of yourself, Herr Jungkinda. I would miss seeing your pretty face however simple it is."

These strangely familiar words and her uneasiness seemed to imply danger and I also left completing the journey home in record time. On the way back however, I had the strangest notion that I was being followed but put this down to paranoia caused by my lady's skittishness. Nevertheless, I decided that on my next mission I would take the Professor's gun even though somehow I sensed this decision may tempt fate.

Returning to my chambers I successfully scaled the stairs without stirring the ever-vigilant Fraulein Warburg. On entering my room I saw the empty truckle bed where Jan would have normally been asleep. He had recently moved out to his own lodgings and I had not seen him for two weeks. I was beginning to miss him and his jokes - jokes that would have started the very moment I came in and told him of my latest adventures. I had been in the habit of trying to make them seem less interesting than they were, as I thought I had detected a hint of jealousy after he had started work proper and realised the drudgery of his days compared with mine. I resolved to go and see him as soon as I had time, whenever that would be. Work was piling up ready for the looming exams in July and I had much revision to do. But I was determined to make time for the sake of my friendship. More urgently, I knew I must rest before my busy day began. I fell into a deep sleep and started to dream.

In the dream I was meeting the mysterious lady-in-black at the usual fork in the road but this time, as she handed me the letter, I grabbed her and pulled her towards me embracing her as she swooned in my arms. I tore off her black neckerchief to finally reveal her beautiful face but to my horror, when I pulled it away, I discovered a hideous skull with maggots spewing from the eye sockets and crawling down the grey teeth. Panting heavily I jumped back into my skin from the world of Morpheus only to hear the bells of Saint Maria's chiming in the distance.

"Was that seven or eight?" I panicked, "Please God, don't let me be late today." For it was Wednesday: Canon law day.

Fearing the worst I sprinted along my usual route determined not be late for Weishaupt's lecture. This grim prospect was not helped by the awful vision of the maggot-filled skull still fresh in my mind as I raced through the university gates.

I realised from the emptiness of the corridors that I was late to the tune of well over quarter of an hour and so well within the zone that would result in major dressing-down. Moments later, panting and flustered, I reached the door of the Doctor's lecture hall. Taking a deep breath I pulled the handle and grimaced as I entered fully expecting a series of scathing taunts. So I was surprised when Weishaupt continued his droning monologue without taking his eyes from the book on his lectern. As I gently closed the door and tiptoed my way in I saw him look up at me and calmly nod towards a seat in the middle of the room which I obediently made for as quietly as possible. Having sat down I still expected some kind of outburst and subsequent ritual humiliation, thinking that maybe he was waiting until his notes allowed it, but still none was forthcoming. My classmates had also noticed this inexplicable suspension of authority and grew suspicious. I was aware of some sneering from those around me induced by this apparent preferential behaviour. My surprise and their distrust carried on until the end of the lesson.

When the lecture was over I took care to leave as surreptitiously as possible, hiding in between some of the more bookish students who had not seemed to notice anything. I was actually through the door when my heart fell as I heard from behind me, "Herr Drechsler."

I turned around slowly to see Weishaupt approaching me and was greatly unnerved to see something I had never actually seen before - a smile on his face.

He spoke disingenuously, "Don't worry young man, you've done nothing wrong. I would like a private word with you in my chambers. That's all."

And then the darnedest of things; the man put his arm around my shoulder directly contravening the accepted rules of behaviour that existed between a student and his teacher. He smiled again and as he did I became aware of the antipathy of the other students for this inexplicable breach of etiquette. He kept his arm there for five more awkward seconds as he pointed me in the direction of his rooms. Somehow I had the feeling that he had done all this in front of everyone quite deliberately but struggled to understand why. 'He really knows how to put someone off balance,' I thought, 'first one way and then the other.' Of course I dared not protest and walked down the hallway to his door which he opened and bade me enter first. My mind raced through the unpleasant penalties I was about to receive; a private dressing-down, a fine or, worst of all, to be ridiculed in front of my fellow students for the remainder of the term. How on earth could I have known what fate actually held in store for me as I nervously edged into Adam Weishaupt's chambers on that morning in June?

Chapter 6

A Fly in the Spider's Web

Weishaupt closed the door behind me and I glanced around the room surprised to discover a treasure trove of antiquities and relics. Books of all kinds, maps, certificates and portraits in fine frames covered the walls. A large globe and a couple of impressive busts on columns stood against the wall behind a grand, old desk flanked with two leather chairs. I also noted, spread out across the entire floor, a beautiful and richly patterned rug.

"Take a seat. Make yourself comfortable," offered my host, sitting in the chair behind the desk. He seemed calm, so in turn I tried to relax and lowered myself into a chair. He carried on, "We have access to all privileges here. I shall call for some refreshments." Picking up a tiny bell from the table he gave it a shake.

I wondered whether this barely audible tinkle would disturb anyone as I hardly heard it myself. But to my surprise a pretty young maid in a tight bodice immediately appeared at the door bearing a tray holding a pot of coffee and two large cups.

Weishaupt grinned like a crocodile that had found a bucket of fish, "It's always best to have a plan for every little detail. The little pleasures in life are so enjoyable, don't you think?"

I didn't know whether he was referring to the coffee or the maid and found it hard to divert my attention from her buxom figure as she left the room.

The Doctor followed my eyes and as she closed the door behind her he commented, "She's very attractive, is she not?"

Whatever he was up to it seemed pointless to lie and anyway I thought she might be listening at the door, as she must have been earlier to hear the pathetic tinkle of the tiny bell. I spoke a little louder than I needed, disguising my general unease with a confident air. Remember this was the Sebastian of the future not the self-conscious soul of the past living in his father's shadow. "Very attractive indeed." I answered with awkward bravado, "One would be blind or a liar to say otherwise."

Weishaupt regarded me with a calculating smile before setting out the coffee. Placing a cup down in front of me he asked, "So, tell me, Herr Drechsler what do you think of my chambers?"

"Very impressive, sir a little treasure from everywhere." I gazed around at the collection of artefacts. Spotting a document on the wall, and noting that I had seen something similar in a book at the library in Count Frederick's castle in Tuffengarten, I attempted to air what little knowledge I had, "That is a Persian calendar if I'm not mistaken."

"Well spotted, Herr Drechsler. You are correct. Though, it is actually known as a Zoroastrian calendar. According to that it is the month of Chardad and the year is 1154 AD."

It occurred to me that two calendars might be an unnecessary complication in a life where keeping up with one posed already enough inconvenience. I asked, "Is it not difficult keeping two contradictory ideas in your mind at the same time, sir?"

"On the contrary, it is the secret of a life where all things have a paradoxical nature - to have two opposing sides apparent at all times."

This man was even more oblique than Professor Van Halestrom and I wondered if all university lecturers had the same disregard for saying what they meant when in private. His eyes ranged around the room inviting me to point out something else. Whatever was going on it was not the dressing-down for being late that I had expected, so I continued to play along. My attention was drawn to one of the busts behind Weishaupt. I mentioned, "One is Vivaldi, I recognise the nose, but the other is not familiar to me and the inscription is too small to read from here."

"Ah, it is a great friend of mine, the philosopher, Immanuel Kant. I believe you will be studying him next year. He suggests that the answer to life lies in three questions: What can I know? What ought I to do? What may I hope for? He considers that the answer to the second and third depends on the answer to the first; and that our duty and our destiny can be determined only after a thorough study of our own experiences."

I was more than aware of Kant's philosophy but now, for some reason, found myself feigning ignorance and it struck me this was not something I was in the habit of doing. Sensing it was the Doctor's odd demeanour that was having this effect on me I hid my real thoughts and hoped that he would not notice. He reached out to the globe next to him and gave it a lazy spin then stopped it with a tap of his finger.

He turned to me as I sipped my coffee. "You're an interesting student, Herr Drechsler. Your grades are excellent and you obviously have a keen intellect."

I was pretty sure he knew at least one of these statements was untrue but again I said nothing and let him carry on none the wiser, if, indeed, he ever was.

"It is in my power to grant any student who possesses a thirst for knowledge entry to an elite band of young academics. This group is known as the Owl of Minerva and within its ranks are many of the local bright lights of education and others from a wide variety of backgrounds. The group comes together once a month at the full moon and meets at the Chapel of Liebfrauenmünster in the centre of town on the Felixstrausser. The next meeting is in three night's time. I would like to extend an invitation to you." *[5]

I was intrigued to hear the name Minerva used again as it had been the code word on my first mission to meet the mysterious lady-in-black. Though a little apprehensive about accepting I was going to anyway out of plain curiosity and to meet these local 'bright lights' when he added, "It is a great honour to be invited to the Minerval gathering. Maybe it would appear rude if such an invitation were to be turned down."

This seemed like a veiled threat but once more I tried to conceal my real feelings and replied innocently, "I would be honoured to attend, sir."

I smiled humbly and gulped down the rest of my coffee, placed my cup on the tray and observed, "I have to be at Professor Lipstad's History lecture in a moment …"

---

[5] The Owl of Minerva. These meetings facilitated an academy in which young initiates to the Illuminati could be selected and groomed for higher positions within the organisation. The class of Minerva was a relatively low rank in the scheme of things. However, it was the soul of the Order and functioned as a sort of assembly line for recruits. Candidates advanced from *Novice* to the *Minerval degree* where they were properly vetted, scrutinised and indoctrinated. Another layer of the owl symbolism was to remind its initiates that the Illuminati does its bidding at night.

He accepted my excuses and stood up offering his hand which I took noticing it to be a little cold. I bowed and turned to go certain that there was no chance he was going to ring his bell once more and summon back the little beauty.

Upon leaving I made my way directly to find the Professor to tell him about what had happened. Though the Professor had never mentioned it intuition told me that a certain antipathy existed between the two gentlemen and therefore I guessed that our brief discussion would be of some interest to Van Halestrom. But when I knocked there was no answer and after trying once more I despondently walked away to my next lecture.

I tried on several more occasions to contact the Professor over the next two days but eventually his clerk told me that he was not due back at the faculty until the start of the next week. This would be after the meeting of the Owl of Minerva on Saturday and by Friday I had become increasingly apprehensive about attending, realising that this might not have been the case had I been able to speak to Van Halestrom beforehand. It was also the night that I had planned to visit Jan. I rued the unfortunate timing but promised myself I would see my friend in the following days.

Had I known what was going to happen on that warm summer night back in 1784 I would have been kneeling and praying on the pavement in front of the Chapel of Liebfrauenmünster instead of innocently making my way up the broad stairs and through the colonnade. As I passed between the pillars, glancing up into the shadows, I remember thinking 'This might be good and it might be bad.' Silly me; I should have known it was all going to be bad. But that's the naive optimism of youth for you and that's what might have saved my life: In the end.

Chapter 7

The Owl and the Pussy

At the chapel's entrance I was surprised to see two maidens in ancient vestal garb standing either side of the large wooden doors. I was now quite wealthy by my usual standards owing to the money I had earned working for Van Halestrom and, after paying off my debts, settling my rent and buying a new saddle and bridle for Petrova I had also splashed out on a dashing new outfit befitting a man of my growing financial status. I was aware the maidens enjoyed looking at it and hoped that they might find their way into the meeting later so they could inspect its tailoring more closely. The fairer sex in general had been increasingly on my mind and, having not even seen the sultry lady-in-black for nearly a week, I was seriously craving some female attention. There seemed to be beautiful young women everywhere in my life but I never had the time or the excuse to become better acquainted. The nymphs smiled rather more knowingly than their vestal garb should have normally allowed. One of them passed me a decorative mask which I inspected briefly before putting on. Before I could think of anything to say, which was as dashing as my outfit, the other girl opened one of the doors and I entered into a dim passageway.

Two rows of candles flickered along the corridor as the heavy door closed behind me. As the reverberations faded I began to make out the sound of many voices coming from the far end of the passageway. I sidled up to a pair of red velvet curtains and tentatively pulled them apart.

'This must be the place,' I thought, seeing forty to fifty other guests in similar masks milling about in a dark cavernous chamber. At the far end of the hall was an enormous wooden owl lit by four huge candelabra around its base each the size of a man. 'The Bird of Minerva' I presumed. The flames threw a dappling of shadows over the bottom of the statue, leaving the austere features of the bird's head shrouded in near total darkness. I slipped between the curtains noticing that everyone was drinking from a silver goblet. As I did I felt a tap on my shoulder and turned to find a man and a woman adorned in the same mock classical garb as the girls outside. The man was carrying a barrel under his arm and the maiden offered me an identical silver cup to those of the other guests. I took the goblet which the man skilfully filled from the barrel creating a large arc of the dark liquid before plugging the spout with his thumb. The pair nodded politely and walked off into the crowd.

Making my way between the guests I sniffed at the claret fluid trying to ascertain its contents. As well as detecting a goodly degree of alcohol I thought I also recognised another ingredient, something sickly sweet that I had smelt somewhere before but I could not remember where.

My interest in this evaporated on hearing a familiar voice ring out, "Of course it's alright to drink it now. I've had my own goblet filled three times already. These chaps are my favourite type of inn keep. They need no pay or any other encouragement whatsoever to go about their business which, as any man worth his weight in beer will tell you, is a damn fine thing indeed."

It couldn't be anyone else but Jan Kohler disguised ironically in an ornamented mask of the nature spirit Pan. Shocked to say the least, to find him of all people here on this night for 'learned academics,' I approached the small group surrounding him. But before I got there I recognised another voice which stopped me in my tracks, like no other could have done.

"Go on, darling, have another. You're so funny when you're drunk and I want to laugh."

I couldn't believe it. Draping herself over Jan and wearing an alluring nymph's mask I was sure it was my-lady-in-black. A surge of envy swept over me as the woman, whose real breath-taking beauty was now revealed by a ludicrously small vestal outfit, began to kiss my oldest friend. I stared incredulously as Jan tongued for Bavaria and nonchalantly held out his silver goblet to be filled by another attentive servant. The embrace lasted long enough to embarrass the owner of the busiest brothel in Babylon and still I held my breath. Twisting my jealously further the group around them cheered as the couple finally parted, some of them eagerly copying their performance and enjoying similar fondlings. I turned away unable to accept what I was seeing. Any other woman with any other man would not have had the same profound effect on me. Reeling from the shock I took an impulsive draw from my own goblet and skulked away behind a column. After a moment I could not help but brave another glimpse and was further mortified to see Jan and my lady in an even more lascivious pose. I turned my back gulping down another slug of the brew.

A drum roll sounded drawing everyone's attention to an opening at the foot of the owl. From the hole wearing a white, hooded gown Adam Weishaupt appeared and came to stand between the tall candelabra. He announced himself to the crowd, "Good evening brothers and sisters. I am so glad to be able to greet those who will carry the light of progress and knowledge into the future. Everyone here tonight has earned the privilege of admission into this renowned sect dedicated to personal empowerment and public freedom. I want you all to share in your beauty and power on this full moon of Gemini. To enjoy one another's company and throw away your cares from the past allowing yourself to move seamlessly into your future." He bowed his head casting it in shadow like the statue of the owl looming above him and chanted, "O thou great symbol of all mortal wisdom, Owl of Bohemia, we do beseech thee; grant us thy counsel." He raised his face catching it in the light of the flaming torches and called out, "Now let the rite begin!"

With this a band struck up and from behind either side of the huge bird musicians filed into the room escorted by two lines of frolicking vestal maidens. The performers and the girls quickly mixed with the guests as general dancing and debauchery broke out. Weishaupt bowed theatrically before spinning round and returning through the doorway in the base of the enormous statue.

The mood of the people in the chamber was rapidly mounting into an orgy. I tried to spot Jan and my lady but their places were now occupied by another pair of lewd revellers. It seemed as though the women dressed in vestal clothing were leading events in the room, encouraging those who were not engaging with the festivities to do so by enticing them with salacious behaviour. As I watched from the relative safety of my column I heard a splashing at my side and turned to see another servant refilling my goblet. As he finished one of the maidens approached me and set about luring me into the cavorting throng in the centre of the hall. Despite myself, I meekly complied taking another swig as I let her lead me on, fluttering her eyes at me in the most seductive of ways. Finally I could take no more and pulled her towards me, holding her round the waist and pressing her body into mine. She swooned in my arms and I leant forward to feel her kiss. I took my advantage, tasting my own lips on hers then suddenly remembered where I had smelt the scent of the potion before; the docks in Frankfurt. It was laudanum! I was certain. Realising this and, also that I did not want my-lady-in-black to see me with this other woman even though I had seen her kissing my best friend, I fought to control my own carnal instincts. Though my head was swimming I could recognise the bite of my pride and the prickle of my orthodox upbringing chiming at the back of my faltering consciousness.

I pushed the maiden away and made for what I thought was the entrance, wondering whether the servants would actually force me back inside to fornicate with one of the revellers. Luckily they did not but as I recovered from this frightening possibility I found myself to be in a different hallway to the one through which I had entered. Rather than return to the pulsating romp that lay behind I carried on.

At the end of this candle-lit corridor were more red velvet curtains. I pushed them apart and stumbled into the chamber, swaying past a collection of ornate statues and large potted plants divided by low ornamental walls. I slumped down on one of the walls feeling the powerful effects of the drugs take hold and spilt the goblet. Clutching my face in the palms of my hands I tried to steady myself as the room began to spin. I felt I was going to vomit and promptly did so - once - then immediately began to feel my head start to clear and took some steadying breaths. As the ringing in my ears subsided it was replaced by a muffled sound coming from somewhere behind me. I could not fathom what it was and rather unsteadily got up to have a look.

Behind a small olive tree to the side of the room I saw them. One was clearly Jan Kohler groaning from behind his mask of pan with his purple trousers round his ankles. The other, still wearing her nymph's mask and kneeling in front of my groaning friend, I was sure must be my-lady-in-black. I began to feel sick again and stumbled back through the curtains knowing that I simply must get away.

Seconds later I fell back in the main hall where the huge owl stood overseeing what had now descended into a full-blown orgy. This really wasn't what I had expected at all. I had thought everyone would be walking around reading books and talking about the age of reason which would have made me the romantic maverick and I could have regaled my fellow sectists with my exciting stories of how I almost used a gun in anger and how I almost wooed a woman, whose face I could almost see, who now had almost all my best friend in her mouth. What a fool I had been. In reality I was just a scared college boy out of his depth, put in a position he had thought he always wanted but whom could now only gawk anxiously around him and not join in at all.

Another drum roll sounded. Weishaupt reappeared in between the flaming torches raising his hands to halt the musicians and announced, "Now, my Minerval brethren, we will perform the Cremation of Care. Come now those who seek the truth of light. Join me in praise for our glorious Molech!" *[6]

I struggled to see what this frightening Canaanite God had to do with the 'truth of light' but still in a state of shock after the scenes I had already witnessed, curiosity got the better of me and I took a couple of steps closer.

Despite the darkness of the chamber I was able to make out a tiny recess in the floor around the base of the owl and noticed that it was filled with a transparent fluid. One of the male servants appeared with a reed basket and set it on top of the liquid giving it a push towards Weishaupt's feet. As the basket travelled across the shallow liquid I could have sworn I heard a baby cry but put it down to the drugs I had taken. Then as I focused on the basket I was sure I saw an infant's arm appear out of the side.

Before I knew it, to my horror and bewilderment, the reservoir turned into a blaze of fire engulfing the basket in a flash. The powerful flames illuminated the huge owl and, as the music began to play again, the party went into an accelerated stage of debauchery. Clasping at my mouth with one hand I used the other to push through the romping mob which writhed before me in every

---

[6] The Cremation of Care Ceremony. Drechsler's recollections bear much in common with similar ceremonies filmed at Bohemian Grove in California and the owl, in this case, is sometimes referred to as Molech. Though, in antiquity Moloch, the Canaanite deity, is represented as a legless bull with arms. This pagan god would be worshipped by the Israelites during times of apostasy (without religion) and is associated with the sacrifice of children. Lev.18:21 'Neither shall you give any of your offspring to offer them to Molech.'

direction. To my relief I found the set of curtains through which I had entered, blundered between them and up the short passage then burst out of the heavy doors at the end.

Stumbling from the chapel I gasped at the cool night air. Feeling a revolting mouthful of bile rise in my throat I gagged as I made my way through the colonnade and down the stairs. There was no sign of the guardian maidens and I assumed that they were back inside giving their all for Molech. I reached to bottom of the steps and wiped the vomit away from my chin.

When I only staggered fifty yards when I was alarmed to see a large shaven-headed man with a heavy, black moustache appear from behind a tree and approach me in the most unsettling of ways. He rudely blocked my progress and demanded, "Are you, Sebastian Drechsler?"

Somehow the question was so simple it threw me for a second until I finally answered, "Well ... yes."

At which the sturdy swine produced a long knife from behind his back causing my innards to turn into gravy. I only had time to see the blade glinting in the moonlight and to consider the night had been bad enough already without this blaggard murdering me in the street when suddenly I heard a swishing sound from over my shoulder and saw a silver arrow appear in his chest with a thud.

The look of total shock on the man's face was almost identical to mine. Except, that from his mouth, spurted a fountain of crimson blood which unhappily splashed across my face. I involuntarily wiped myself - again - as the man reeled backwards ending up propped against the tree. I stared in sheer astonishment at the macabre sight for a moment not knowing what to do, until looking over my shoulder towards the chapel in the direction from which the arrow had come. There was nothing behind me to suggest who might have fired the shot that had doubtless saved my life. Unless, of course, they had been aiming at me? My heart began to pound even faster.

'What in God's name is happening tonight?' One thing was certain - I wanted it to end right away. I gulped apprehensively and glanced down at my hand seeing that it was covered with blood. What was I doing here? That was an easy question to answer; nothing that would lead to any good – and so, without further ado, I fled.

It was an excellent piece of fleeing, of which I am still proud to this day. I recall sprinting past a well-to-do couple going the other way who wished me 'Goodnight.' This, as you will understand was hard to reciprocate knowing that they were going to find something up the street that was certainly going to ruin their evening stroll. I ran all the way home in a blind funk and stayed up till three o'clock washing the blood from my clothes. Though I scrubbed hard I could not remove the stains nor the vision from my mind which still persists to this day and will always serve as a bloody reminder of the worst time I've ever had at a student's night.

Chapter 8

No Rest for the Wicked

I awoke with a start on my bed. By now I was getting used to waking up covered in cold sweat after being terrorised by horrific dreams. In my latest vision I was being chased by a huge owl that was trying to kill me for stealing its laudanum. Even sleep was not allowing me a safe haven and I was certainly not finding one in my waking life. As I lifted my head from the pillow the look of horror on the bald man's face shot back into my mind and all at once the harrowing events of the previous night came back to me in a flood of dark recollections. I shuddered and half-swooned with emotion then buckled with fear and remorse as the entirety of the ordeals returned to haunt me.

"Jan," I sighed, 'how could it possibly be?' I shook my head trying to cast out the odious memories. It didn't work and I got out of the bed which now somehow seemed dirty.

I fumbled across the small chamber and doused my head with water from the bowl by the window then gazed out across the rooftops of the old city. It was a pretty view. Green trees and neat houses nestling under the city wall all basking in the pleasant morning sunshine. Here and there the pleasing vista was punctuated by one of Ingolstadt's many church spires, the sounds of their chiming bells filling the summer air. 'That's what I need,' I thought, 'a church.' Not being the most pious of Christians (unlike my devout parents) I hadn't been to church since I had moved here ten months ago. Now I noted how much had changed in that time. I felt my soul yearn for something that seemed every day, normal - something that reminded me of home. And as I came to a happier state of equilibrium I remembered; it was Sunday after all.

As I collected these thoughts there was a commotion downstairs. The sounds of someone arriving echoed up from the hallway and I could hear my petulant landlady lambaste the unfortunate soul who had made the mistake of coming so early in the morning. The complaining steadily came closer until I realised that the caller must be for me. Whoever it was had come so high up the stairs that there could be no alternative. As the steps approached my stomach churned and I imagined the authorities or another bald man with a knife, or even Jan come to boast which might be worse. What if it were my lady?

"Control yourself Sebastian." I murmured and strained to hear the man's voice that was mingled with Fraulein Warburg's constant protestations until the knock of a cane landed twice on the door. I timidly made my way over. Then considering I had nowhere to run and, indeed nothing to hide, I flung open the door only to find - Professor Van Halestrom.

Well, it was my door this time so I spoke first and heard myself indignantly ask, "Forgive me, sir, but what in God's name are you doing here?"

He smiled inscrutably and replied, "I was going to church and I had a feeling you would like to come along."

I frowned deeply as it seemed that whenever I saw his face it was always calm and wise while mine usually had its mouth hanging open in stupefaction. His smile turned to a grin as the ringing of church bells wafted in through the window.

Five minutes later as we walked down a street bustling with townsfolk dressed in their fresh Sunday clothes I was pestering him for all I was worth. "One day, sir you will have to explain to me how you perform the miracle where you tell me what I'm going to do before I know I'm going to do it myself."

"Ah but then, Herr Drechsler you would never have the chance to surprise yourself and that would be permanently disappointing, believe me."

I frowned at this unsatisfactory answer but carried on undeterred, "I'm sorry, sir, but as I understand it, nearly everything that comes from your lips seems to be a riddle."

"Is not all of life a riddle, my friend, and life's purpose to understand it?"

He had been prevaricating in the same infuriating manner whilst I had got dressed and we left the house. Now, as we walked along in the clear light of day, I felt that I must find out what was going on in my new life and that somehow his timely appearance had something to do with it. I pressed on, "But, Herr Van Halestrom, I feel there are several extremely pressing matters of the gravest concern to which I must find explanations."

Finally he stopped and looked me in the eye. "Alright, Sebastian, I believe it is time. I think that you are now ready to attain another level of understanding. You have had time to grasp what you have already learnt and now you realise that all is not what it seems. I believe that you truly know this because you have seen it for yourself. Also I believe you have changed your behaviour to adapt to this new uncertain environment and, that at times, you have pretended to be something that you are not to gain some sort of control. This is the way we learn, through our own experiences."

This was true enough. I had seen some unbelievable things and also I had pretended to be something that I wasn't though how the Professor knew of it was a mystery to me. Never mind. For once there seemed to be a fairly logical progression of ideas. Maybe things were finally starting to make sense. We set off again and I relaxed as I felt I was about to find out something I needed to know. We continued walking and came to a pleasing avenue, the maple trees of which created a canopy of shimmering green above us. One hundred yards up ahead I saw the spire of St Bartholomew's Church. Regarding the building's uncomplicated symmetry a calm fell over me as we strolled along.

"So you think you can tell me what I want to know, Professor?"

"I will try, Sebastian."

I took a deep breath and tried to think of the first and most pertinent question out of the hundreds rampaging through my mind. Suddenly I couldn't think of one I could fairly ask which I could reasonably expect him to answer. I became frustrated. All this time in the dark and now with the possibility to find out what might be going on in my new and overly-complicated life and I couldn't conceive of one good question to ask. Let me explain.

Yes, I had attended the meeting at the temple but what would he actually know about a party organised for lusty, drunken students? Also our lady-in-black was *obviously* her own woman and entitled to do whatever she wanted, with whomsoever she pleased. That she chose to do it with my oldest friend was of no consequence to the Professor. What should he know or care of such things? What about the ceremony itself? Well, I had been drunk, or worse, drugged and as a consequence I had no idea if the things that I thought I had seen were real. Also I had grappled like a randy sailor with a young maiden and though I had enjoyed her for only a short while; it was still during an orgy. I was not proud of any of these things and I believed they were excesses of which he would not care to hear. As for the killing of my assailant; I had no wish to incriminate myself in a murder if I did not have to and what would the poor old Professor know of such wickedness anyway?

I tutted to myself and tried to order my thoughts as we neared the church. I watched the priest welcoming his congregation one by one and prayed my questions would arrange themselves in such a neat fashion.

"Relax and it will come to you," assured the Professor and I had a moment of clarity as the most important of the events from the previous night surfaced once again, its significance out-weighing my personal plight. I knew I must tell someone.

I squeezed my eyes together and sighed, "Last night I watched a man die after he was shot in his chest with a silver arrow."

He didn't hesitate not even for an instant.

"I know. It was me. I killed him. He was going to murder you."

"What!" I shouted, inadvertently alerting the priest and his parishioners to our presence.

Annoyingly Van Halestrom repeated himself, "I said, I know. It was me. I killed him. He was going to murder you."

"Yes. Yes. I heard you the first time," I hissed self-consciously.

"You did ask, Sebastian."

"I know I did, sir, but forgive me ..." I noticed the churchgoers staring in our direction and whispered, "I'm sorry but I am still a bit surprised. How did you ...?"

"I have a crossbow - a really good one. Take a man's head off at fifty yards. I use the silver arrows so they know who has done it."

Bewildered yet again, I staggered through his points, "They? Who are 'they'?"

"The Illuminati: I kill the Illuminati with silver arrows so they know who has done it," he nodded to check I knew what he meant.

"Yes, yes. You kill them with the silver arrows so that they know who has done it. I assure you, sir that is the part I understand."

We were drawing closer to the line and I didn't want to cause a scene on this pleasant Sunday morning but Van Halestrom seemed oblivious to these sentiments, "Look here's an arrow." He fumbled around in his pocket before producing one of the lethal darts and pushing the cursed thing in my face.

"They are not solid silver but plated, see. This increases range and accuracy whilst, of course, ensuring they know …"

This time I anticipated him, "Know who has done it. Yes!" I leapt in front of him attempting to shield the bolt from the line of the churchgoers, suggesting, "We should probably put that away now."

"Perhaps you're right," he conceded, "Look. You told me you wanted to know what was going on. So I'm telling you. I believe I owe you that much."

He replaced the arrow in his pocket and we carried on towards the church. I took a deep breath, gathered my thoughts and continued, "So what were the Illuminati doing at the Chapel of Liebfrauenmünster?"

"They were all Illuminati. Adam Weishaupt is the leader of the whole operation. He is probably suspicious that you are in league against him and tried to compromise you by drugging you and getting you to indulge in a lustful act. When you failed to perform, as it were, he arranged to have you killed. That's when I made my entry."

"So you're telling me that you knew I was going to that ... that orgy at the chapel and that I would be in terrible danger but you let me go anyway?"

"Oh yes."

We had reached the back of the queue by now but I still could not help my anger boiling over until, unfortunately I finally snapped, "Damn you, Van Halestrom!"

Infuriatingly, he kept as cool as an Eskimo's water closet while I was obviously extremely agitated. So much so that by the time we shook hands with the priest the nervous clergyman looked at me as though I was an escaped patient from the asylum when all along it was the Professor who was the real mad man; with the crossbow and the silver arrows so they knew who had blasted done it.

We entered the church and took our seats near the front below the pulpit. I was still shaking my head in disbelief and attempting, with difficulty, to calm both my outer and inner selves before the service began, But Van Halestrom made this impossible chattering beside me, "Did you know Benjamin Franklyn, one of the fathers of the United States of America, which, by the way is also being infiltrated by the Illuminati, says that his favourite part of going to church is the quiet period before the preacher starts to deliver the sermon? I would have to agree. It's obvious that you don't need a spiritual leader there in front of you acting as some sort of conduit to your God. If you are going to achieve spiritual union you're going to do it on your own. Anyway that's another way they control you, through the church." He made an arc with his eyes and finished, "They're Illuminati too y'know." *[7]

Someone shushed him from behind as if to prove a point. At last he was silenced and we bowed our heads in quiet contemplation. After a moment a dreadful memory flashed into my mind. It was the sight of the baby in the burning crib. So much had happened last night, most of it whilst I was intoxicated, that I had forgotten about it until that moment. I whispered, "So you were actually in the chapel, in the hall, with that ... that odious bird?" He nodded. Though confounded to hear this I carried on, "Well what about the infant? At one point of the ritual I thought ... it was real."

"It was. That's why I hunt the murderous scum down and kill them whenever I get the chance."

"Sweet mother of God!"

Not surprisingly my ear-splitting outburst caused a church warden to come over and ask what was wrong. Van Halestrom lied telling the man that I had a dementia known as, "Terretsia lacrobia. A vile sickness of the mind which forces its victims to make uncontrollable calls," as he put it and assured the warden that he was in full control of the situation and that he had brought me to the church as all scientific medicine had failed me and all we could do now was to throw my ravaged soul on the mercy of the Lord.

"A good Christian can never resist a challenge," he muttered, as the warden went to sit down and the priest appeared in the pulpit. The opening hymn began and the congregation was soon in full

---

[7] The Illuminati & the Founding Fathers of America. The extent to which the Bavarian Illuminati had penetrated revolutionary American politics via the Freemasons, of which all the founding fathers were members, is unknowable. However, Thomas Jefferson, as Ambassador to France between 1785-1789, knew Weishaupt and wrote sympathetically about his professed basic aim of '*making men wise and virtuous*' and contended that, unlike the new American republic, '*secretive methods were a necessity under the religious and aristocratic tyranny of Europe*'. Hundreds of conspiracy theories persist to this day concerning the Order's involvement with revolutionary America as many have noted the Masonic symbolism stamped into the Great Seal of the United States and even upon the street layout of Washington DC.

swing. Even if I had screamed 'bloody murder!' at the top of my voice no one would have been any the wiser such was the heartiness of the singing. I stood there in a motionless fit of delirium uselessly humming along. At one moment I felt as if I was losing my mind. Presented as I had been with these outrageous allegations to which I could think of no other reasonable explanation but that they might be true, when all around me was such innocence, was horror itself. A sweet little old lady smiled at me from the pew ahead. I gulped at her and stared out of a stained glass window depicting our Lord Jesus dying on the cross for our sins. After the hymns the priest delivered his sermon, of which I remember nothing, and soon the prayers began.

A small confessional was opened ten paces away at the side of the hall. For some reason Van Halestrom elbowed me towards it until I almost fell from my seat. I resisted at first irritably shaking my head at him but he seemed to insist. Eventually I gave in considering that at least in the cubicle I might be able to get some peace and solitude. If I were to let the Professor go before me I would still be here at Christmas waiting for him to receive absolution for his dark deeds. An old lady appeared from the door pausing briefly to cross her chest and I made my way over, let myself in and settled down on the bench.

After a moment the priest entered and sat down behind the screen. Another quiet moment passed before he spoke.

"It wasn't really me in the chapel last night."

I yanked my head away from the screen. Not only did the priest seem to know me but he had a woman's voice. I voice that I recognised. Though I knew it was impossible I was sure it was the lady-in-black. I clutched my forehead and wondered if this madness would ever end.

There was a pause before she spoke again, "I said, it wasn't really me at the chapel last night … Well it was but ...then it wasn't. Oh, I wish I had time to explain. Is that you, Herr Jungkinda?"

How could it be her? In the church of all places, in the confessional, impersonating a man of the cloth? When the last time I had seen her she was literally hanging off the end of my oldest friend. My mind was swamped with waves of conflicting emotions. It seemed as though it was becoming impossible to tell the difference between my irrational dreams and my absurd reality. I stumbled for something to say and ended up asking, "So, what are you doing here now, in a confessional, in St Bartholomew's Church?" On hearing my question I became determined to receive a proper answer and pressed on, "On a Sunday morning, two streets from my house, impersonating a priest? Why? Why? Why?"

She whispered breathlessly, "I came to see you. To explain what happened last night."

I lent closer to the screen desperately trying to see through it. "Well, I cannot see you - as usual. So you might as well tell me."

"There is no time. I must leave right away."

I sighed, "Well, sorry, but it all seems a bit of a waste of time, doesn't it, really? I mean; if you wanted to talk to me, why did you not come as a normal parishioner? We could have done that, like normal people do, probably - somewhere in the world." Realising this sounded perhaps too wistful I pulled myself together and pulled my ear to the screen listening intently for her answer.

It came quickly, gasping, "I could not risk being spotted. There are Illuminati agents everywhere. You must be careful and do whatever the Professor tells you."

"We are already at the stage where he tells me what I will be doing in the future anyway. It would seem in many ways," I tried to hint as to my feelings for her, "... that I am no longer in possession of my own freewill."

I waited for a reply but this time here was none. After a moment I put my nose up to the screen and peered between the lattices but there was no one there. She had gone. It was the last straw for me that morning and I fully lost my mind.

"For the sweet love of Christ! Will someone tell me what in Hell's name is going on?"

I shouted this outrage so loudly that when I flung the door of confessional open the line of prospective confessors fairly jumped out of their shoes. In a frenzy of bewilderment I went to the first of these individuals and shook them violently, shouting, "Where is she? What have you done with her?"

Seeing my psychosis deepening Van Halestrom approached, obviously not wanting to cause any more of a scene than we had done already, if that was possible by this point, which admittedly it was probably not. He took hold my shoulders and insisted, "We should go now, Sebastian. There is nothing more we can do here."

"What do you mean, 'there's nothing we can do here?' We have to find her. She was here! Just now! I heard her voice speaking to me!"

Having lost control of my senses I was unable to realise how bad this sounded. Managing to break free from Van Halestrom I turned back to the confessional and threw open the door of the other side only to see, to my deepening confusion, an innocent looking priest adjusting his cassock. He smiled up at me oblivious of my irrational quest to find a vanishing woman and was therefore shocked as I hauled him up by his dog collar screaming, "What have you done to her? What have you done to that poor woman?"

The church has its limits too and this last particularly humiliating imposition on my behalf exceeded nearly every one. Considering the potential seriousness of my indiscretions I was lucky that the town's watchmen were not summoned once more. Who knows what the fine is for assaulting a priest? I'm sure it's a lot more than breaking a window and some chamber pots. We were eventually asked to leave although I'm certain we would have been forced to go had the Professor not dragged me out of the place kicking and screaming and shouting oaths like a Prussian troubadour.

"Perhaps a different church would be best next Sunday," coughed the Professor as we walked away from St Bartholomew's. "There are actually seventeen churches in Ingolstadt."

I frowned at him ungraciously as he carried on, "Right, my lad, you probably need a proper meal and a good rest. You shall come back to my humble abode where, if you'll permit me, I shall try and make amends for the predicament you believe yourself to be in."

I had already endured enough of his riddles for one day and I shot him a glare to show it. He smiled, regardless of my disdain and concluded, "Do not fret, my lad. Everything will start falling into place soon then nothing will surprise you except what you are prepared to do about it."

With this he tapped his silver-headed cane twice on the cobbles whereupon; an expensive, black carriage drawn by a matching pair of fine black horses appeared from behind us. Of course this was a total surprise in itself thus ruining his promise and simultaneously removing any remaining credibility that he may have had. I sighed and raised an eyebrow as the driver promptly opened the door below him before resuming his impeccable posture. Van Halestrom gestured at the open door and begrudgingly I got in. He followed after me and I heard the crack of the whip as the carriage pulled away up the avenue of maple trees.

Chapter 9

The Castle Landfried

The black carriage quickly passed through the city gates and soon the walls of old Ingolstadt were far behind us. We carried on north travelling at a decent rate for the next hour. The flatter farmland, typical of the Danube, slowly changed into a series of steep sided valleys and presently we took a turn at a fork in the road and made our way into the hills. After a few miles I glimpsed a fabulous castle which we seemed inevitably headed toward for there was no other road than the solitary dusty track on which we journeyed. Half château, half splendid fortress, the building clung precariously to the top of a daunting shard of rock. Its turrets and pointed towers made for an impressive view set against the pine-covered valleys and the distant misty mountains to the East.

The Professor nodded at the imposing fort. "The Castle Landfried: Built some four hundred years ago by a local nobleman of the same name. According to all accounts he was the most evil of men who was in the habit of locking his detractors away in the castle dungeons, many of the poor souls never to be heard of again. He was a complete homicidal maniac but also an excellent architect. Though, perhaps unsurprisingly, you never hear about that."

The carriage swept ever upwards until finally passing over a spectacularly high bridge spanning a fearful canyon. Rumbling over the chasm I felt my habitual fear of heights briefly manifest itself before, with another insistent crack of the driver's whip, we reached the other side. After the bridge we came to a pair of black wrought-iron gates surmounted by a crest of a two-headed eagle. I watched as the heads miraculously split in half and the gate opened by itself. Peering through the dust that kicked up behind us I stared on as the gates closed again. Intrigued, I turned up ahead and gazed at the castle's incredible towers reaching up into the sky like fingers of an enormous armoured glove. The carriage rattled under a portcullis into an outer courtyard and through a second archway set in a thick wall. With an abrupt "Whoa!" from the driver we slowed to the foot of a broad stone staircase leading up to a pair of gigantic oak doors.

From a smaller door set within these a smartly dressed old servant had appeared and was making his way down to us.

He was by the carriage door when we stopped and opened it, greeting his master, "Good day, sir." Upon seeing me he added, slightly condescendingly, "I see you have brought a guest, sir. Does this mean you would like me to set the table for two?"

"That's right, Bacon. Our guest will be staying the night. Please prepare the Günter suite for him."

I stepped down from the carriage staring up at the awe-inspiring castle. The masonry seemed perfect in every detail. Splendid fortified walls surrounded the courtyard which was all but empty apart from an old magnolia tree scattering the last of its blossom across the cobbles. Van Halestrom jumped down from the coach and called to the driver, "Klaus. You may take the rest of the day off. We shall not be needing you any longer."

With a wry smile the driver led the carriage out of the courtyard.

After admiring the fort's exceptional architecture for a moment longer I could not help but declare, "It is a truly extraordinary building, Herr Professor."

At which his older servant, who was making his way up the stairs, muttered, "That costs a fortune to heat in the winter."

I faced Van Halestrom in consternation. His servant had publicly cheeked him. Surely he should be immediately reprimanded so as to set an example to the other staff. I had already noticed the Professor's relaxed attitude to his driver. I was determined to tell him that this wouldn't do.

I piped up but out of earshot of the elderly rogue, not wanting to overstep my mark, "Surely, sir you should punish your servant for his impudence?"

Somehow the old fart still heard me from twenty paces away and replied, "I'm a butler, not a servant, and he knows there's no point in complaining. I'm too old to change."

This rudeness was intolerable and I went to argue my case for reprimanding the scoundrel. But before I could Van Halestrom raised a finger, "He's from England. Very good really, couldn't run the place without him. Remember, Sebastian, nothing is *ever* truly what it seems."

I couldn't imagine what this had to do with letting your servant back-chat you and gave up with a shrug of exasperation. We climbed the stairs behind the old man and filed through the small door and into a long hallway, the stone walls of which were covered by the stuffed animal heads including wild boar and antelope and a few species that I did not even recognise.

"I didn't kill them," mentioned the Professor gesturing at the wild, frozen faces. "Hunting animals for pleasure is not a pastime I would whole-heartedly encourage anyone to partake in but they do give the place a certain ambience."

"But how is a man meant to test himself and hone his skills for the battlefield, to say nothing of feeding himself, without the thrill of the hunt?"

"There are many ways to simulate the hunting process, Herr Drechsler. There is also other much more important prey than helpless animals."

We turned into a cosy study off the hallway. He offered me a deep leather chair set in front of a fireplace so big that both of us, and even the obnoxious servant, could have easily stood up in it had there not been a fire already blazing on the hearth. The Professor lit his pipe with a taper and took down a handful of papers from the mantelpiece. He went through them muttering to himself "Bill, bill, bill." After a while he sighed, "Sometimes, Herr Drechsler, I feel like old Luther."

I didn't understand this remark and urged him to explain with an uncertain nod.

"Wherever I go there seems to be a huge bill in front of me," he mimed hammering an imaginary nail into the wall.

"I think I understand. Do you mean when the protestant reformist fixed his proclamation of religious freedom to the door of Wartburg church in 1517?"

"The very same, lad: You are obviously well educated though your sense of humour sometimes also reminds me of old Luther."

To my surprise he threw the papers into the fire.

"Is that not a little rash, sir?" I asked, worried by his irresponsible behaviour.

"Why do you think I live in a castle?" he replied bluntly. "The truth of the matter, Herr Drechsler is that the vast proportion of the money being sought from me by my debtors is, in fact, payment for the unnecessary war fought against Austria for the succession and, as such, is a financial illusion. A monetary phantom dreamt up by economic vampires who wish to suck out the life blood of the country. I have spent much time and effort confiscating money from my enemies and do not intend to give it them back in the form of taxes."

With this he picked up a poker by the fire and agitated the coals sending a cloud of glowing embers flying up the chimney.

"But surely," I contested, "The state cannot function without the taxes of the people of whom it is the master."

"There's no master to it, my lad. The taxes claimed merely service usurious levels of interest on a series of unnecessary loans. The criminals who own this debt also control the amount of money in the system which effectively turns the 'people,' as you put it, into fiscal slaves. This is the hidden conspiracy of capitalism. I believe that somehow it was the reason for your foreboding dream and it is also how the Illuminati plan to rule the world."

I shuddered recalling my hideous nightmare and ventured, "Sir, it would seem that every theme I begin upon quickly leads back to the Illuminati."

"That's because everything does lead back to the Illuminati. They are the sprawling evilness behind most that is bad on this earth, possessing the power to corrupt even international heads of state and royalty from the shadows. As one tentacle of their evil order creates war and revolution another causes stock market crashes while yet another swoops in to collect the debt. Like a deathly plague they will continue to ravage all they infect until they are stopped. That's why you are here."

"I don't understand, Herr Professor. Why am I here?"

"To learn how to fight them."

"Me? Fight against them? How and with what? All you gave me was a single flintlock. How am I expected to stop an international gang of murderers who can supposedly control the Kings of Europe?"

"With a little help from your friends." He flashed an optimistic grin. As he did his servant appeared at the door.

"Dinner is served, sir."

"Thank you, Bacon," Van Halestrom gestured to the next room, "Shall we?"

We moved to a banqueting hall overlooking the fabulous mountainside and sat at opposite ends of a large oak table. Over dinner the Professor was at pains to direct the conversation away from more pressing matters and we talked in depth on a host of different topics. These discussions lasted for so long that the sun was already going down by the time we withdrew back to the cosy study where the large fire continued to blaze. Sitting in the pair of leather chairs we digested what had been a fully comprehensive meal with so many courses I had lost count. I must have eaten more that day than I had done in a week back in Ingolstadt. I tried to hide a rather large and vaporous fart not wishing to offend my host.

Without taking his attention from the fire the Professor murmured, "No need to hold them in, my lad. There's only me here and I don't mind."

I was still finding it difficult to keep a secret from the old man. Glancing at the gloomy portrait hanging over the fireplace I attempted to change the subject. "Who's the character in the picture, Herr Van Halestrom?"

"It is the old landlord himself. Count Theodor Vladimir Landfried the third, a thoroughly ruthless villain of Russian extraction. During his heinous life he tortured and murdered hundreds of innocents terrorising the local population with a series of horrific pogroms and witch-hunts. In fact, such was the blood-curdling callousness of his atrocities, that they were responsible for perpetuating the myth of the vampire in the area."

I shifted uneasily in my seat and stared up at the painting as a blast of wind moaned in the old chimney. "It's not the sort of painting one would normally hang in the room they visited before going to bed, Professor."

"Ah, but mad aristocrats and even mythical vampires are nothing compared to the monsters that we face. For unlike the madman they are cunning, organised and extremely sophisticated and unlike vampires, they are real and not invented."

The flames threw flickering patterns across his face as a lone crack from the fire cut through the quiet. I leant closer and whispered, "You mean the Illuminati?"

"Yes my lad. The Illuminati," he turned to me with the fire dancing in his hawkish eyes and began. "The real vampires are descendants of a people known as the Thirteenth Tribe who originated from a region east of the Black Sea known as Khazaria. In 740 AD, it is thought that their ruler; King Bulan adopted

Judaism as a political strategy to protect his country from the threat of Christian warlords to the West and Muslim hordes to the East. But the real truth is that, unknown to his people, King Bulan and an inner circle of occult priests worshipped the wicked mysticism of the Kabbalah and, somehow during their dark rituals, discovered the secret of setting the great civilisations of the earth against each other enabling them to take control of the world. Though, it is no secret but simply a devastatingly effective plan. You see they believed that Adam, God's first man, is simply a microcosm of the entire human race and that, as Adam was led to dissolution, then so can man be. For like Adam man is fundamentally weak and by using his frailties against him; greed, lust, wrath, pride he can be led astray. In the macrocosm of the world the Illuminati plan to achieve this by providing mankind with sets of opposing and flawed political philosophies. All the time secretly funding both sides from behind the scenes with the great power of capitalism accrued over many centuries through fraudulent money lending. In time these ideologies, containing ever larger parts of civilisation, will annihilate each other until, in the end, only pure capitalism remains. It will then be offered as the only possible solution to cure man's material and philosophical woes. Wrongly believing this to be his true destiny, man will accept the cult of money and with the Illuminati controlling the world's wealth they will become the master and mankind will unwittingly become the slave. Man, like Adam, will have been led astray. As man becomes illuminated he will thus succumb to the doctrine of Lucifer but instead of being brought into the light the world will actually slide into darkness and total oblivion." *[8]

A timely crack from the fire punctuated the Professor's monologue and he sat staring into the flames. By this point the hairs were standing up on the back of my neck but he was not finished and after a breath he carried on, "Even as I speak Weishaupt seeks to

---

[8] Khazaria: Birth of the Illuminati. As S. Drechsler describes the thirteenth tribe originated from Khazaria and King Bulan oversaw the country's conversion to Judaism in 740 AD. Much speculation exists about the 'secret hand' of the Khazarians and these conspiracy theories also include more radical claims; for example that descendants of the tribe have a controlling influence over modern history and contemporary geopolitical events. There is also a wealth of information concerning Illuminati and Luciferian interpretations of the Kabbalah.

ferment revolutions around the world, creating new republics in France and the Americas so as to balance them with the ancient regimes of Europe. Soon these states will be turned on each other so that after endless wars and suffering their peoples are eventually brought to their knees under the yoke of his rancid order."

I was struggling to absorb the magnitude of such evilness, though for some reason it was the theological points that seemed to sink in first, and I could not help but ask, "So, you are saying, sir, that the Illuminati are Luciferians?"

The Professor stroked his beard before carrying on, "It is, perhaps, not as simple as you may first think. The Illuminati believe that Adonai, or the Biblical God to you and me, is, in fact, the God of darkness and ignorance and that their God is the bringer of the light and wisdom. For it is he who bears the light revealing man's true nature is one of sin. In the eyes of the Illuminati dark is light and light is dark: Deus est Satan inversus or God is Satan reversed."

Only the sound of the fire stirring in the hearth filled the silence that hung between us. Though I understood what the Professor had said, I was sure he had not actually answered my question and so, with growing trepidation, I asked once more, "Sir, are you saying that the Illuminati are Luciferians?"

"Oh yes, my boy: They are definitely Luciferians."

"Good God!"

This was definitely not what a man wishes to hear before finding his bed in an old castle; that the madman and the evil organisation bent on killing him and taking over the world were Devil worshippers. Is this what Weishaupt had meant when he had said 'God of Nature'?

The Professor, seeing my growing consternation, dismissed it with a wave of his hand. "Look, my lad. Whatever you believe, whether you believe there is a God in Heaven and a Devil presiding over Hell, what we are actually fighting against here on earth possesses a much greater threat than Lucifer or even vampires ever could. No. The enemy which we face is the most cruel, vicious, resourceful, relentless, selfish and determined in the world. For what we are up against is the very weakness of man himself and remember, Sebastian that includes the weakness in me and in you."

This final point was lost on me such was my rapidly increasing sense of foreboding. Thunder and lightning! Was it true? The

Illuminati: Luciferians? I could not help but stare back at old Theodor's forbidding portrait, the whites of his mad eyes still terrifying after hundreds of years. And this mass murderer was apparently *nothing* compared to the real enemy that we faced.

Feeling decidedly uncomfortable I sat listening to the crackling fire and the wind rushing up the chimney while Van Halestrom slipped into stern contemplation. It had already been a long day and for once my urge to discover more about my new world seemed to wane as it dawned on me that I had probably heard enough for now. I finished my brandy and, after a small bow, wished Van Halestrom goodnight. Taking a candlestick from the next room I recalled the directions I'd been given and found my way to the Günter suite at the top of the most remote tower in the castle.

On opening the door I was startled by an eerie shadow of a grand old four-poster bed cast on the wall by my candle. But after undressing I snuggled in between the sheets which, to my happy surprise, had been warmed and were of such fine quality that they caused me great feelings of comfort especially after the unsettling stories I had heard. I prayed that the old building could protect me from all the darkness that lurked outside. Though my mind was seething with evil visions my body yearned for rest. I yawned deeply wondering what new revelations were to come the following day. Whatever it was it meant missing several lectures at university so at least I could take solace in that. This must have been the last thought I had before falling into a long, deep and thankfully dreamless sleep.

Chapter 10

A Little Education Can Be a Dangerous Thing

I was woken by a swish as Bacon pulled the curtains apart filling the room with bright morning sunshine. Lifting myself on one arm I used the other to cover my eyes as the servant informed me, "Good morning, Herr Drechsler. I believe the Professor has something to show you on the main terrace."

I got up, washed and dressed then went to find Van Halestrom. Annoyingly the butler, as I had been told to refer to him, neglected to tell me exactly where the main terrace was, no doubt out of sheer bloody mindedness and such was the size of the castle it took me a full ten minutes to find my host. In the end it was the noise that gave away his location. Whilst searching about I heard a series of commands wafting down an arched hallway and followed the sounds out onto a large sunlit terrace overlooking the valley.

"Pull!" Called the Professor and I saw a small plate fly into the azure sky then explode into myriad pieces after hearing the same swishing sound from over my shoulder as I had heard two nights before. I turned to see Van Halestrom armed with an elaborate crossbow of a type I had never seen. After a quick inspection I noticed it had four bows and therefore, I guessed, the capacity to fire several bolts without having to be reloaded. 'That looks like a handy bit of kit,' I said to myself as the Professor beckoned me over. I strolled toward him and spotted Klaus, the driver, on the other end of the terrace loading some sort of catapult with a pile of plates.

"Good morning, Herr Drechsler," greeted the Professor. "What a splendid day to begin your first class. I think you'll agree weather conditions are perfect for the ancient and most noble sport of archery."

I inspected the fascinating weapon closely. It had what I believed must be a sight fashioned from a telescopic monocular mounted on the top. I was quite itching to have a go. The Professor recognised this, as would a child, and offered me the bow. "She's all yours, my lad. Remember, squeeze. Don't pull. Just like a woman."

I placed the heavy crossbow under my chin and peered down the telescope at Klaus's magnified and rather anxious expression.

"Steady, Herr Drechsler," directed Van Halestrom, "Remember we are simulating the hunt."

"Of course, sorry, sir." I pointed the weapon at the blue yonder. "But there is nothing else on which to focus. Not even a cloud."

"We shall produce a target. Now try to follow the plate in the viewfinder and shoot a little ahead of it."

"Ready when you are," I replied.

Van Halestrom called, "Pull," and I saw the plate flash beyond the lens. I over-compensated, passed back in front of it, pulled instead of squeezing and shot my bolt too early. The arrow missed and flew harmlessly by.

"Remember, just like a woman," reminded the Professor.

I frowned at the crossbow. "I'm glad to see these arrows are made from wood, Herr Professor. How many more shots do I have?"

"Only two left. Try not to waste the next one. Here it comes," he paused momentarily before crying, "Pull!"

This time I anticipated the trajectory more successfully but still fired a touch too early. The arrow clipped the plate slightly altering its direction before falling away.

"Good shot, lad! You're obviously a natural," he cheered and nodded, "Had a feeling you were. Here," and beckoned at the bow which I passed back.

"Put a double in this time, Klaus, if you please."

Van Halestrom reloaded the bow with its clever system of levers and pulleys then placed a couple of arrows on their stays. He composed himself before calling out, "Pull!" This time two plates flew out in opposite directions. For an older man Van Halestrom's actions were remarkably agile. In a flurry of movement he rapidly let off two shots successfully destroying both targets. To my astonishment he then span on his heel and fired again, this time one-handed and from his waist; the last bolt cleanly removing the head of a small stone statue on a plinth behind us.

"Excellent!" I clamoured, thrilled by such murderous dexterity. Who would have thought this old scholar could be such a deadly marksman and armed with this weapon he was certainly a formidable opponent. It seemed like some secret to have and I felt myself rethinking my opinion of the man yet again.

As these thoughts coalesced, I suddenly realised Bacon was

standing but four paces from the decapitated statuette with a look of complete contempt on his face. I was surprised when he did not flinch but simply rolled his eyes and announced, with an air of thorough disdain, "Breakfast is served, sir."

Van Halestrom went to appease the veteran servant. "Sorry, Bacon I didn't see you there. Anyway, you never did like that statue of Cupid. You said it yourself, the other week, remember? That it was a revoltingly salacious piece of pot only fit for a vulgarian."

The impudent butler had already rudely turned his back on his master and was making his way inside. He replied idly over his shoulder, in his excruciatingly condescending tone, "Yes, of course, sir."

Although his master had nearly shot him it was still a bare-faced piece of impertinence and I couldn't help but complain, "Can you not condition that man of yours, Professor? It would seem that this fellow has the upper hand in nearly all your relations with him."

Van Halestrom answered firmly, "First, Herr Drechsler, he is not mine and second, in my affairs no one is high and no one is low. We are all employed here in our labours as equals, if not in wealth then in favour. I believe the working man must have the same rights as all others. Anything else breeds discontent and eventually irreconcilable differences. Bacon is the finest of stewards, Sebastian and you will find that out in time. For now you must get used to him. After all it is just his way."

It seemed to me that the servant had enough bad manners to fill both St Mark's and Peter's square. I mulled over this unnatural social order trying to appreciate the concepts the Professor had attempted to explain to me but I was having difficulty. In the Professor's position I would have simply sacked the insolent old rascal and brought in a more servile replacement. Then I remembered Van Halestrom's words, 'Nothing is *ever* what it seems,' and tried to reserve judgement for another time.

While we ate a hearty breakfast the Professor explained to me that his plate-launching catapult was inspired by Archimedes, his favourite of the ancient Greek scholars. He told me of the great battles the inventor had helped win in order to defend his home city of Syracuse from the might of the Roman Empire before tragically being killed by an invading centurion for refusing to stop his studies. Also how, before his untimely death, he had produced many incredible leaps in technology and thinking that have furthered the ascent of man; the water pumping screw, the lever, and the mathematical formulae for density and volume, both miraculous achievements in themselves.

Listening to the Professor speak was like being showered by a great fountain of knowledge; a constant flow which never once decreased through our long friendship. Even to this day, some sixty years later, I still remember the wisdom he bestowed on me across the table in that sunny room in the Castle Landfried.

After breakfast the Professor led me through to the next room where a blackboard had been erected. Written upon it was a timetable for my week's indoctrination into his crafts which Van Halestrom took time to explain. I was to spend the rest of this first day becoming fully familiar with the quadre bow. On Tuesday I was to be introduced to explosives, poison and a variety of other dark weaponry. Wednesday would be taken up by a hike through the countryside culminating in a rock climb where I would familiarise myself with the use of safety ropes and basic mountaineering techniques. Thursday I was to be taught by Klaus to master the reins of the carriage and receive a course in evasive driving skills then on Friday I was to have a five hour fencing, axe and knife lesson. When it came to Saturday the Professor was much vaguer in his planning and suggested that the activities for that day had not been chosen yet but that I should expect something a little different. I was to be paid ten thalers a day for my time at the castle receiving this money at the end of the week and every night, after my lessons, I would be taught in the ways of the Illuminati.

As we went through the week's activities I became increasingly excited, feeling that fate had placed me in front of a door that would lead to my new self. All I had to do was to go through it. When the Professor had finished he asked me if I had any questions and I told him, "My only reservation, sir, is that my studies do not suffer as a result of my time here in your service and that my parents do not discover my absence from the university."

"Those matters have been taken care of, my lad," he said, with a confident wave of the hand. "I have made the necessary communications with your lecturers and a plan has already been resolved to alleviate the need for you to attend your classes this week."

I wondered what he meant by this but relaxed knowing that Van Halestrom had enough influence at the university to make his claims a reality.

"There is one more thing, Professor," I asked sheepishly.

"Oh that. Of course, I wondered when you were going to ask. Yes, Sebastian, do not fear you will be seeing her again very soon."

Remarkably, he had done it again. The wily old bird new exactly what was on my mind – the-lady-in-black. I nodded at him acknowledging that I understood. We made our way back to the main terrace where a large bucket of wooden arrows were now placed next to the daunting crossbow. Forty paces away Klaus knelt by the horizontal catapult with several stacks of the plates piled up beside him and I noticed three round straw targets on stands set up at different ranges along the patio. 'This is what studying should be like,' I said to myself and walked over to the weapon flexing my fingers.

The next five days were some of the most hard-working, terrifying, and enjoyable times of my young life and during this time I formed a deep bond with the amiable Professor. It was hard not to. Although he was my social superior he actively encouraged my dissension with laughter unlike my father who was definitely not of such a disposition. While at times it was impossible not to exchange harsh words due to the nature of the training, it was always in a way that left no ill feeling between us. As I came to understand this strange social order I relaxed and began to learn more quickly. The good Professor actually seemed to enjoy the lively back chat which he regularly induced in me after making one of his seemingly over-simplistic remarks with regard to how easy something should be.

For, although I did find a natural empathy with the quadre bow as he had predicted, some of the other skills were a lot harder for me to perfect on such a rapid basis. And so his constant over use of the word 'just' frequently aroused my temper; 'just' hit the target, 'just' mix the potion, 'just' climb the rope while I swung around helplessly at the end of a pathetically thin piece of twine four-hundred feet above the village of Bisenhard from an escarpment he had informed me was known locally as, "The fissure of death," and responsible for, "the demise of many a poor mountaineer throughout its gruesome history," with my fear of heights making me consider suicide a veritable pleasure.

In the evenings in front of the fire the Professor carried on teaching me about the Illuminati. He told me of their strange accordance with occult religious practices such as the Zoroastrian calendar like I had seen in Weishaupt's room. Also he explained that to aid the secrecy of the organisation the leaders had chosen code names for themselves after the greats of antiquity; Philo, Cato, and Hannibal with Weishaupt arrogantly titling himself Spartacus. They also had coded words for locations too; Munich was Athens, Ingolstadt was Ephesus and Bavaria was Achaia. *[9]

After a while I felt I was beginning to understand the sinister workings of the order and he explained to me how such knowledge sets one aside from the man in the street who is typically unaware of the fraudulent powers that are really manipulating the rulers of the world right under his nose. In turn, this great ignorance in the populous can produce a kind of madness in the recipient of the information. A feeling such as I had experienced in the church. Because so many folk are not prepared to believe in what you know, by telling them you run the risk of alienating those around you, so it was generally best to be clandestine about such beliefs.

It was unnerving at times but I took to the subject with great interest and soon found myself becoming greatly intrigued by the conspiracy. Though I felt somehow Van Halestrom's obsessive will for its destruction still remained something of a mystery.

On the Friday night it occurred to me how quickly my time at the castle had gone by. I knew I was going to miss the lessons and the challenges that had been so enjoyable to overcome. Another thing I was going to miss were the three large meals a day, a fire in every room and a huge four-poster bed that was inexplicably warmed for me and always covered in the finest, fresh smelling linen. I grimaced at the thought of having to return to my more modest lodgings back in town. The thought of splashing cold water on my face in my draughty little room at Frau Warburg's made me shudder.

---

[9] Weishaupt's Illuminati codename. S. Drechsler's recollections are accurate here. Adam Weishaupt's codename in the Illuminati was Spartacus, after the revolutionary Thracian gladiator who led a slave uprising against the Roman Empire. Other leading lights in the order also took their secret titles from antiquity: Baron Von Knigge; Philo. Baron Barrusus; Cato: etc. Ancient pseudonyms were also used for cities and states. For instance Munich was known as Athens, Frankfurt as Thebes and, as the author points out, Bavaria was Achaia.

I sat on the end of the four poster bed in my nightshirt holding up my candle to look around the room for the last time. I was to leave the castle tomorrow and perform my next errand for the Professor as soon as the lesson of the day had been completed. After this I was to return to my own lodgings and begin going about my normal business as I had before.

I sighed contemplating the end of my temporary life as a gentleman when oddly there was a quiet knock at the door. I made my way over to see who it could be at this late hour. It was well past midnight and the house was usually asleep by this time. On opening it I was surprised to see Bacon's ghostly old face lit by his lantern. Before I could speak he offered me a thick folder of manuscripts saying, "I think you'll find that it is all up to date, sir."

I took the papers and inspected them. On the first page was a résumé of my timetable at university with a list of subjects covered. I hastily began leafing through the documents. Though the hand writing was that of another and the language was slightly different to my own they were copies of the essays I had been set over the last week. As the revelation dawned on me I unthinkingly murmured, "These could be handy."

As soon as I said it I realised it was too much of a coincidence. But before I could explain myself the sardonic butler pointed out, "That was, indeed, the intention, sir." I frowned, somewhat upset that I had not understood quicker as he carried on, "I think you'll find these writings sufficiently robust to deceive your tutors, sir. I have also taken the liberty of rewriting some of your earlier work that had not yet been handed in. You were quite wrong, I believe, in your theories concerning the philosopher Aristotle and his opinions on freewill so I have made the necessary amendments."

I stared at the stack of papers as his words sank in. Was it true? It seemed to be. I looked closer. What everything? Yes! It was all there. Reaching the bottom of the pile I was astonished to discover all the remaining work I was to have completed before my exams. Elation swept through me as I realised the butler's role in it. He must have done this himself. The Professor and Klaus had been too busy teaching me; he was the only one who could have authored the manuscripts. While I had been leafing through the folder he had quietly slipped away. I peered down and watched the faint ball of light descending the spiral stairs still bright enough to make out his wiry frame.

"Thank you, Bacon," I whispered.

The ball of light paused for a second and I heard a derisive, "Yes, sir," waft up to me before the glowing sphere gradually faded and disappeared. I returned to my room with the bulging folder squeezed tight to my chest. Van Halestrom was right again. Bacon was indeed an excellent steward!

Chapter 11

The Serpent was the More Subtil

I could not have been in a better frame of mind on the morning of my last day at the castle. With the year's course work complete, a full month left to prepare for exams, plenty of money in my purse and a week of healthy exercise and top nosh under my skin to boot I was as happy as Ludwig. The dreadful events of the previous week had faded from my mind, even after the lessons I had received about the evil Illuminati. Their threat somehow seemed very far away and I sat up in the bed with my hands behind my head confidently greeting Bacon as he opened the curtains. My mood was further buoyed by the fact I suspected another rendezvous with my lady-in-black was imminent. After her pleas of innocence in the confessional at St Bartholomew's I felt I could once again enjoy the promise of her enticing sauciness. Yes, it was true, like the sturdy castle around me I was on top of the world that sunny morning.

The day began well enough with breakfast as usual, though Bacon had told me the Professor would not be joining me for some unknown reason. After eating alone I made my way to a veranda that had become a favourite place of mine. It was a small balcony complete with a telescope on a stand overlooking the winding track leading up to the fortress. I strolled up to the telescope and bent down with my hands behind my back placing my eye to the lens. As I did I was shocked to see in the viewfinder, a beautiful woman wearing a powdered wig and a stylish yellow dress. I looked again but now frustratingly her attractive features were partially obscured by a white parasol though, in an extraordinarily low cut frock, her sweet and heaving bosom was all but fully revealed to me. It appeared that the damsel was in some distress as she anxiously waved a gloved hand in my direction.

'Good Gracious,' I thought, 'a beautiful woman in trouble all the way out here? And no one but myself to help her for miles around.' This was true. I had no idea where Bacon or the Professor was. I moved the telescope slightly to see that the maiden was standing next to a driverless carriage that looked as though it had been ransacked. Rising from the telescope I waved back in the lady's direction but as I squinted into the distance I realised it was too far to see her without the benefit of the lens. In a flash I decided it was time for action and ran down to the stables.

Within two taps of a tinker's hammer I was trotting under the castle's portcullis on a fresh young filly determined to rescue this woman from her dilemma. I was sure the grateful lady would be inclined to let me charm her with my new sense of confidence and apparent wealth. Maybe even give me a little reward as well. After making sure that I had the key to the gate in my back pocket - having found out that only the Professor's coach automatically opened it - I rode off down the path and over the bridge pushing the horse to a gallop as the enticing possibilities revealed themselves.

I soon found the abandoned coach by the side of the road but disappointingly there was no grateful maiden to thank me for my trouble. I got down from the horse and seeing several discarded garments on the ground, idly lifted one of them with the barrel of a pistol I had brought along. I checked around for the lady then led the filly along the path with the gun at the ready just in case there were bandits skulking round the next bend. That's when I saw her. Somehow she was now standing on a huge boulder on the far side of the road which meant there was a mountain stream running between us. I remember thinking, 'How did she get there?' but there was no time to ask.

She excitedly waved at me obviously relieved to see her saviour and squealed, "Thank heavens above; a fine and decent man who can properly come to a woman's aid. Oh, it is my great good fortune you are here, sir." She blew a kiss from under her parasol and waved again. From this close range I could not help but see how her bosom heaved. Her accent was Spanish but she had quite a good command of our language and spoke breathlessly before I had chance to reply. "I waved at the castle because it was the only place I could imagine there would be someone. As you can see I've been robbed. There were two beastly villains with guns. They took everything I had and chased my pathetic driver away. Now the coward has not returned and I am stranded here helpless."

Time to play the hero I reckoned. Unusually for me, I lowered my voice a little to further impress the woman and reassured her, "Fear not, my good lady. I shall soon make everything better. The first thing we must do is remove you from that rock."

"I cannot get down. I have already tried, sir. I think I will need to be carried."

There was a short pause as I looked at the stream then back at the woman. She seemed to share my concern and after glancing down at the river then back at me she asked, "You do think you can do it don't you?"

"Of course I can," I declared, proudly speaking from my chest. Taking one more look at the stream I stuck the gun inside my belt figuring that I could jump the stream to the delectable woman then sort the rest out when I got there. I took a few steps back, made a run for it and leapt onto the boulder landing at the woman's feet with a slap. Unfortunately, I could not grip the rock's smooth face and slowly descended into the stream. The temptress looked down at me with a finger on her dainty lip and sighed, "Oh," as I felt the cold water chill through my lower half. Once at the bottom I looked up at her with a frown and steadily managed to inch my way out, pulling myself with great effort back to her feet. When I raised myself up onto my haunches she immediately knelt down to me brushing her breasts across my face as she did.

"Oh, thank you, thank you, kind sir." She squeezed me while I was still on my knees fully enveloping my face in her cleavage. I slowly stood up as the woman chattered, "Oh but, sir, when the robbers came they threw my vanity case over this rock behind me and it has my jewellery in it. Will you find it for me?"

She was already helping me up the boulder with a hand at my waist. I glimpsed at her pretty face under her parasol but I could only see her lips pouting coquettishly, "Oh, thank you, sir. You *will* be my special one for this favour."

Motivated once more by this encouragement and another firm push on my backside, I carried on up the boulder and quickly reached the top. Whereupon I saw a small wooden chest banded with iron. 'That was easy,' I thought and knelt down beside the box giving it a shake to see if it was empty. There certainly seemed to be something inside so I undid the clasp and lifted the lid.

'Boom!' There was an enormous explosion, I think. I'm not really sure what happened next; it seemed as though it was an enormous explosion but it was probably tiny for if it had of been of any sizeable proportions I probably would not be here today.

However the blast was strong enough to throw me backwards and, after falling head over heels, I inevitably repeated my slide back down the face of the boulder before splashing into the brook fully submerging this time. When I resurfaced, coughing and spluttering for air and nursing my wounds - damn it if the blasted lady, if indeed she ever was one, was sitting on my horse with her legs crossed spinning her white parasol on her shoulder and laughing at me. I pulled the gun out of my belt even though it was soaked and therefore useless. Seeing the pathetic weapon she laughed even harder and I looked down at the gun in disgust and threw it in the stream. She howled uproariously at this and I pulled myself from the water.

"You've obviously still got a long way to go, Herr *Wunda*kinder. It seems you have a simple face and a simple mind to match it."

I couldn't believe it. My-lady-in-black was now the seductress-in-yellow! I looked again. She blew me a kiss and chuckled to herself as she held out her beautiful face, now for the first time fully apparent to me, theatrically posing her hands around it in a mockingly provocative manner. This was extremely galling. She knew she had tricked me with her womanly ways and I had been a chump. I had even changed my blasted voice to impress her. How ridiculous. She had obviously greatly enjoyed the deception and the willing part I had played in my own downfall. To compound my humiliation the crafty wench slowly pulled the castle key from the depths of her cleavage and winked at me. Blast! She had managed to pickpocket the damn thing off me whilst I thought she was sizing up my athletic frame.

"Let's go back and see the Professor shall we? I'm sure he'll be interested to hear about this." In one graceful slide she dismounted my horse and marched off to the carriage. "You can take me there. That is; if you can drive?"

And so I had to suffer the ignominy of driving her back to the castle in her carriage and also the embarrassment of retrieving the key from her to re-enter the gate. The Professor had told me that I would be seeing her again 'very soon' but I had not expected this. Over the past week he had told me that the cocky woman was a most trusted member of our organisation and that they had worked together many times before. But I was mortified by the way I had been duped by her and the easiness with which this had been accomplished. With my head still hanging in shame we met with the Professor in the library some twenty minutes later.

"He's not good enough and you know it," griped the lady.

"He'll be fine on the night trust me. He always does the right thing in the end. Don't you, Herr Drechsler?"

I neither appreciated Van Halestrom patronising me or my lady's obvious doubt in my ability. I didn't want to lose the Professor's faith in me or the job which had been so profitable.

"If you merely need a messenger then I'm sure he's fit for purpose. But c'mon, he didn't even think it was strange that the telescope was already focused on me. Yet he couldn't have seen me without it. And once he was down there I could have tried a lot harder than I did to get him to open the box. My God! He didn't even know I had stolen the key to the castle. It was too easy. I don't want him around if he's going to be a liability."

"Yes, well he'll have to watch out for that won't he? But I'm sure his experiences this morning will make him think twice about doing something just because a beautiful woman has waved a dainty glove in his direction."

I hadn't been appreciating the way they were talking about me since we got to the library and finally showed it by petulantly folding my arms. There was a lingering pause as we all considered our positions. I could not help but glimpse at our gorgeous ally who had changed into a bright white shirt, riding breeches and knee-high leather boots. She was indeed a beauty; almost beyond compare. Tall, about five foot and nine inches, with flowing chestnut hair, a full but athletic figure she was as attractive a women as I had ever seen. There was also something else about this girl; a grit and determination and damn-it-all attitude that I had rarely met in any man let alone a woman. Her soulful eyes pierced through everything they beheld and she spoke passionately through a pair of glistening, cherry lips, the curl of which only a dead man would not enjoy.

She broke the silence, "So what are we going to do?"

"We carry on as planned. Sebastian will complete the task and we shall say no more about it. I need to be elsewhere and there is no other we can trust."

Fed up with my lowly position in the proceedings I snapped, "Is it fair that this person knows my name and that I do not know theirs?"

"It's Francesca. I have no care who knows it," she snorted,

rearing up like an imperious filly.

"Alright you two," arbitrated the Professor and took a deep breath turning to me. "Tonight, Sebastian, as you may have guessed, your task will be a bit different to the one I usually ask you to perform. I wish you to go to Weishaupt's secret lodge, known as the Golden Dawn situated twenty miles west of Regensburg and once there steal a manuscript. This document is known as the 'The Thirteen Protocols' and is of great importance to us. I haven't asked you to do anything like this before but it is my belief that you are ready to go to the next level. As an indication of my faith in you I will also double your wages to complete this task. We already have other agents there to aid you in your mission. They have been instructed to leave a window open for you and we believe there will be no one else there to hinder you. Because of this your safety will be assured. You will gain entry into the lodge after the papers are stored and Weishaupt and his cronies have adjourned to a meeting elsewhere in the building. After securing the manuscript you will take it to Frau Hoffmeister's safe house whereupon you will be instructed what to do next."

'Sounds easy enough,' I thought, 'don't know what all the fuss is about.'

Van Halestrom leant closer his eyes filling with stern resolve. "Remember, Sebastian, we cannot afford any mistakes tonight. This manuscript is of the utmost importance because within its pages are contained the proof of the devilish scheme to divide and conquer the great tribes of the world and lead them into eternal slavery."

"Right then," I said, looking between their serious faces.

Maybe that *was* a bit different after all. *[10]

---

[10] Weishaupt & The Lodge of The Golden Dawn. It is interesting that S. Drechsler recalls hearing this. It is hard to trace the exact origins of this sect. While mainstream historians record its inception as being in England in 1887 under the auspices of William Wyan Wescott there also exists some speculation that Weishaupt was responsible for its invention and that the order was a satanic cult which provided a meeting place for those with designs of spreading the Luciferian doctrine throughout the world.

Chapter 12

The Spear the Axe and the Arrow

The weather had turned as bad as the atmosphere between me and Francesca as we rode back to Ingolstadt on that Saturday evening. We had not exchanged a word since leaving the castle and the rain was beating down harder with every stride of our horses. At last we reached the Northern crossroads before the city gates and she pulled up her mount saying coldly, "This is where I leave you, Herr *Blunder* kinder but I'm sure I will have the misfortune of seeing you again somewhere soon."

With this she left and I watched her canter away with an unhappy sigh. Absolutely beautiful but, like most women I had met, totally impossible to understand. Though there was never another that had quite the same effect on me as Francesca Nicola Kropotkin. I trotted into the city and went to exchange the horse I had borrowed from the castle's stables for my own Petrova. Next, I visited my rooms around the corner as I wanted to find my lucky hat and the pistol the Professor had given me.

Leaving Petrova tied up outside I dashed up the stairs and into my room. Picking my hat up from the dresser I noticed a piece of paper wedged in the mirror. I stared at it for a moment before grabbing it and turning it over. My heart filled with horror for on it was the sign of the spear the axe and the arrow.

How was this here? Who had done this? I spun around half-expecting to see Adam Weishaupt standing there behind me. I glared at the paper and threw it away before flying down the stairs, bursting out of the front door, jumping on Petrova and galloping off.

This frightening invasion of privacy had introduced a new level of threat to my life and unsettled me to the core. Things were getting personal. They weren't just trying to kill me in the street now they were coming to my house - maybe to do it there. It was also this fright that caused me to make my first mistake working for the Professor. In my haste to leave my room I forgot the gun. It seems stupid now but I had been so surprised by the sign on my mirror that I neglected to find the pistol in my drawer. What a fateful error that was to prove. All I could think of at that moment were the atrocities at the chapel and everything the Professor had told me took on a sharper focus. But unaware of my foolish mistake I went on with my mission without a weapon. I leant down over Petrova's mane and squeezed my heels into her flanks urging her on; on to Weishaupt's Lodge of the Golden Dawn.

I arrived at the rendezvous a little early, as was my habit, to check the lay of the land. At least I believed it to be early; the star clock was useless as the weather was so abysmal. Looking up amidst the rain I could make out a procession of black clouds filling the sky. Not only was it pouring down but a tumultuous wind had also risen and howled through the branches of the trees under which I sheltered. I peered into the darkness barely able to make out the two flags that marked the lodge's location behind a thicket up ahead. My orders were to wait there until seeing a lantern flash twice, whereupon I was to move in and find a window that had been left open for me. At this point I would enter the building, grab the manuscript and make my getaway. At no time during my mission was I to actually see any of my accomplices so as not to compromise their identities but Van Halestrom had assured me that these agents could be relied upon to complete their tasks. This was comforting but I was certain that my lady Francesca would be also be there in some guise or another. No doubt wearing lewd attire and draped over some poor unsuspecting fool to trick, deceive or simply insult them as part of the plan. Though I was glad that she was on our side I hated the thought of her probable licentious behaviour, however feigned it was.

Staring towards the lodge in the darkness I wondered just what *was* going on in there. The Professor had been unspecific about the details of the meeting. Mentioning only that the manuscript was to be discussed by the assembly at the beginning of the evening then the party was to descend to another part of the building and this was to be the moment of my action. I waited nervously for the signal huddling in the rain behind the row of trees.

After what seemed like an age I finally saw the lantern flash up ahead, once, then twice. It was time to move. I led Petrova through the short meadow that lay between me and the thicket. As I grew closer I tried to make out the insignia on the flags hovering above the lodge as they thrashed around in the gale. I shuddered with fear when I realised they were emblazoned with the same ominous emblem of the spear the axe and the arrow that I had seen before. Most notably two hours ago on a parchment stuck to my blasted mirror. *[11]

For the first time I was scared. What was I doing? I glanced around uneasily. Was I really sneaking through a field in a storm in the middle of the night to steal something off my own lecturer a man of great importance who, not only could ruin me academically, but on good authority had also tried to and kill me and *especially* after I had received a mysterious warning note?

I squatted down, the seriousness of the situation suddenly forcing me to the ground. I took a swift breath of the damp night air and tried to bolster myself. 'C'mon Sebastian. The bastard did try to kill you. You at least owe it to him to pay him back by ruining his party.' Also, if I was successful, it might shut up the high and mighty two-faced 'Princess Francesca*lina,*' whilst proving my real worth to the Professor. Then who knows what I might achieve within his organisation? Though the bigger conspiracy was on my mind, at that moment I was more motivated by the respect that my heroism would engender from my colleagues. Especially Francesca, and obviously the small matter of the money had also to be considered. My thoughts coalesced into those of action. I had come this far all I had to do was walk into a room, pick up a piece of paper and leave fast. I could definitely do the last bit and I pictured myself sitting in the castle Landfried nonchalantly reading the document in front of a fawning Francesca who I imagined in a ridiculously alluring frock to give myself extra impetuous. That did the trick.

I rose with fresh determination and pulled Petrova behind me up to the edge of the thicket. After tying her to a tree I made my way

---

[11] The Spear the Axe and the Arrow: I can find no record of this particular combination of symbols being attributed to the Illuminati though the individual insignias go back to antiquity. The spear mounted with the Phrygian cap has had revolutionary symbolism for centuries. Since ancient Roman times the cap has represented those who seek liberty and was made infamous during the French revolution of 1789 with the red of the cap also being linked to Bolshevik and other communist insignia. The axe surrounded with the bundle of birch rods or fasces also has its roots in ancient Rome and was the symbol for strength and authority: Through many; strength. In the context of the story it is interesting as these insignia were to be used by opposing political ideologies; Communism; the red cap: Fascism: the fasces or bundle and the basis for the word 'Fascists.'

through the soaking undergrowth towards the lodge. The Professor had been right as usual and sent me on the correct course. For, although the foliage was so thick that I lost sight of the flag posts, when I appeared on the other side I was directly facing the building.

The storm had been worsening by the second but as I gazed into the darkness a flash of sheet lightning that lit up the scene as clear as a summer's day. I trembled at the sight seeing a dozen ghoulish figures in strange hooded robes in the driveway attending to a queue of carriages. I stared at the strange vision for a moment until instinctively ducking down as the proceeding thunderclap roared overhead. As far as I could tell there was no one else around the rest of the house. I strained in the gloom to see the gable end of the lodge where I was to make my entry. Sure enough, through the thicket, I spied an open window. The light from inside shone through the shutters which had been left slightly parted.

To my dismay the window was on the first floor which seemed a disastrous oversight. But after closer inspection I saw that, because the lodge was built into the side of the hill, the side of the thicket forty yards to my right was at the same height. I pushed my way up through the thorny bushes until I was level with the window. As I had guessed the bank was at the same height but it was still six feet from the wall leaving an alarming gap maybe twelve foot deep in between. After inspecting the various dimensions I realised I was going to have to jump for it. The leap would be difficult but not impossible as the large window had a deep ledge on which I could land.

Shuffling round I tried to make way for a run up but this was made difficult by the bushes which were very thick in all the wrong places. I checked to see if there was another option. There wasn't. I crouched down peering in through the opened shutters. Inside the room I could see a long table surrounded by several chairs. As I looked closer and at the far end of the table I spotted a parchment resting on a scroll box. It had to be the manuscript. I stood up. Right all I had to do was complete the jump. The rest was simple. If I got this bit right I would be back in Ingolstadt drinking at my favourite tavern before I knew it and another hundred thalers richer into the bargain. I took a deep breath and flexed my knees. Forcing my right leg back through the bushes as far as I could I steadied myself, put my head down and went to make my leap.

Chapter 13

The Lodge of the Golden Dawn

I landed on the window ledge with a grunt. Surprised at my athleticism I decided to congratulate myself. After all it was an impressive jump. 'Well done Seb!' I thought and of course that's when I lost my balance. So confident had I been that I was in equilibrium I had not bothered to hold on to anything and to my horror I started to fall backwards desperately flailing my arms around in an effort to stop myself. At the last moment I snapped out my hands and grabbed on to the shutters anxiously gasping, "Concentrate Seb!" before taking a couple of deep breaths and pulling myself inside. A feat in itself for the shutters swung heavily on their hinges as I went in the window and landed on the floor. I slowly stood up finding my bearings and took a few steps into the room.

Glancing down I saw my muddy footprints covering a beautiful Persian rug similar to the one in Weishaupt's office. I tiptoed round the chairs trying not to foul the carpet and approached the head of the table. The parchment was rolled into a cylinder containing several pages and tied with a broad red ribbon decorated with hieroglyphs.

As I leant over to pick it up and a mighty blast of wind slapped the shutters against their stays with a crash. I snapped my head round and as I did - damn it! I heard voices, lots of them, approaching fast. I hesitated and glanced at the manuscript then back at the window. Could I make it? I grimaced at my dirty footprints on the rug and bit my lip as the handle of the door on the far side of the room slowly started to twist. 'Not now! Not now!' I panicked, turning around to find a pair of handles in the wooden panelling of the wall behind me suggesting a small cupboard. I flung the doors open and slipped inside closing them as the voices entered the room.

My heart was banging along like a skeleton pleasuring itself in a biscuit tin, 'dang, dang, dang, dang!' I tried to control my panting to not to give myself away and also so I could hear the talking in the room. It was pitch-black inside the cupboard and I stood frozen like a statue listening to the muttering men milling around. I heard them taking their places and gradually a silence fell over them. I squatted down whereupon I was surprised to find a keyhole. Pulling my eye to it this was the amazing sight I saw.

There was a ring of thirteen men sitting around the table, all of them dressed in black gowns with pointed hoods and slits for the eyes. I thought this was handy as it might prevent them from seeing my footprints on the carpet. To my frustration I heard someone complaining about the draught and saw the shutters at the far end of the room being closed. Then with a sinking heart I heard a bolt brought down to lock them into place.

'Capital!' I whispered to myself and let out a silent groan. The talking died down and everyone settled in their places leaving a few sentinels in red robes standing behind the seated members. I guessed these men were of a lower order as they weren't allowed to sit. Now there was only one empty place; the chair directly in front of me at the head of the table behind which lay the document on the scroll box. I heard the door from the hallway open as the last of the mysterious bunch came in and sat down. When this particular individual entered a hush fell round the room and even from inside the cupboard I felt a presence had come amongst them.

There was a short pause before this man, dressed in a golden robe and sitting barely six foot away from me, addressed the meeting, "Good evening, Brothers." It was Weishaupt. I recognised him instantly. The blood chilled in my veins as he carried on, "This is a great night for this esteemed lodge and for the whole of our glorious organisation. Since the modern inception of our order in 1776 we have directed our labours towards this moment which we will look back upon in centuries to come as a pivotal point in the quest to reach our goals. Seven years ago you tasked me to revise the document in front of us: The Thirteen Protocols. The sacred text handed down through our sects' holy bloodlines through the ages which cite the methods by which we will rule over the Goyium and tonight we shall accept these new directives into our mighty fraternity as law. We shall do this in the usual way."

'What's the Goyium?' I wondered. Certain I was about to hear the secrets contained in the mysterious document I struggled to get a better view. However, to my frustration, it soon dawned on me that Weishaupt was reading it to himself. My suspicions were confirmed when after a couple of minutes I saw him pass it to the next hooded man on his left. Thunder and lightning! There must be some solemn vow of silence. I calculated two minutes each, thirteen of them. Damn it! This is going to take an age. Just my luck. *[12]

And so it was. I watched and waited as the parchments were passed slowly round the table in virtual silence as the members of the lodge coughed, scratched themselves and farted. Eventually, after what seemed an eternity, the protracted ceremony was over and Weishaupt spoke again, "Brothers, now that we have familiarised ourselves with the sacred text we shall move to the altar to sanctify the rite."

Finally the 'Brothers' got up and filed out of the room behind Weishaupt followed by the red sentinels and the last of these closed the door. "Thank God for that," I whispered and let out an extensive sigh of relief. I waited for a moment before coming out of the cupboard and putting the document in my satchel. Now I was more than ready to leave and darted over to the shutters but to my nightmarish terror found a huge padlock holding the bolts in place. I shook them to make sure but it was useless. They were locked tight.

Surely I was done for! Curse the stupid Professor! Curse this bit of paper! What difference could it make anyway? Apart from removing me from the rest of a life I had planned so hard to enjoy. I desperately retried the shutters but they were immoveable. I would have needed an axe to break out. What was I to do? I prowled round the table like a rat in a trap. How had I let this happen to me? I was about to drown myself in self-pity when I suddenly spotted some black robes hanging in the cupboard where I had been hiding. My heart leapt as I realised the chance this might afford me. I pulled open the doors revealing three robes in all and took the first. After checking I had no other option, which was obviously the case, I pulled the garment over my head.

A minute later dressed in the robe I peered out from the room down

---

[12] The Goyium. It is odd that Drechsler recalls Weishaupt using this term which originates in the Talmud and is not part of Bavarian (Austro-Prussian) dialect. Though, it is believed that Weishaupt was originally from Hebraic stock which might explain the usage of language here. There are many translations of this word. These range from 'nations', 'people', 'gentiles' and perhaps most unfortunately a derogatory slang usage of the word which translates as 'cattle,' though it is not mentioned on the Wikipedia site.

the empty hallway. Luckily there was no one around and I sneaked down the corridor leading to the top of the stairs. 'Where is everyone?' I asked myself, hastily descending towards the front door and freedom when to my eternal displeasure one of the hooded brothers came out and told me.

As I got to the bottom of the stairs he appeared from the shadows and grunted, "Hey. They're all waiting for you in the cellar."

I stood fixed to the spot not knowing what to do.

"Well what are you waiting for?" demanded the man.

I shrugged inside my robes which I was starting to realise were perhaps a size too big.

He thrust a tiny purple cushion at me that I involuntarily took and when he pointed to a door in the wall to my right I quickly ran over to it stupidly calling out, "Thanks."

Once through the door I carried on down a flight of stairs lined with lanterns, holding the cushion out in front of me like an idiot not knowing what to do from one moment to the next. I stopped at the bottom of the steps in front of a pair of curtains sensing this might be a good opportunity to turn back. Glancing behind me I was dismayed to hear some more voices coming down from above. Cursing my luck I took a deep breath, held out my cushion and went through the curtains.

Seeing thirty full grown men in hooded robes with slits for eyes all turn round to face you at once when you have just broken into their secret underground ritual is a sight that doesn't ever leave you. It's the sort of scene that has the visual potency to burn its way onto the retina of the mind years after many other memories have faded. Believe me.

Although utterly terrified at that moment somehow I did not pass out or go down on my knees begging them to, "Make it end. Make it end!" The robed men formed two lines in front of me as another came over and placed a horrible curved knife on the cushion. Remembering not to say 'Thanks' this time I slowly made my way between the lines of men towards the far end of the chamber. Out of the shadows ahead Adam Weishaupt appeared in his golden costume and went to stand behind an altar. With my heart pounding like a cannon at Waterloo he bade me approach and I wondered in what possible way this abhorrent set of circumstances could be any worse? I found out immediately as two red sentinels emerged next to him pulling along a beautiful naked woman in chains with a black silk bag pulled down over her head.

And me carrying a sacrificial knife! I nearly screamed inside my hood and barely managed to control myself. As I reached the altar the woman was put down on her knees. 'Sweet Jesus Christ save me from this horror!' I prayed as it suddenly dawned on me that this poor girl could actually be Francesca. Perhaps she had been caught and was now to be slain for her deception. But I could not tell. This was the part of my lady that I had never seen up to now so I simply did not know. Weishaupt took the knife uttering some rot about divine spirits of the irreverence's. I could not concentrate on his words such was my shock as I saw the girl's head tipped back by one of the red-robed devils.

I couldn't bear to watch anymore and shut my eyes tight. God save my mortal soul for not stopping that evil ritual but if I had reacted then both the girl and myself would have been lost. What could I have done? By thunder I was so scared I nearly wet myself. Perhaps I could have knocked Weishaupt over, even got the knife off him but there were thirty others who would have rendered any lone struggler useless. Anyway - it was already too late. There was a gruesome but swift slitting noise, the sound of the ruffle of the robes followed by the soft thud of a slumping body. Then even with my eyes closed I felt something sickeningly tangible. It was the gawping, perverted pleasure and awe of those who had witnessed the disgusting ritual.

I felt the weight of the weapon return to the pillow and squinted out of my slits to see Weishaupt wash his hands in some water from a golden bowl on the altar. There was a group sigh and the sound of some shuffling followed by the voices of a small choir droning a medieval chant. I turned back the way I had come and carrying the pillow with its blooded knife in front of me proceeded to move towards the door. By the grace of God no one tried to stop me. Lord knows what I would have done if someone had? I walked straight in between the curtains, up the stairs through the door at the top, placed the cushion on a chair by the door in the hallway then stepped outside into the storm - which was raging with such power that the wind and rain almost blew me off my feet.

Nervously glancing around at the sentinels loitering outside the lodge my blood froze solid when I spotted one who had removed his hood and was vainly stroking back his orange hair in the gale. Holy

Christ! It was Jan Kohler or I was the Mayor of Ingolstadt! What on God's earth was my oldest friend doing at this depraved ritual? Something told me that it would be a bad time to ask. So I ducked my head, wrapped my hands in my sleeves like a monk and walked swiftly past the front of the building before disappearing round the side.

Quickly finding a convenient tree root under the window where I had broken in I frantically hoisted myself up the bank and fled. Finally free from the dreadful place I tore through the undergrowth in a blaze of fear discarding the robe as I crashed along. I floundered on at full pelt not caring about the branches slapping me in my face or the sting from grabbing a thorny vine in my hand. The pain didn't matter. The only thing that mattered was to get away from that place as quickly as possible and those evil, murdering Satanic fiends.

Moments later I was galloping Petrova through the black Bavarian countryside in the driving rain and tumultuous wind as if all hell itself was coming up behind me and licking so close that my heels were starting to smoulder. All the time encouraging her with my calls, "C'mon, Girl! Let's fly tonight!" while the lightning flashed and the thunder roared around us.

It was all true. Everything the Professor had told me. I was living in a tragic play of terror; a fantasy world more nightmare than reality in which, even my friends were characters in the horrendous plot. I prayed to God that he would let me be the hero of the piece and that I might get to live happily ever after. Now that I had the documents I figured I must be halfway to understanding this new crazed reality of mine. Had I known how far I had left to go I might have given up right there and then. One thing was certain and I shouted to confirm it, "I take it all back, Van Halestrom!" As it would appear that the only thing that was consistent in my new life was that he was right again.

Chapter 14

The Four Horsemen of the Apocalypse

This was the perilous night when I really started working for the Professor. Up until then I had been involved in the adventure but only as a messenger. Now I was deeply in it. As a thief for one thing and for a raft of others it would take a whole page to list. It was then as I rode on through the storm asking God to help me and wrought with fear for my life that the nightmare intensified further still. For, as I picked up the road back to Ingolstadt pushing Petrova to her top speed, we came across four of the ghoulish red sentinels on horseback travelling the other way.

What they were doing riding four abreast down a narrow country road at night in a storm I will never know. What did they expect? They were lucky I did not run them down. It was only my riding skill and Petrova's instinct that prevented a major collision and we barged into them knocking two of the horsemen asunder. Perhaps it was this that made them suspicious or the fact that I offered them a finger when one of them called out, "I hope you can ride your mother better!"

If there's one thing I can't abide it's someone insulting my mother. Not that I was about to return and demand satisfaction by slapping the biggest of them round the face and insisting that he get down off his horse while I thrash some respect into him. Anyway, that was of no bother now because to my utter dismay they were going to give me a chance to have a fight with them whether I liked it or not and came chasing after me.

"No! No! No!" I wailed, at least I had the pistol. Then as I felt for the gun in my belt I realised that it was back in my desk, in my room. All I had was a bag stuffed full with this murderous gang's precious documents and my stupid lucky hat. Shit! Shit! Shit! This was turning into another seriously bad night. I tried to think of what I, Sebastian Drechsler, humble, foolish student would normally be doing on a Saturday evening. It certainly wouldn't be this and I banged my heels into Petrova's flanks urging her away from the wall of red robes and snorting black stallions behind me.

For, though I was hurtling along somehow my pursuers had managed to turn and catch me up. Sweet mother of God they were fast. I could not help but glance behind as a flash of lightning illuminated the terrible vision further; the bridles of the four horses glinting in the unearthly light. Even with their hooded robes masking their faces I could sense their determination to catch me. It was the four horsemen of the apocalypse incarnate three lengths behind me and closing in. But damn it! The cocky swine still rode four abreast as they tore down the lane with the black mud splashing up from the pounding hooves.

This was my advantage and I knew best how to take it. As another burst of lightning lit up the road ahead I swerved Petrova straight towards a narrow dip in the hedge and asked her to jump for me knowing they could not all follow at once. We landed with a solid thump and sped on through the field. I had seen the route when I came this way and spotted that a small advantage could be made taking this shortcut and rejoining the lane on the other side. Even in the slippery conditions faithful Petrova flew over the gate at the other side of the field and we galloped off into the night. I glanced behind to see that I was now pursued by only one red-robed horseman. The others were nowhere to be seen as yet and I felt myself relax slightly as the odds had been made a little better in my favour. But after tearing on for another mile and through a small hamlet I considered screaming for help at the unlit buildings because the red demon was gaining on me with every stride of his powerful black stallion. Damn it! I glanced over my shoulder once more to see that the human phantom was barely a length behind and even in the darkness I was sure I could see his eyes glaring out of the slits in his hood.

Petrova was tiring fast as we galloped along the winding country lane with the hooded sentinel inexorably closing in. I finally realised I would have to fight him. It was the only way. The moment the red devil caught me I would try and strike him off his steed with my riding whip. I desperately geed Petrova on raising the whip and hoping beyond hope something would save me when, to my complete amazement, amidst the furious wind and beating rain something did. For incredibly, at that very moment, a mighty bolt of lightning shot down from the heavens and struck my foe squarely in his chest, lifting him from his horse and propelling him backwards in a fiery, screaming ball of cinders and death. I rode on for a furlong in pure disbelief staring backwards at his galloping riderless horse as the rumbling thunderclap subsided around me.

Up to then I was sure God had never intervened before in my favour at any time of my life, especially when I needed him. But despite his obvious protection of me I suddenly clutched the bag containing the manuscript and flung it into the muddy road. Why I did it I will never know? Surely if I was being looked over I could have made good my escape along with the papers. But that very second I saw a cluster of glowing lanterns amongst the approaching shadows. Certain the other cultists had circled me and were closing in to avenge their colleague I turned Petrova into a small copse by the side of the road. Shaking, soaked and panic-stricken I dismounted and tried to keep us both as still as possible.

There was a shout and the pack of riders pulled up where I could see them. Despite the atrocious weather they had spotted the bag and one of them lifted it up and inspected its contents. I relaxed slightly when I realised it was not the three remaining red devils but another group of men. Although they also looked tough and purposeful so I squatted down further, not knowing what to think. *[13]

After a short discussion the horsemen rode off towards the fallen cultist and I stayed quivering in the dark for a moment before pulling myself together and setting Petrova in the opposite direction. Now I wasted not one minute in getting away. I have honestly never ridden faster in my life but if sheer terror could have propelled me along that road I would have reached the safe house of Frau

---

[13] Abbot Jacob Lanz struck by lightning. Incredibly, though there seems to be some conjecture about the precise timing of this amazing event, according to one of the most notable sources ***Pawns in The Game*** by W. Carr published 1958 this top ranking Illuminati official was actually struck by lightning and killed on 10th July 1784 near Regensburg Bavaria. When the authorities discovered his body they mistakenly decided that he was carrying the incriminating documents. Now it has become widespread belief that the abbot was, in fact, on a mission to deliver the papers to Paris where they would be used to aid the French revolution and that the papers were sewn into his robes. If we are to believe S. Drechsler's version of events it is fascinating to uncover the real truth behind what is already an incredible, but little-known, historical event. Either this is the event chronicled by so many historians and conspiracy theorists or we are party to an absolutely astonishing coincidence.

Hoffmeister even quicker than my faithful mare could have carried me. Cantering up the driveway I was spotted by the stable lad sheltering from the rain under the branches of a tree. He whistled up ahead and when I reached the farmhouse the old frauline was already outside with a lantern.

She busied the stable lad to attend to Petrova and I entered into the warmth of the cosy house. But as I came through the door I was thrown back onto my heels by a familiar voice from the shadows, "What took you so long, my lad?"

Sitting by the table in the dappling light of the fire I was astonished to see Professor Van Halestrom. Shock fully stunted my next sentence, "How … on … earth?"

He regarded me intently, lit his pipe and without taking his hawkish eyes off me carried on, "I see that you don't have the satchel. I presume the papers are lost too. But judging by the look on your face our enemies are not in possession of them. Am I right?"

He was always blasted right. I didn't know why he bothered asking.

"Am I right, Sebastian?"

I squirmed with embarrassment, furious with myself for discarding the satchel. Eventually with my head hung low I muttered, "I threw them in the lane. Some riders came and picked them up."

He shot forward in his chair, "How many riders? Were they serious looking men?"

Surprised by his intensity I held up the fingers of my soaking gloves to show him, mumbling, "Five: Maybe six."

He thumped his fist down on the table scaring me out of the few wits I had remaining and cried, "By Jupiter! We may be the luckiest men in Bavaria!"

"But surely, sir, I have failed you. Tonight is a total disaster."

Springing from his chair he grabbed my shoulders and smiled, "On the contrary, Sebastian. By the grace of good fortune I think we still have the advantage."

"But how can this be, sir?"

"Tonight, Sebastian I believe we have been party to a remarkable turn of fate. You see, I think it was the sheriff's men you saw find the satchel. They had been out patrolling after receiving reports from a concerned privy councillor of hooded ghouls on the prowl."

He gave me a knowing wink to indicate his own part in this deception and, as I stared agog, he carried on, "If this is so then the authorities already have the protocols which, after all, was our main objective. It would seem serendipity in this case is the mother of good fortune. Well done, Sebastian. Well done!"

My bewildered spirits soared as this news sank in. If he was right, as usual, then somehow my honour had been saved by this most virtuous of coincidences. Good grace indeed. It was a blasted miracle! But suddenly remembering Francesca's possible plight I could not help but gasp with exasperation, "But maybe, sir, everything is still lost."

"Relax, lad," replied Van Halestrom, obviously misunderstanding me and tapping his forehead with a finger, "I managed to memorize the papers before you stole them. See. I have made a copy."

I followed his eyes to some papers next to an ink pot and quill on the table. My scrambled thoughts raged for a moment until I asked, "Please, sir, tell me how is it possible that you managed to *memorize* them?" I looked about the room reconsidering his presence at the farmhouse before eying him suspiciously. "And how are you here at all? Explain this to me. Are you somehow ... omnipresent?"

"No, my lad, I was there."

It was impossible! What was he talking about? I stared him in the face and wailed, "Where? Where were you? In my blasted hat!"

"No. I was in a robe at the table disguised as an elder. I saw your footprints on the rug. I guessed you were in the cupboard behind Weishaupt?" He slapped me on the back and laughed, "I must say, I felt for you when they bolted the windows but I knew you would get out of there. And get out you did."

It was as though I were being followed by a fly that watched me from a wall wherever I went. "But ... how? How were you there in a robe at the table? How is it possible?"

He raised a finger declaring, "Everything is possible, Sebastian. Even to pose as an Illuminati elder and attend the evil ritual of the Golden Dawn then get away undetected as we both did this evening."

"You mean you saw me! You were at the ritual too?"

"Yes, Sebastian, I was at the ritual too. After reading the protocols I was trapped in the procession with the others and forced to adjourn downstairs where I was also waiting for the moment to escape."

"But ... but," By now my thoughts were roiling about in my head like the contents of a butter churn worked by a hysterical dairymaid.

He tapped his pointed nose and carried on, "Now I can explain, Sebastian. You have just taken part in a vital mission that has been planned ever since we heard Weishaupt's revised version of the protocols was going to be revealed the Lodge of the Golden Dawn. This document is the incontrovertible proof of the Illuminati's devilish scheme to take over the world. Therefore, it was imperative we got the original to show to the highest authority. It had originally been our plan to intercept one of the elders as I did tonight and for me to use his personal effects in order to gain access to the protocols and hopefully steal them. But this was a risky strategy and it meant I would have to be the last to leave the room. As you saw tonight it would have been impossible without putting up a serious fight. Then two days ago we discovered a servant who was prepared to leave a window open but who would not risk removing the documents himself, even for a price. This is where you came in - so to speak. I was sure that one of us would be able to seize the protocols and this meant we could still get our man. I knew that one way or another we would succeed. And one way or another we did."

I was incredulous to hear of his elaborate scheming and could not help blurting, "But ... surely ... you could not have planned it all."

"No. Of course not but my liquidation and impersonation of Herr Franz Lange did prepare the way for you as his inadvertent understudy at the ritual as it was Lange who was supposed to be carrying the cushion. Do you see, lad? Your unintentional heroism has saved the day twice. Once ensuring the sheriff obtained the protocols and then again by playing the part of Lange. For as his imposter I should have taken the cushion. I was simply unaware of it and might have even been discovered had you not entered when you did. I must say I was most surprised to see you walk in wearing those robes. They must have been three sizes too big. I thought you were going to trip up and bring us to shame. I left moments after you and Klaus brought me here in Lange's stolen carriage. Simple."

"Simple!" God's breakfast this man needed a dictionary. "So you were there posing as them? Killing them?"

"Hunting."

"Killing, hunting: It's the same isn't it?"

"Councillor Lange was a very evil man, Sebastian: A head of one of the Illuminati bloodlines. His ticket had been marked for some time. He had to go." *[14]

Shocked to hear of another unsettling murder and remembering the evil scenes at the ritual I stumbled, "Then ... sir, why did you not kill them all?"

"You were there, Sebastian. There were thirty of them. What were we to do? It would have been hopeless and you know it. Like you I also closed my eyes."

He *had* been there! He had noticed that I had not watched the sacrifice even behind the slits in my hood. I eyed him with frantic apprehension, beseeching, "Well if you know all, sir, then please tell me ... is ... is Francesca dead?"

He put his hand on my shoulder and solemnly answered, "No. She is safe." I gasped with relief and finally the grief and worry overwhelmed me and I collapsed down into a chair. The Professor sat too and Frau Hoffmeister appeared placing a couple of tankards of beer on the table. Such was my thirst I grabbed one of the tankards and half-emptied it in two enormous gulps. Wiping the foam from my mouth I went to drink again. After taking a goodly swig himself Van Halestrom muttered, "It was her sister, Montarese."

"Holy Father!" I exclaimed, coughing out my next mouthful of beer.

Kindling his pipe the Professor carried on, "There was nothing we could do in the end. We tried to rescue her from the Chapel of Liebfrauenmünster last week where you saw her with your friend. Unfortunately, we failed and I believe her fate was sealed. Though Francesca valiantly tried to find a way to save her alas it was all in vain. Montarese had been involved with the Illuminati for many years and was a tortured soul. In the end I fear it was inevitable."

"Good God!" I shook my head in astonishment remembering the

---

[14] Franz Lange Councillor of Eichstatt & the Illuminati. S. Drechsler's recollection of this character's gruesome death would seem to explain an anomaly from the official stories. This member of the Illuminati is often confused with the Abbott Jakob Lanz (very similar to 'Lange') who it would appear, after being struck by lightning, also perished on the same night. Interestingly I can find no official date for the obituary of F. Lange so it is certainly possible that the author's version of events is true. Also the similarities in the names and histories go a long way to account for conflicting reports of the men's deaths.

events last weekend at the chapel and also Francesca's deep preoccupation on our way back to Ingolstadt earlier that day. I was utterly incredulous to hear of these shocking details. To say nothing of my alarm at the danger in which my own life had actually been placed. As the entirety of the night's events finally became apparent to me I could not help but jibe, "Professor, I feel, that at times, I have been used as a pawn in your lethal game of chess."

He leant back in his chair sucking on his pipe, "Given your movements tonight, Sebastian, maybe not a pawn but a knight."

Having the evenings' many horrendous and death defying deeds likened to a board game was the last straw and finally I lost my temper, "A confounded knight, sir! I was almost killed - more than once! Why did you not tell me of the mortal danger that I faced?"

He sat forward leaning across the table. "You might not have done it if you had known of the peril."

"Of course I might not have done it if I had known of the peril! Surely that goes without saying. Imagine suggesting that I should go to Weishaupt's lodge and steal the protocols but that if I am caught I will definitely be killed and me agreeing to it. You said nothing of sacrifices or crazed cultists. You lied to me. I thought you were against the lies and the treachery of our enemies?"

"If it was a lie, Sebastian, it was a small one and employed to defeat a falsehood of much larger proportions. In terms of morality this is a fair transaction."

"A fair transaction, sir! It is a miracle that I am alive! Four of the red maniacs chased me … I was nearly struck by lightning!"

He held up his hand granting, "You have obviously been through a lot tonight, Sebastian. I can see that but now it is over. Things may seem very confusing right now but if I am right, sometime in the future we may well look back on tonight as a great victory for us."

Francesca's sister had been murdered and nearly me too and I had found out Jan was working for the bastards who had done it. As far as I was concerned the night was teetering on catastrophe.

"If it is a victory, sir, then please tell me what we have won?"

He pushed the papers into the middle of the table.

"As I have said; I'm sure the sheriff has the original and for our own benefit I have used my perfect memory to make this copy so we may know the details of their evil scheme. Now we understand their plans we can understand how to fight. For now we too are the

Illuminated Ones."

He turned his attention to his documents puffing away on his pipe. Although terrified, angry and thoroughly confused, I could not help but marvel to myself, 'Perfect memory, assassin, imposter, mind reader. Is there anything this wizard cannot do?'

I took another long draw from my tankard and wiped my mouth with the back of my glove. It was over. I had lived to tell the tale of the incredible night of the lightning strike hand of God when others had been far less fortunate. While I sat there dripping wet and trembling with fear I could have never known the implications my inadvertent heroism was to have on the future. No one could have: Except for the Professor of course. Looking back now I realise he knew well what to expect and the profound effect the robbery of the protocols would cause. For did the wise old bird not cleverly predict, 'we may well look back on tonight as a great victory'? Prophetic words indeed.

As I played out the evening's unforgettable events in my mind it was impossible for me not to think that somehow God had been watching over us, guiding and protecting our plans through the ordeal. I prayed that He would keep up his vigil but worried that we might not be able to count on his timely intervention forever.

After watching the Professor studying the papers for a while I took the opportunity to find out some more of the riddle and asked, "So when can I read them, Herr Professor?"

"Soon," he murmured, "Very soon."

Chapter 15

The Thirteen Protocols

I read the Professor's copy of the Protocols on Sunday morning back in Ingolstadt in the park near my lodgings. Afterwards I went immediately to a church and prayed for a long time. I didn't go back to my rooms but sent someone round to pick up my things and I moved into new lodgings that very evening. I no longer felt safe at Frau Warburg's - and neither would you have.

It is not possible for me to relay the whole document within the pages of my story as time will not allow. However, to give you an idea of the devilish venom which lay in the fearful passages, I have recalled one of the protocols that struck me most forcefully. I was not surprised Van Halestrom had remembered them; perfect memory or not. Seventy years on parts of the text are so frightening that they are still seared onto my mind. This is number twelve entitled 'Tyranny of Power.' As I recall it went something like this;

…While the peoples of the world are still stunned by the accomplished fact of our revolution, still in a condition of terror and uncertainty brought about by the chaos we have created we shall restore our own order by destroying all the other mechanisms of their inferior civilisation;

Aristocracy: Family: Inheritance: Property: Government: Nation: Religion.

Once these obstacles are removed the people of the world will be forced to recognise, once and for all, that we have seized everything we wanted and that we are so super-abundantly filled with power, that in no case shall we take any account of them, and so, far from paying any attention to their opinions or wishes, we are ready and able to crush with irresistible power all expression or manifestation thereof at every moment and in every place. Then in fear and trembling they will close their eyes to everything, and be content to await what will be the end of it all.' *[Protocol 12]* *[15]*

I spent the rest of the day in a daze staring into a tankard at a bierkeller in town. It was not only the ominous protocols that crushed my spirits to a pulp but now the other monumental events of the previous day began to weigh heavily on my mind: Three gruesome deaths, the lightning strike, the sacrifice, the chase and to top it all Jan, my oldest friend, an Illuminati servant. Not even he could joke his way out of this and I wondered, with much vexation, what we would say to each other next time we met. Altogether it was impossible not to let these thoughts drag me into a whirlpool of dark machinations and I spent that night tossing and turning on the bed in my new rooms unable to sleep. Monday morning wasn't much better and I walked into university like a ghost, my mind in turmoil. A sharp voice snapped me from my stupor.

"Herr Drechsler."

It was Weishaupt. His cold blue eyes glared at me from behind his spectacles and his square mouth fired off the words, "I wish to see you in my chambers after your morning lecture. You will be there."

I was too scared to run off and stood transfixed (which by now had become my default modus operandi). He spun on his heel and strode off with his shoes clacking down the polished corridor. 'I'm done for now!' I panicked, certain that he knew it was me who had stolen his precious documents. A couple of students dodged out of his way as he marched past them, ducking their heads in fear of catching his eye. This was not your typical Monday morning at university; being killed by your lecturer in the free period before lunch. Understandably, it was hard to concentrate through my next lecture and then, almost without knowing it, I was in front of Weishaupt's door some three hours later in a blind funk.

---

[15] The original writings of the Illuminati. The original documents found with Abbot Lanz's body after the lightning strike have not survived so unfortunately there is no record of the text to back up S. Drechsler's account. Although other papers seized from Illuminati agents on later dates bear strong similarity to those the author describes. These documents were reprinted and released by the Bavarian authorities in 1786 to warn foreign countries about the Illuminati and their political intentions. Interestingly the text also bears a strong resemblance to the Protocols of the Elders of Zion. The mother of all conspiracy documents, this text is widely believed to be a hoax produced for political ends. Though it is an inexplicable coincidence that the document S. Drechsler recalls bears such close resemblance to this text released over a hundred years later, forged or not.

'You can do this,' I tried to convince myself, unconvincingly. He couldn't prove anything and even he wasn't mad enough to kill me in his rooms. Or so I hoped. Finally with my heart in my mouth I found the courage to knock.

"Come," wafted a gentle response. Dreading what was to follow I shuffled inside closing the door behind me.

"Ah. Herr Drechsler. Please sit down."

Confusingly he had reverted to his ingratiating style which threw me even further off balance. I lowered myself into the chair as he eyed me up and down from behind his desk.

"How is everything going, Sebastian? Getting on all right?" He put a finger on his chin, continuing with a hint of insincerity, "Exams coming up soon. I suppose you're ready for them aren't you? Fine student like you will have no trouble passing. No. Not you, Herr Drechsler. Which is good, I'm sure your parents would be very disappointed if anything were to prevent you from completing your studies here at the university. To say nothing of drunken antics, being locked in the city gaol and bad time keeping. "

There was a long uncomfortable pause before his demeanour darkened and he muttered, "I've got my eye on you, boy. And remember my eye sees everywhere." Without taking his icy stare off me he nodded at the door, "Now, I have two funerals to arrange."

Having been given the chance to go, I nearly fell flat on my face in my haste to leave his chambers. Hurrying down the corridor I went through what he had said: 'First he is fearsome then polite then fearsome again.' It was enough to send me mad. Well at least it had been brief and I hadn't been given the opportunity to condemn myself out of my own mouth. Thank God! Damn him and his all-seeing eye. I wondered if one of the funerals was going to be mine. Then I remembered the Professor's assassination of Councillor Lange and the lightning strike 'Hand of God' that sent someone, or at least what was left of them, straight to the grave. Surely Weishaupt must have known these individuals. Though, I still could not tell if he knew of my involvement with the theft of the protocols. But would he have confronted me about it if he had or would that have meant he risked exposing himself? The game of cat and mouse had too many permutations for me to think of all at once. It was like playing six simultaneous games of chess with the Professor.

Whatever he knew he was certainly suspicious and he had already tried to kill me once before. So I resolved to stay as far away from the faculty as possible and study for my exams at my new basement room on Spitalstrasse about which I had not told a soul.

Later in the week when I reported the meeting to Van Halestrom and he laughed saying, "He's just playing mind games with you, my boy: The old thesis/antithesis technique; otherwise known as blowing hot and cold. It is simply an attempt to destabilise you. Don't worry, Sebastian. You have nothing to fear from that creature whilst in the confines of the university. He cannot prove a thing so do not concern yourself with his threats. We will see to it that your exams are successful legitimately and, if we cannot succeed like that then, my lad, we shall cheat."

He gave me a hearty slap me on the back and I thought him quite the rogue. I relaxed then as his positive words did reassure me. If Van Halestrom said he could do something I was thoroughly prepared to believe the man.

Chapter 16

Tribulations and Examinations

And so it was settled. I was to study hard in my basement trying not to twitch whenever I heard something go past the window and keep my head down until my exams started. This was made easier because my coursework had already been completed by the admirable Bacon alleviating my need to visit the university. So I threw myself into my books and seldom left the house for three weeks. In this time I saw no-one but my ill-mannered landlord and at times sorely craved any company especially that of the Professor and, of course, the mysterious and tragic Francesca of whom I dreamt frequently.

Then, as with all periods of waiting, the day eventually came when it was at an end. I paced down the lanes towards the university frenetically going through the facts I had crammed into my aching head. My exams were to be conducted over three days; history on the first, philosophy the second and on the third, the one I was really dreading, canon law. It wasn't only because my examiner to-be was a murderous Luciferian maniac with designs on taking over the world, though it was hard to keep this salient fact from my mind completely, it was because the subject itself was as complicated as Byzantine bureaucracy, which come to think of it is exactly what it was. The endless lists of statutes and over complicated laws would not settle in my mind as I had no care of what one priest had to facilitate for another nor how their infernal Bishop would feel about it if they did not. It wasn't like history where the dates and events were naturally fixed in the memory by the drama of the narrative they told. History I could do.

So I was not surprised to find myself walking out of the university some three hours later happy at the way my first exam had gone and relieved that the first part of the ordeal was over. Something that did surprise me was the sight of the Professor's black carriage parked in the street outside. Klaus spotted me and with a discreet nod signalled that I should carry on down the road. Presently, the pair of black horses appeared at my shoulder and I heard Van Halestrom offer, "Hop in my lad. We can give you a lift."

I pulled myself in through the door and hearing the whip crack plopped myself down facing Van Halestrom as the carriage pulled away.

"That went well did it not?"

As usual he read my mind and continued to do so, "You'll probably be all right tomorrow as well as you rightly expect. But the third exam looks as though it will pose more of a significant obstacle."

"Why is that, sir?" I asked, fully expecting another horrid complication approaching - which of course it was.

He unceremoniously answered, "Weishaupt plans to destroy your papers before they are marked so you will not score at all. Thus ruining your results and making your expulsion from the university a certainty. My clerk overheard him discussing the plan with one of his cronies at the faculty."

"What!" I bleated.

He held up a finger. "Do not worry. A plan is afoot to foil his wicked scheme but it relies entirely on two significant points which are directly under your control."

"What? What must I do?"

"As you know the exam is to take place in the old cloister rooms. You must occupy desk number seven and as soon as Weishaupt reveals the questions on the blackboard you must immediately write them down. Otherwise our plan fails and with it your university career."

My mind was reeling like the town drunk, "But why?"

"It is unimportant, Sebastian. Just do as I say and everything will be fine."

There was that infernal word 'just' again but I let him go on, "Now, we cannot take you to your house as we do not wish to give away its location. Also there are matters of great importance to which I must attend. I have not wished to concern you with these events because of your studies." He flashed a grin then balanced it with a stern look of determination. "Although I can tell you this much: Due to recent events some Illuminati dignitaries, including the influential Baron Von Knigge, have chosen to distance themselves from the order. Also an injunction has been sought on Weishaupt in the high court after the documents you stole were handed in as evidence to the Prosecutor Royal. So if we are successful, my lad, it will be in no small part down to you."

He banged his cane into the roof bringing the carriage to a halt and put his hand on my shoulder. "Now we must leave you, Sebastian. Remember, desk number seven. Good luck." *[16]

I dismounted and heard him call out, "Farewell, my lad. Don't give up now," and watched the carriage rattle away.

I scuttled back to my basement and locked the door behind me. I sighed deeply reflecting how the complicated things in my life were now even more so. I wondered with much trepidation if Weishaupt had found out that it was me who had stolen his precious protocols exposing him to the authorities. Surely he would kill me if he had.

Unsurprisingly, that night I had a terrible dream. In this nightmare I found myself sitting at my desk in the exam in front of a blank sheet of paper. From nowhere Weishaupt came at me with the same curved knife from the sacrifice but the other students did not look up and kept scribbling away. I tried to to scream but could not call out because of the strict rule of silence during the test.

To my credit, even after these nocturnal hauntings, I did not buckle and the following Philosophy exam went as smoothly as the previous day's History had. That evening I lay in bed praying for the swift resolution of the final test and that I could get to the correct desk. With these worries churning in my mind I hardly slept a wink. Exams were bad enough anyway but this was getting ridiculous.

Then the most awful of beginnings: After spending the whole night listening to the chimes of St Maria's slowly drawing closer to the moment I had been dreading for so long, when seven o'clock finally loomed half an hour before I was to rise, I finally fell asleep.

I awoke minutes before the start of the exam in a state of absolute delirium and ran so fast through the streets that I would have

---

[16] The first edict against the Illuminati. In June1784 the first edict banning membership of all Bavarian secret societies was passed though these measures were only seen as half-hearted. Tellingly, the authority's suspicion of the Illuminati continued to mount after this date which may well be explained by the author's exploits. Charles Theodore, the Prince Elector, presided over these hearings. Obviously those who were in charge took a dim view of an organisation which sought to bring about the overthrow of governments. Baron Adolph Knigge was a highly influential aristocrat who notably fell out with Weishaupt halfway through 1784. Despite other explanations being given in the official accounts for the Baron's defection it was definitely true that Weishaupt had suddenly become unpopular at this time.

flattened anyone unfortunate enough to fall into my path. If the sight of a wild-eyed student charging along with his nightshirt flapping over his breeches was not enough to stir the good townspeople I resorted to shouting at the top of my voice, "Get out of the blasted way!".

I bolted down the colonnade leading to the old cloister rooms nearly exploded with fear. The students were already going in. No! No! No! I envisioned my disappointed father shaking his head while my mother openly wept behind him, the old man's mouth moving in a slow motion, "Boy you are a failure."

'Aargh!' I hurled myself into the queue barging my way through the other students and bursting inside to see a couple of individuals already selecting their prospective desks. Quickly getting my bearings I spotted desk number seven bathed in sunlight falling from an adjacent window but noticed portly Grubber three paces away and closing in fast. I nearly screamed at him but, remembering the strict rule of silence that should I break would mean instant expulsion, I flew towards the desk coughing as loudly as I dared and kneed him in the back of the thigh. A technique I had been taught by the Professor when wishing to incapacitate someone from behind.

And incapacitate him it did. For in my eagerness to get into the chair before my learned colleague could park his ample rump in the same position I used quite some force. The ill-fated Grubber writhed on the floor in agony as Weishaupt appeared at his door eager to see the cause of the commotion. I smiled innocently and pointed to my throat. He frowned at me and glanced down at Grubber floundering by my feet before pulling his crocodile grin obviously aware of something he thought was unknown to me. Little did he know; I knew of his trickery and had a plan. I secretly scoffed before realising, 'What was the blasted plan?' I had no idea. I hadn't had either the time or straightness of mind to consider it.

Feeling suddenly sympathetic I offered my hand to Grubber but he pulled back in fear and went to find another desk. Looking around I now felt helpless in the bright morning sunshine and gazed at the empty white sheets of paper on the desk. Weishaupt looked out over us and after signalling the start of the test removed the cloth from the blackboard revealing the questions. I picked up my quill and as instructed wrote them down.

Well I'm not going to tell you what happened over the next three hours for its very mention would probably bore you to death, as surely as cataloguing every grain of sand in the world and then doing it again - thrice. Suffice to say that, in the end, I thought it went quite well. Not a stunning account of canon law by any extent of the imagination but enough to get me through. Or so I thought.

The bell sounded and Weishaupt came round collecting the papers and dismissed us. As I was one of the last to leave, being the furthest from the door I was almost alone with him when I saw him locate my paper and, with a look of pure devilment stare me straight in the eye whilst removing it from the pile.

"Damn you pig dog!" I cursed under my breath. But how could I complain? He would merely deny his intentions and he knew I was unable to speak as the conditions of the test were still being observed. He left through his own entrance and gave the waiting clerk the papers. The frustration was maddening. I wanted to go and spin the bastard around and smash his face in. I barged out of the cloister rooms in a rage of furious spite swearing that in some way I would get my revenge however long it took. For now I was definitely ruined.

As I planned many gruesome acts of violence where Weishaupt was the screaming, blood-covered victim I was amazed to see someone I had not expected to see in the slightest. In fact, so stunned was I to see him there it momentarily stopped me considering the outrage that had befallen me. Although he had his collar unusually high and was wearing an incongruous hat, the brim of which was pulled suspiciously low, I could still tell it was snooty old Bacon making his way along with the other students. He stood out like a sore thumb amongst the throng leaving the gates and turned the other way. I jogged up behind him bursting with a mixture of intrigue and anticipation and asked gently, "Herr Bacon? Is that you?"

He acknowledged me with a tip of his hat, answering in his usual considered drawl, "Ah, Herr Drechsler, how pleasant to see you, sir." He carried on walking seemingly as unsurprised to see me as if he were back in the castle bedroom pulling back the curtains.

I wondered, desperate with hope, "Pray, sir what is it that you have been doing at the university?"

After inhaling for a painfully long time he announced, "I believe, sir that I have had the rather dubious privilege of coming here and fighting my way through herds of malodorous students in order to sit in a drafty room all morning peering through a telescope and writing your exam paper on canon law."

I couldn't believe it. Although it was now totally obvious: That's why I had to be at desk number seven because it was the only one that could be spied through the window. He carried on in the same grating monotone, "I understand, sir that the clerk is our man, so to speak, and will place my manuscript in the pile whence it will be marked as usual. Weishaupt suspects nothing and will not check for he believes he has destroyed the original."

While he delivered this astonishing, life-changing news the black carriage pulled up next to us with trusty Klaus at the reins. In a deceptively graceful movement for a man of his age Bacon boarded the coach closing the door behind him. Leaning out of the window he tipped his hat and bid me, "Good day, sir."

Klaus gave me a friendly wink rousing the horses and the carriage trundled off up the street. I watched them leave in joyful rapture crying out at the top of my voice, "Yeehaa! Up yours Adam Weishaupt!"

That was a good day from then on. Horrid exams completed the last of which by a veritable genius, the sweet smell of summer in the air, pretty girls everywhere making themselves available for the throngs of young students celebrating the end of term and, above all, the thought of Weishaupt's angry face distorting with apoplexy as I strolled back into university on the first day of term next September.

"Hurrah!" I cheered to myself and supped the head off a frothy tankard of beer. It had been a long time coming but that evening, for the first time in what seemed like an age, I did relax. Although as was becoming my habit totally on my own. For, due to my enforced self-incarceration in my new lodgings and the solitude which moving to a new town had already brought, compounded by the fact that I no longer saw Jan, I had become quite alone in Ingolstadt. Though it was not a concern at that precise moment, I had noticed it start to happen generally in my life and considered that this was because no one else seemed to have the attraction of the new band of twilight folk that I was coming to know.

Chapter 17

Summer Holidays

The summer holidays happily passed without incident. After receiving the confirmation of my successful examinations I returned home to Tuffengarten for three weeks during August to see my parents. Mother was overjoyed to see me and instantly began to fatten me up complaining that, 'the food of Ingolstadt was only good enough for town folk and not enough for a country boy like you who needs more energy than those idle people of the city;' Which was the utter illogicality of my French mother that I had missed so much.

Father, on the other hand, was his usual abrupt self. Having become used to the relative informality of university society, and especially my new band of friends, I found it hard to remember to bow to him, in the morning, before and after lunch, and when I was going to bed. It started to make my back ache in the end but it was nice to see him anyway. Although he tried his hardest to cover his real feelings with those of worry, concern, and stern contemplation, I was sure that somewhere deep down inside the old man there was a glimmer of pride that his only son had survived his first year of university. Heaven knows what he would have thought if he had even an inkling about the life that I actually led.

I spent much of my time fishing at my usual place by the river and noticed how sorely I missed the companionship of my old friend Jan. This was the first summer we had spent apart since we were boys. I worried that the different paths we had chosen toward manhood would mean that would we would never see each other again. Since seeing him at the Golden Dawn I had been making a lengthy detour on the way back from university to avoid walking past the money-changers and his lodgings.

These distractions aside I was in good spirits and five pounds heavier when I returned to my basement room in Ingolstadt and saw a note pushed under my front door. It was from Van Halestrom. He wanted to meet with me. This of course was not what the message said because it was in code and read: 'Game of chess. Monday: Six o'clock my chambers.' My heart jumped at the news and the possibility of seeing Francesca again.

I was in fine fettle that fresh September morning as I entered the university on the first day of term. Indeed, so good was my mood that it was not even dented when I saw Herr Weishaupt lurking in the corridor in his black gown watching the year's new undergraduates file by him. Shocked to see returning me he threw me the most malevolent of stares. To my eternal pride I strode confidently past and did not cower but held my head high and even braved a whistle. I could see that this act of defiance truly made his blood boil. It was even better than I had endlessly pictured. What was he to do? Send me down for whistling? Much as he would like to even he couldn't be that strict. One of my colleagues behind me, a morbid but insightful lad called Frankenstein or some such, witnessed the exchange wittering, "You don't want to get The Doctor upset. He'll have your guts for garters." *[17]

I laughed off his comment but through the day the idea dawned on me that my hiatus from danger was over as Weishaupt was now aware that I had thwarted him. Even though he would only be lecturing me once a week and I could always hide at the back having him lurking round the university and head of the law department was enough to set my mind whirring in a series of dark machinations. Now he would surely be planning his revenge. By the end of the day my fine mood had evaporated and I consoled myself with my up and coming meeting with the Professor.

At six o'clock sharp I entered Van Halestrom's room noticing the chessboard on his small table was prepared for a game. 'No need for code.' I thought and sat down as he welcomed me with a wave. After drawing white he made the first move.

---

[17] Frankenstein and the Illuminati. This must be S. Drechsler's little joke though possibly an insightful one. Being a scholar he would have been familiar with Mary Shelley's novel ***Frankenstein*** of 1818 set in Ingolstadt University three years later in 1787 so maybe it was a nickname given retrospectively to one of his more morbid fellow students. He also may have been trying to be cryptic given the context of the story as there is much speculation about the symbolic connection of the Illuminati and Frankenstein. It is rumoured that Percy Shelley, Mary's husband, may have been a member of the Illuminati and that there are many fascinating metaphorical connections between the novel and Weishaupt's order.

"Good to see you, Sebastian. I hope you have your wits about you for there is much to tell." He made himself comfortable in his chair before beginning, "Firstly, work is still carrying on in the courts to bring about the trial of Weishaupt's organisation. This is excellent news as we worried that they may have already managed to achieve control of the judicial system. Though, whether the courts are successful or not, at the end of October it seems there will be another opportunity for us to further bring about the Illuminati's downfall. I will have more to tell you as this comes to pass. In the meantime, I have another job for you. Are you interested?"

I moved a knight into play replying, "Of course, Professor. What is the task?"

"Not so much a task but a spot of paid extracurricular activity: Something for the weekend if you will." He moved a pawn into attack and smiled, "That's right; just a spot of extracurricular activity."

It was that word 'just' again but I missed it this time. What was to happen to me on my next mission was a shock indeed: A real eye-opener for sure. Extracurricular activity, my Bavarian arse!

Chapter 18

The Slave Trader

At sunrise the next Saturday morning I was huddled behind a frosty blackberry bush on a freezing hillside rubbing my hands together to keep warm. I spied between the brambles along the high forest pass winding past our position.

"Here they come," whispered the Professor and ducked down a few yards away. Presently two huge white horses came into view pulling a heavy, covered wagon over the brow of the hill. On the footplate sat three tough looking characters wrapped in stout coats and large hats with their collars turned up to the extent that their faces were all but totally hidden. They scanned the surrounding scenery as their breath condensed in the cold air. I glanced over at the Professor and was mortified to find that he was no longer where he had been hiding.

My heart began to thump like the fist of a man who's woken up in a coffin. As usual Van Halestrom had not told me what I was to expect. This lot looked serious and the possibility that he was going to confront them was thoroughly alarming. We had travelled a fair distance to this place and I was pretty sure that he had not come all this way to deliver these brutes some flowers. My fears were confirmed when I heard the Professor shout, "Halt or I shoot!" I couldn't help but peep over the bush to see the Professor standing thirty feet in front of the wagon with his menacing bow pushed tightly under his chin. The three ruffians looked at Van Halestrom then amongst themselves as if doing a quick bit of mental arithmetic. On finding the result obviously in their favour they chuckled before the biggest of them brought up a blunderbuss and fired off a mighty shot.

'Boom!' The explosion rang out through the forest and the shot tore huge splinters from a silver birch tree where Van Halestrom was standing. Expecting to see my friend struck down in mortal agony as the smoke cleared I was startled to see him twenty paces to his left. Suddenly a hail of silver bolts spurted from his bow and I heard the sound of the arrows slicing through the air and hitting their targets. 'Zut! Zut! Zut!' I watched aghast as the three men fell from the wagon all of them ending up lying perfectly still but awfully contorted on the icy ground. Van Halestrom made his way towards the wagon, keeping the murderous bow trained on the corpses. When he was sure the brutes were all dead he called out, "Come over here, Sebastian."

I crept over to the carnage seeing a plump old man emerge from the front of the wagon nervously keeping his hands over his expensive wig. He regarded the Professor with abject terror in between glancing at his hired help, who lay all around and were obviously no help at all. I came up behind Van Halestrom as the quivering merchant got down from the footplate. He was about sixty-five years old and wore a fine blue coat decorated with rows of buttons and huge elaborate cuffs over a pair of gleaming white breeches stretched tight round his spherical middle.

The Professor spoke clear and earnest, "Martin von Speer, I accuse you of the heinous crimes of slavery, murder, piracy, kidnapping and the wilful violence you have committed upon thousands of unfortunates whose lives you have ruined. On behalf of those individuals and for freedom and liberty throughout the world I, Peter Van Halestrom, commit you to death by firing squad and may your God have pity on your pathetic soul."

I heard the click of the trigger and the punch of the arrow and watched the merchant's face stare at us in horror. I glanced down at his stomach expecting to see the arrow sticking out but incredibly it had disappeared inside him. He clutched at his midriff it would seem also looking for the arrow and raised his head in disbelief as a large crimson stain appeared on his trousers. He fell to his knees with a gasp. A position he held for a moment before collapsing face down on the ground with a crunch.

"That's that, then," said the Professor and without batting an eyelid moved to the wagon and started unfastening the canvas.

"Would you help me here?" He asked. I joined in though in absolute shock at the violence I had seen. We lifted four heavy strongboxes out of the wagon and placed them on the roadside. Whereupon the Professor produced a sturdy, silver-handled knife and prised one of them open like an oyster although the treasure in this case was a hefty pile of coinage.

After moving the wagon and the corpses away from the track we freed the horses and walked our own from the forest. Once into the open we cantered for a couple of miles before slowing again to preserve our mounts as the weight of the coinage in our saddlebags was of such a burden. We did not return to Ingolstadt but travelled north to Nuremberg. Van Halestrom had told me our mission would last the whole weekend and that I should come prepared for all eventualities. He might say that but to prepare 'for all eventualities' when on a day out with the Professor was difficult to say the least. After half a league of bumping along through the pine trees I asked, "Could you now explain to me what the hell is going on, Professor?"

"Of course, my lad: I'm sorry that that happened the way it did. I would also like to promise that there will soon come a day when these nasty surprises will be a thing of the past. It is in the nature of the teaching that they are performed in such a manner so that they have the right impact."

"Well they certainly had impact." I replied sardonically.

"Herr Speer was an important member of the Illuminati and was being groomed for inclusion into the top level of the order. He supplied many of its members with slaves throughout Europe, England and the Americas. If I had not killed the man another six hundred men, women and children would have gone missing from the coast of West Africa in two month's time. Two hundred of these would die, maybe more depending on the conditions of the crossing. The rest would suffer the endless humiliation and degradation of a lifetime's enforced servitude at the hand of a master who possessed limitless capacity to further their woe and suffering. I am simply not prepared to stand idly by knowing that these disgusting crimes will continue when I could have stopped the perpetrators of this evil. The courts will do nothing about these men, so I have taken it upon myself to become their judge, jury and executioner."

He sighed and solemnly continued, "Slavery is one of the most abhorrent crimes of all and anyone who even considers it a possible career has already negated their right to be treated like a human being. There is nothing that can be done about such people and that is why they must be eliminated like dogs that have gone mad. It is true that in life there are opposing sides of good and bad. All inherently evil systems rely on there being a host, i.e. the good, and a self- appointed parasite which feeds from it, i.e. the bad. When a man becomes as bad as Von Speer, he is doubtless a murderer, a pervert, a liar, a cheat and a total immoral deviant who should not be let near normal gentlefolk who credulously project their own peaceful qualities onto him. Historically, the problem of the good is that, unlike the bad, they dare not strike first. This reluctance of the good to act creates the symbiotic cycle of their own suffering and in turn, also produces creatures like Von Speer. That's where we come in; to strike first, to hunt down the evil scum and redress the balance. This is the big lesson, Sebastian; in order to save the lives of others sometimes it is right to kill. This known as moral calculus and you need to embrace the concept before you can advance to the next level."

"Right then," I said, somewhat dismayed at this seemingly bleak assessment of the human condition and wondered out loud, "What level am I at now?" calculating the further horrors I would have to witness to achieve subsequent 'levels' of understanding.

"When you no longer need to ask what level you have attained you are sufficiently initiated and, of course, it no longer becomes a priority to know. You will come to understand this."

'More paradoxical thinking,' I thought, unappeased by this and still troubled after seeing such unprovoked and unsettling assassinations. I couldn't fathom the justification for the slaughter of these men who were after all merely going about their lawful business, however cruel it was. How could this be right?

Though you may find it shocking I was to come to understand these acts of violence not only to be fully justified, and more than necessary, but a necessity. These stark conclusions were brought into focus by many things that were to happen in the future but especially the events of the following day when I was to witness one of the most remarkably uplifting experiences of my life. Although the Professor had not forewarned me of his plans, as usual, so there was much for me to consider as we continued on down the road to Nuremberg.

We reached the city at sundown and found suitable lodgings before the two of us turned in early as the ride, along the other events of the day, had been of such a testing nature. We awoke early, breakfasted heartily then rode to the centre of town to an old building next to the river. Van Halestrom left me to look after the horses and, as I pondered why we had come to this place, I noticed a sign over the door that read 'Slaves for Sale.' After some time Van Halestrom returned with a most incredible crew in tow. To my utter astonishment the Professor, using Von Speer's papers, had collected all the slaves who belonged to our freshly deceased friend and was marching them out of the building in full view of the other traders. This demanded no small act of valour on the Professor's part as there would have been hell to pay if someone who knew Von Speer had realised what was happening. We lined the slaves up, one of us on either side, and marched the poor souls away from the market and off through the town.

A strange sight we made indeed: Thirty men women and children of all colours, and origins, young and old, with me and the Professor showing them the way. We got to a haberdashery in town where Van Halestrom went in and, so help me God, if he didn't clothe every single one of the hapless folk using the money he had taken from the boxes. There was much happiness amongst our brigade as they started to relax in their more hospitable circumstances. They had been cold in the autumnal weather having nothing about them but rags at best, so these clothes were greeted with much relief. Next I was sent to buy food and in such quantity that I brought it back in a wheelbarrow before handed it out to the throng.

With our friends now fed, watered and clothed in decent fashion, the parade continued to the docks where the Professor troubled himself for some time arranging and paying for journeys for the freed slaves. He handed out maps and money trying to divide the group into parties which could travel together with some sort of natural leader who could understand what was best to do. In some cases the Professor booked guides and companions, telling these people that if any of the individuals put into their care came to any harm he would hear of it and be back to track down the culprits and prosecute terrible punishments upon them all.

After several long hours, with the last of our abused individuals either booked on a boat or already travelling down the river, the Professor and I left the docks behind us. There had been some earnest and emotional farewells at the riverside as the slaves thanked us for what we had done for them. Van Halestrom himself left the city with not a penny left of the money that we had taken from the merchant. I calculated this generosity had made some of his freed charges very wealthy indeed. There was a small but solid community of mulattoes at Mainz, several days travel west along the river Pegnitz where I believe many of our group settled and that their descendants are still living peacefully there today.

"We have made some people very happy this day," ventured the Professor.

"And others slightly less so," I noted. Sarcasm aside the events of that day and seeing the different looks in the eyes of the murdered merchant and of his slaves when they were freed would not leave me and, I might add, are still there to this day. Van Halestrom may have had unusual teaching methods but this lesson in moral calculus was impossible to forget. And what an important lesson that was to prove.

Chapter 19

The Art of War

The next few weeks were very busy for me as the Professor's demands on my time increased. At the weekends I visited the Castle Landfried and was given more combat lessons in various disciplines. Van Halestrom taught me how he had moved so quickly in the forest and how to use the awesome quadre bow to great effect. After much practice I became able to cut one of the large straw targets in half with a series of shots placed together in a line. The Professor roared with delight to see this destruction and commented that I was becoming 'a veritable William Tell.'

In the castle gymnasium I learnt many acts of brutalism; how to break an arm with a twist and how to kill with a kick or a punch and even how to slit a man's throat. I worried that I would not be able to carry out such extreme acts of violence. I had fought before, yes, in a bar room fight but only once or twice with any real conviction and always in self-defence. So this was all very serious stuff and I looked with a growing concern to the future when these skills would be called upon to order. Needless to say the Professor understood this and told me that if I felt uncomfortable at any moment we could call a halt. But this never came to pass and the teaching carried on and on.

I was sure this training had something to do with the event the Professor had told me about that was to take place at the end of October. It was already nearing the end of the month and brown leaves were swirling around the door of my basement room on Spitalstrasse. As the nights drew in I became both apprehensive and excited in equal measure. I had also been told that Francesca would be deeply involved in this mission. I had not seen her for so long as to make her memory induce a painful longing in me. It was impossible for me to gauge what she would do when I next saw her. Would she embrace me and tell me I was a hero, as I dreamed, or ridicule me because I was a pathetic fool? Though profoundly unbalancing I resigned, in the end, to envisage the possibility of both outcomes simultaneously.

By now I had taken to avoiding my lectures with Weishaupt altogether. Despite there being eighty other students in the hall I could not bear to be near the man. The Professor assured me that Weishaupt was under far too much scrutiny to attempt revenge, especially on a student of the University. But once or twice I caught him glaring at me and knowing what he was capable of it was too much to bear. I knew it was a risk not going to my lessons and something I would not always be able to do but I felt that somehow things would not stay the way they were for long. There was much gossip round the campus of Weishaupt and his Illuminati and the courts and like a storm on a hot summer's day it was as though something had to break. I just prayed it would not be me.

On the last Friday of October I was stowing my hat and scarf in my locker when I found a note on the inside of the door that read; 'Chess match 11.00am.' Suspecting I was about to receive the details of my next mission I found it impossible to concentrate on my morning lecture. As soon as it ended I hurried down the echoing corridors towards the Professor's study. A moment later I was sitting at Van Halestrom's desk brimming with anticipation as he greeted me in his usual affable way.

"Tea, Sebastian?" He set out two cups of steaming brew and lit his pipe before rummaging around in a drawer of his desk. After a moment he produced a circular medallion and tossed it on the table where it landed with a resounding clunk.

"Have you ever seen this before, my lad?"

I picked up the medallion and as I examined it I received a fearful jolt of deja-vu. Embossed on the face, surrounded by some Latin phrases, was a capless pyramid and at its summit the awful eye radiating beams of light. It was the ominous vision from my ghastly dream. The precursor of all the life-changing events which had befallen me over the past six months and I almost threw the thing down in revulsion.

"It is the vision from your dream is it not?" probed the Professor.

What to say to a man who has asked you to agree with the thing you had thought yourself but had not yet had the chance to mention was still an annoying mystery to me. I tilted an eyebrow and muttered "You know it is."

As usual he carried on regardless of my displeasure, "This symbol has recently been selected by the American Congress as the

Republic's great seal proving the Illuminati's rot is spreading. Notice; there are thirteen layers to the pyramid. This is a metaphor for our society. The bottom level is you and me and every other uninitiate in the world; the 'Goyium' or 'the cattle.'"

'So that's what it meant,' I sat up in my chair with growing annoyance to be referred to as cattle. I remembered Weishaupt using the word when I was hiding in the cupboard at his beastly Lodge.

The Professor continued, "As we go up the pyramid the levels indicate the layers of Weishaupt's vision of civilisation until here at the top, the penultimate level represents him and the elders and crowning it all, The Eye of Horus, the Egyptian God symbolizing the underworld and Lucifer by which all in the movement are ultimately controlled. Note the date at the bottom, 1776 the year of the order's most recent reincarnation under the oversight of our good friend Adam Weishaupt or Herr Spartacus to you and me. Now the Latin, if you would translate."

I read out the phrases, "Annuit Cœptis - Novo Ordo Seculorum. He approves of the beginnings and new order ... of the ages?" *[18]

"Or, 'New order of the World.' Yes, very good, Herr Drechsler. How's that for coming straight out and saying it? This technique is called 'hidden in plain sight.' It is indeed their plan to have a new order for the world: Their Order. And this is what we plan to do about it."

He rolled out the plans of a building on the table and carried on,

"In Munich this All Hallow's Eve will be the most important meeting of the Illuminati since its modern inception eight years ago. At this rite which will be attended by the entire oligarchy, including the elder heads of the bloodlines, the magic Eleusinian Mystery will

---

[18] The Pyramid & The All Seeing Eye of Providence. This infamous symbol with its intriguing Latin phases remains perhaps one of the most famous conspiracies of all time. Though the engraving S. Drechsler describes would have been slightly different to the one we are familiar with, as the author claims an early version of the symbol did already exist (created by **William Barton**) and had been accepted in 1782 by the US as the Great Seal of America. Today its most celebrated expression is on the reverse of the US one dollar bill, first printed on the notes in 1933 under the auspices of President F.D. Roosevelt. Speculation about this esoteric symbol and its usage, meaning and history would appear to be almost endless (perhaps even more so after its mention in this memoir) and a great deal of time would have to be set aside to research this one topic alone such is the volume of literature written about it. Good luck!

be performed, summoning the spirit of their order to bestow on them power and guidance to win their current battle with the high court. Things are coming to a head. The Illuminati are running scared but are going to perform this rite anyway simultaneously mounting a coup d'état on the state before it can move on them. They already have many top officials under their control and also a dignitary of extremely high office who is part of their plan to take over the realm. It is no coincidence that there is another meeting in Munich that night at the Chancellery where the high court will sit to make judgement on Weishaupt's organisation. The Illuminati plan to wipe out all who attend this meeting and then fill their places with their own men thus becoming the rulers of Bavaria."

Struggling to take in such treason I scoffed, "And how do they intend to achieve this miracle, sir?"

"Ah, that's the interesting part of the plan." He sipped his tea and annoyingly at the point when he was to finally elaborate forcing me to ask, "Which is?"

"Blow up the chancellery building with them all inside."

I looked around the room for a sane person to confirm that I had heard him say what I thought he had.

"I beg your pardon, sir. I thought you said …"

"I did. Blow up the building with them all inside."

"Yes, yes, Professor that is the part I heard. It is the act of the demolition itself that sounds a little far-fetched to me."

"On the contrary, my friend, it is simple. The explosives are already laid deep within the building's foundations but are so well hidden they cannot be found. So we must lie in wait for the conspirators to arrive and attempt to trigger them." Noticing my stupefaction he raised an eyebrow. "Is it so surprising, Sebastian? Remember, a similar plot has been tried before. In 1605 Herr Guido Faulkes the English catholic planned to blow up the Houses of Parliament in London. Though I fear the Illuminati may be more successful than old Guido. That is; unless they are stopped."

Was this possible? My mind was spinning like a whirling dervish, a feeling I was getting used to experiencing every time I was in Professor's company.

He surveyed the plans on the table carrying on, "During the mission Klaus and I will be across the city at the chancellery ensuring it isn't destroyed while yourself and Francesca will lead the ground assault at the temple. She is to infiltrate the organisation using her particular skills and seduce the aforementioned dignitary then to extricate him from the ritual before the arrival of the magistrates who have been informed of the conspiracy. He is of such significance to the state that his exposure as an Illuminati member could mean the overturning of our entire monarchy. Although it is a great moral difficulty of my own we must help him flee before the arrival of the magistrates. Your task will be to look over Francesca and her charge during their time at the ceremony. You will break into the temple and maintain a vigil over the pair making sure she comes to no peril and that she escapes with our target, whereupon you will also leave and we will meet at a safe destination. Any questions?"

Quite understandably there were thousands shuffling like multiple decks of cards in my mind. I tried the first, "What ... should I do if someone tries to stop me?"

"Of course it will be better to remain undetected throughout the mission although, if you have to, you can kill as many Illuminati as you wish. We only need twenty to secure the conviction including some of the bigger names and perhaps Weishaupt himself. Although, if they are already dead, my friend maybe we need not trouble the courts at all."

I felt myself tense at this thought, still apprehensive at the potentially huge deviation in my behaviour that killing another human being would represent.

Van Halestrom carried on, "But you'll have your work cut out achieving such innumerable slaughter as over two-hundred members are expected to attend. Yes, the whole kit and caboodle will be there. This is our chance to catch them all red handed so to speak."

I understood his irony recalling the gruesome sacrificial slaughter that I had witnessed at the last of their demonic rituals and shuddered at the thought of seeing such horror again. He picked up his cup of tea without taking his eyes of the plans and I grasped the opportunity to get some more detail.

"Tell me, sir how were the Illuminati able to achieve the positioning of the charges in the Chancellery?"

"They infiltrated the Masons charged with constructing of such government buildings a long time ago. It is the reason I left. I used to be a Grand Dragon myself but the Illuminati's influence over the fraternity forced me to retire. For many centuries the Masons have been a fine tradition but now they are manipulated from within by a few crazed radicals. I fear their hidden hand will besmirch the organisation's good name far into the future. Anything else?" He finished his tea. *[19]

I was surprised to hear that Professor had been a Mason; A Grand Dragon no less. He was still full of secrets. I tried to focus on the task at hand and for which I had been training so long. Surely I could not go back now? Perhaps I could manage to stay undetected as the Professor advised then hopefully I would not have to kill anyone at all. Still, if I was going to play my part guarding Francesca I wanted to be able to do it properly.

I stuck my chin out with grim resolution and trying to sound as confident as possible mentioned, "I might be a little low on hardware for such a night out, sir. All I possess in terms of weaponry is the single shot pistol you gave me three months ago. I haven't fired that once."

"Ah yes, that reminds me." He got up and made his way over to his library shelf which was packed to the ceiling with hundreds of books. Pulling back a volume which I noticed was 'The Art of War' by Sun Tzu, he stood back and fascinatingly a door cut into the bookcase smoothly opened revealing a secret cupboard filled with enough weaponry to start a small war - even arming both sides. I ogled the incredible arsenal stunned at the inappropriateness of such an armoury on university premises.

"Is it really safe to have all this equipment here?" I gasped, counting at least twenty muskets and a couple of serious looking blunderbusses.

"Of course, Herr Drechsler, surely it's the last place anyone would think of looking." It wasn't what I meant though in one way

---

[19] Freemasons & the Illuminati. The belief that the tradition of Freemasonry has been infiltrated by the Illuminati has existed for hundreds of years. This claim is given historical credence by the official ratification of the two organisations at the Congress of Wilhelmsbad 1782. It is rumoured that the leaderships' true goals are only revealed to adepts at the higher degrees while the lower members are unaware of these plans and naturally defend the integrity of the institution. It is interesting that S. Drechsler recalls his mentor describing its influence like a 'hidden hand,' a term which has now become commonplace.

he was certainly right. Who in their right mind would expect to find such a deadly battery in a lecturer's study?

Sometime later I nervously shuffled away from the Professor's room carrying a huge suspicious looking black bag. A series of heavy palpitations swept through me as I considered its contents; one quadre bow, forty silver arrows, sixty wooden ones, two knives, two pistols, a short sword, four grenades, a file of poison, a knuckle duster, forty feet of silk twine, detailed plans of the temple and a truly fascinating garment of Japanese origin which was made from one piece of black material incorporating many pockets and designed to cover me from head to toe. Such was the haul there were several boxes I hadn't even had time to open. Altogether the bag, which was made from heavy black canvass, weighed at least sixty pounds.

I struggled under its weight and bulk with such difficulty that even getting it out of the university and off towards my lodgings was a chore in itself. Although my basement rooms were not far the bag was so heavy that I worried I would not complete the journey without doing myself an injury. Also there was the further complication of the detour I had to make avoiding Jan's lodgings. I stopped next to a tree by the road and pulled my collar up to keep out the murky fog that hung in the air that evening. Rubbing my hands together I wished that I had a nice warm carriage to take me home. Well sometimes in life you have to be careful what you wish for, especially to avoid labour or difficult confrontations because many moments of indolence and reluctance have led to a fall. And oh, how far we have to fall.

Chapter 20

Pearls before Swine

When the carriage I yearned for appeared out of the fog and pulled up beside me I could not believe my luck. Certain it was the Professor coming to my aid I had already half opened the door and was preparing to climb aboard when I heard Weishaupt exclaim with feigned surprise, "Ah, Herr Drechsler, fancy seeing you here. Why don't you get in? I'm sure I can take you wherever you wish to go."

I stood dumbstruck with the opened door in my hand peering into the shadowy carriage. Weishaupt's face appeared like a ghost out of the darkness. "Maybe it would seem rude to turn down a lift from your lecturer, Sebastian."

Though he was on his own except for his wizened old driver and I was carrying enough weaponry to arm a platoon, I still felt uneasy.

He forced a smile. "Jump aboard. To show you there are no hard feelings."

What could I do? Social etiquette prevented me from slamming the door in his face and telling him to go to blazes. After all, as he said, he was still my lecturer. I checked up and down the road feeling the comforting weight of the bag in my hand before taking a deep breath and pulling myself into the seat opposite him. He raised an eyebrow as the enormous bag crashed down beside me but overlooked it and asked, "Where to?"

I may have got into the carriage but even I wasn't so stupid as to reveal my address and called to the driver, "Just take me to the convent on Donaustrasse."

We set off with a jolt and he regarded me balefully. "I'm sure you don't live in a convent, Sebastian. Though it is a shame that you don't trust me enough to tell me where you live, at least you will share a carriage with me. So I think this marks an improvement in our relationship, don't you?"

He smiled and eased back into the gloom. "Now, I know we didn't get off to a good start."

'You can say that again!' I nearly shouted but bit my lip and let him go on.

"I also know that you are somewhat aware of my situation, as it were, and I yours. But, instead of this being a problem, I think it might lead to a greater sense of understanding between us."

With this he pushed a small box toward me with his foot and I peered down at it. After a moment he joked, "Take a look. It won't bite you."

I glanced at his untrustworthy grin barely visible in the shadows remembering what had happened the last time I opened a case such as this. I leant down examining the casket. It was the size of a large brick and had an elaborately carved lid. I slowly ran a finger over the intricate patterns.

"Go on, open it. You know you want to."

Not sure what he was up to but certain it was not a trap I gingerly opened the lid. As I did I felt my gasp reverberate around the carriage for inside the casket were ten beautiful glowing pearls. As it dawned on me that I was expected to take this treasure trove, enough to buy my mother and father a huge house in the country and provide me with wealth far beyond the dreams of most hopeless romantics, I felt all my blood flow straight to my groin. The women, the splendour, a carriage of my own, wait, not one! Two, three! C'mon, Sebastian, enjoy yourself. You can afford it. I fell back in my seat with my heart a flutter prospecting the fine life of a gentleman which I had tasted at the Professor's castle could be mine forever. Then I suddenly realised that paradoxically it would have no Professor in it at all. Weishaupt butted into my thoughts, "I'm sure there is enough there for a man of your tastes to have everything he could wish for."

"How do you know what I wish for?" I sniped, finally finding my voice.

"I see it in your face, Herr Drechsler. I see it when you look at my carriage. I see it when you look at the pearls. I see it when you look at my attractive maid. You know, you could just say the word and I would have her sent to your house. I'm sure you would appreciate that. Of course she would be fully willing to complete any task you set her, accommodating your every whim. All these things are within your grasp, Herr Drechsler. All you have to do is bend over and take them."

"Why don't you stick your pearls up your evil arse!" was, of course, what I should have said but alas, to my never-ending shame I didn't and the coach pulled away leaving me standing outside the convent on Donaustrasse with my bag of guns, bombs, knives and poison; all rendered useless because I had been bought off by my mortal enemy. Even after he had tried to kill me and ruin me I had let him get away with it because he'd given me a box of pearls. I felt all things at the same time; revulsion, joy, rage, sadness, calmness, anxiety. Everything from one extreme to the other to the stage where my ideas became a spinning wheel of confusion with me watching from its hub as the feelings blurred past me bewildering me with their polarity.

To add insult to injury I still had to lug the heavy bag back to my basement room a few streets away. After an exhausting haul I opened the front door and almost jumped out of my skin when Bacon greeted me from the shadows, "Good evening, sir."

"What on God's Earth! How the hell did you get in here?" I could make out his wiry frame sitting in my favourite chair.

"I see you took the box, sir. The Professor told me you would. Well, no matter. At least Weishaupt thinks he has bought you off."

I wasn't at all happy to find Bacon in my quarters spying on me. Now my secret was out. At that moment all I had wanted was to be alone with the loot and work out what I was going to do.

I enquired with some annoyance, "Why has your master sent you and not come here himself?"

"If we were to be fully correct about the matter, sir, he does not know I am here. Also, I feel that I should tell you, in reality, for whatever it is worth, it would appear that I am in fact the master and not the other way around."

My mind tried to untie this knotted sentence. Releasing the bond I realised what he was insinuating. But this was ridiculous! This man was merely a servant. Van Halestrom was the true heir and guardian of the castle. It was the Professor who had the job and reputation and distinctions. He was the obvious master. How could he dare make such a claim? I went to put him in his place once and for all. But as I went to speak my mind I remembered the Professor's words, 'Nothing is *ever* what it seems,' and how he had let Bacon speak to him and asked myself; could it be true?

It was at that moment as I stared at Bacon's impossibly enigmatic old face covered in shadows that I realised it simply must be. Just as every other thing that I had once believed was one way was, in fact, the other. As was becoming my habit I let out a huge sigh and prepared myself for the revelations I was no doubt about to endure before wearily begging, "For goodness sake, man just tell me the truth."

He took a measured breath and began, "The truth, sir, is that I was once the Professor's mentor and before that someone else mentored me. When the Professor's turn comes another will replace him and so on. That is the way our system works. And I should tell you, sir, we were also offered the bribe. It is something that happens to us all in the end."

He raised himself from the chair and went to leave.

"But ... what happens now? I stumbled unsure of my next move.

"Now, sir, I believe we are at the moment the Professor told you about; the moment where nothing surprises you except what you are prepared to do about it." He walked passed me and opened the door, politely bowed and bade me, "Good night, sir," then left. Damn the impertinent, unfathomable, unpredictable Bacon and his blasted riddles. Thunder and lightning! This bunch were an infuriating gang of constant liars. I sat on a stool looking at the box wondering how long it would take for Weishaupt's pretty maid to get there.

Hell's bells, what was I to do? If I took the pearls and fled, as Weishaupt obviously wanted, wouldn't the Professor or Bacon come after me? What a terror that would be. Even if I was armed to the teeth with a bag full of military hardware, I still wouldn't fancy my chances against Van Halestrom in his undergarments with his hands tied behind his back. No thank you. Anyway, I would miss him terribly, inconsolably, and the rest of them, especially Francesca. The thought of a life without her was unthinkable. And what would I do anyway? Wander around aimlessly, a member of the idle rich but one that must constantly look over his shoulder. And how would I explain it to my parents? My father would get the truth out of me in two minutes flat and my mother even faster. Of course I knew what the right thing to do was or else I wouldn't have been sitting there looking at the box in the first place but galloping Petrova toward the jewellery quarter in Augsburg to exchange the pearls for good old hard cash.

Added to this was the complexity that I was seen as Van

Halestrom's apprentice and heir. Could it be true? Of course, I had fantasised about this but up until now I had kept these fanciful notions at the back of my mind. After what Bacon had said this seemed more like an impending certainty rather than a distant possibility especially if I didn't get killed in the meantime. Though the responsibility of this inheritance was of such enormous weight at that moment I could not even consider it. I closed the box but not before taking one of the pearls, for my old age you understand, in case I lived that long.

The following morning I received a letter from my mother. It read; 'It was so good to see you recently. You know that your father and I both trust you to be good but that whatever happens we will always be proud of you.' I'm not ashamed to say that I cried for some time after reading it. It was profoundly touching just then to be reminded of the tenderness of my loving and decent parents especially after all I had recently been through.

The next day I galloped Petrova through the southern gates of the city but instead of going to Augsburg I was headed for Munich. I had decided to carry out my mission to help my friends thwart the evil Illuminati. With these thoughts at the front of my mind I began to feel a steely resolve forging within me to carry on to the next level for it was there that I believed I would find my new self.

Chapter 21

The Eye of Horus

All Hallow's Eve 1784 was a strangely balmy night but as I huddled behind the parapet on the roof of the Imperial Exchange in the heart of Munich, I could feel the cold hand of fear on my shoulder. Twenty feet below me in the darkness stretched out the Temple of Eleusis. I peered through my crossbow's telescope watching the dignitaries being greeted at the entrance. My nerves were as taut as the strings on my bow as I waited for my Lady Francesca's appearance along with her new secret friend. Despite never meeting the man I already despised him enough to punch him in the face - knowing that his face was probably, even as I thought it, being pushed into her heaving bosom in the back of some expensive carriage. Trying to shake the discomforting image I concentrated back on my mission. The Professor had said that he would, "Let me know," when he was in place at the Chancellery but I couldn't understand how as it was over a mile away.

As I pondered this there was a bang in the sky as a rocket exploded exactly over Van Halestrom's position. I watched the flare slowly burn out before peeping back through my telescope. The distant chime of a church clock rang out and exactly on time Francesca appeared in my lens with her companion in tow.

Good God! The scheme was like the workings of a clock. I reflected that they must have done this many times before then immediately prayed they had not because my sweet Francesca was stuck to the lips of her new, and I hoped pretended, beau like a hungry leech. Indeed, such was the intimacy of the embrace and the size of the presumptuous swine's enormous feathered hat, that I could not even see his face. I tried to convince myself that she would never fall for a ponce who would wear such a thing. Only to observe them clutch each other even more licentiously and move rather unsteadily into the temple. The other guests had looked similarly relaxed and I wondered if they had all been drinking the same sickly potion with which I had been drugged at the Chapel of Liebfrauenmünster a few months before.

But there was no time for such ponderings: It was time to move. I hoped that my training had prepared me for what was about to come and, aiming my crossbow at the raised porch on top of the temple roof, squeezed the trigger sending an arrow flying into the night. Trailing a silk twine behind it the bolt found its mark in the porch's wooden structure with a resounding thud. I tested the line, giving it a really hard pull to make sure it was secure as it had to bear my weight as I slid across to the other side.

I had practised on a similar rope slide back at the castle. But this would be the first time I had done it in earnest, on a mission, at night fifty feet from the ground. I stopped thinking about it and tied the other end of the twine round a chimney. Trying to get the better of my vertigo which was erupting inside me like a volcano I reloaded the empty stay of the bow, as I had been trained, before throwing it over my shoulder on its strap. After making sure the rest of my weapons were secure I took a deep breath, put a loop over the twine, grabbed it with both hands and prepared to do what seemed like the most foolhardy thing I had ever done in my life and threw myself off the side of the five-storey building.

I couldn't have been more pleasantly surprised. Maybe it was because of the intense worry I had suffered beforehand but once I got going I rather enjoyed the brief mid-air ride and slid towards the roof of the temple at exactly the right speed with my black cloak fluttering heroically behind me.

What I enjoyed less was the unmistakeable sound of the chimney giving way over my shoulder. Luckily the line stayed tight long enough to let me land safely and I turned around in time to see the chimney stack totter then finally come crashing down in an immense cloud of dust and ash. I glanced about in fretful anguish as the tower of masonry poured into the street. Like an idiot I put my finger to my lips as if to tell the tumbling stonework to make less noise - because it was very noisy, very noisy indeed. Certain my presence would be given away by this terrible racket I cowered listening to the last brick come to rest and waited for the alarm to be sounded.

To my relief none was forthcoming and I pulled in the twine with shaking hands trying to retrieve as much of my stealth as possible. I crouched down getting my bearings. Having been over the plans of the temple I had a good understanding of the building's layout and quickly found the door leading from the roof. Finding it open I wasn't a bit surprised. Who would expect somebody coming in from the roof? I descended the stairs and arrived, as planned, in a corridor running the width of the building's top floor. Van Halestrom had told me that the dignitaries including Francesca were to retire to individual chambers in the basement and change into their robes before attending the main ceremony which would begin at exactly nine o'clock.

I knew there was a service ladder at the end of this corridor that led down to the cellars where the chambers were located. I ran along the corridor to the end and found the door of the shaft then got inside. After mounting the ladder I closed the door and breathed a sigh of relief. So far so good, I had penetrated the lion's den and I hadn't had to kill anyone - yet. I climbed down hoping to find Francesca and to check to see that nothing untoward was happening to her – whatever that meant on this strangest of nights.

Reaching the bottom I dismounted the ladder seeing that I was in a corridor which ran behind the dressing chambers. As I crept down the narrow passageway I quickly saw its real purpose. There were spy holes drilled through the walls of the dressing rooms. Some of the holes even had chairs placed below them where I presumed the spying had become so constant the peeping tom needed extra support due to his fatigue.

I put my eye to the nearest hole. Good Lord! I got a shock when I did. For inside the room a naked young woman sat astride a large man in a chair and was enthusiastically riding away. Rather whimsically she was wearing his hat – a bishop's mitre! I pulled my eye away then quickly placed it back thinking, 'lucky old bastard.' Before realising, with a fright, my good lady might be up to something similar. Rushing to the next hole I stared through it and instantly wished that I had not. For two men were having the most strenuous of physical intimacies with each other which, to me, was a purely repellent thing to behold and I yanked my eye away. Shuddering at this last scene I shook my head to rid me of the foul vision. I was certain that during my quick glance into both rooms I had seen a similar flask to the ones containing the toxic brew that had drugged me so heavily before. I thought it might explain the exuberance of the sexual acts that I had witnessed. Also I understood that this Dionysian celebration used alcohol and other intoxicating substances to increase the level of revelry and excess signifying the descent of Persephone into the underworld.

Two hoots to Persephone! I wondered if I actually wanted to see what was going on in the following rooms. My mind was made up when I heard voices approaching from around the corner. I ran back to the ladder and climbed far enough up it so as not to be seen by whoever was coming. The voices came closer before passing right below my feet. There was some dirty laughter as the owner of one of the voices spied through the next hole and my jealous mind sprang back into action producing a vivid scene of incredible sexual paranoia that only one's own consciousness can generate. After a while the first voice let the owner of the second take a look and he jeered dirtily too. The two perverts stayed in their positions for so long I feared that I must go back upstairs as the time was fast approaching for the ceremony to begin.

Reluctantly I scaled back up the ladder annoyed that I had failed in my mission to keep a watchful eye over Francesca. Trying hard not to imagine what she might be up to I quietly closed the door of the shaft and sneaked back along the corridor to the central staircase to check the lay of the land. Below me I could see a solitary guard at the archway leading to the balcony above the central hall where the ritual was to be held. I did not want to do away with him unless absolutely necessary so I waited for a full two minutes trying to avoid the grisly act. But when I heard the fanfare announcing the start of the ceremony and still the idiot had not moved I unsheathed one of my daggers and prepared to do what I had trained for so many times.

I took a deep breath holding the blade out in front of me and took three ninja-like steps toward him. But when I was only two paces away - stone me - if the sentinel casually strolled off. Like a startled pheasant I turned and ran behind a column with my heart pounding so loudly that I was certain everybody in the place would be able to hear it. After a few seconds I peered round the column. Luckily the guard had gone off in the opposite direction so after a quick glance up and down to check the coast was clear I dashed through the archway.

The balcony was exactly as I had pictured it and overlooked the large domed hall which was steadily filling with cultists. What I didn't expect to see was the huge capless pyramid in the middle of the room which stood nearly as high as the balcony. I stooped to a crouch behind the stone balustrade and crept along until I was directly overlooking the open head of the pyramid. Peering in between balustrade's pillars I watched as the last of the cultists filed in wearing their identical hooded robes and suddenly realised: 'How the devil am I going to see my lady when she is dressed in the same fashion?' To my utter horror I immediately found out. For with her head swaying as if in a trance she appeared from the shadows at the back of the hall supported by two red-robed sentinels.

Although it had taken a long time to see the parts of Francesca that I had already viewed, I now saw pretty much all the rest of her at once. Apart from her nipples and groin which were covered in a skimpy piece of black material forming a 'V,' she was absolutely naked. I say it now but despite the terrible fear I felt for her at that moment, I could not help thinking how incredibly beautiful she was. Indeed, more beautiful than anything I had ever seen. I gasped at her gorgeousness before bringing myself around in a fluster of self-control. I wondered why they had afforded her the dignity of letting her wear even this smallest of garments and not placed the same terrible bag on her head as her poor sister. My question was promptly answered. They didn't! One of the attending sentinels pulled a black bag down over her head and tightened the drawstring round her throat. Her head swayed languidly as he did this convincing me she had been drugged. If not she would have kicked him so hard in his potted potatoes that he could have eaten them mashed for his supper. I gulped as the sentinels pushed her towards the base of the pyramid where another figure had appeared. I instantly recognised his golden robes and arrogant striding posture. It was Weishaupt. Francesca was forced to kneel at his feet and a silence fell around the hall.

Weishaupt raised his arms and addressed the crowd, "Tonight my brothers, for we are all brothers on this mystic eve, we have come together to celebrate our spirits' return to the underworld for the winter. But this is not a time of decline or death for us, for death becomes our life as night becomes our day, illuminated by Venus our guiding light. Tonight we will perform the Eleusinian mystery and its power will be passed through all levels of our brotherhood from the ultimate one, our celestial master. Now prepare to behold his awesome and eternal light."

What the blazes did that mean? I was half-inclined to leave at that point having such little wish to find out but of course my sense of duty and honour, and the fact that I was scared rigidly to the spot, made up my mind for me. Droning incantations began with the emergence of four Cabalist priests wearing large breastplates. *[20] I recognised their chanting from somewhere. God knows where! This was not the time to try to remember. The shamans took up their positions at the four corners of the pyramid, swinging golden bowls of smoking incense around their feet. Now came the next terrible shock. Twenty paces behind Francesca appeared the devil with the purple cushion. Already on it the same curved knife that I had seen before. I rolled onto my side freeing the crossbow from my back and placed it under my chin. Peering through the weapon's telescope at the cluster of men surrounding Francesca I prepared to take the head off the first or last evil bastard who went near her.

What in Jehovah's name was I going to do now? The situation was utterly desperate and getting worse by the moment. I had fifty arrows in my quiver and there were at least two-hundred deviant lunatics downstairs all capable of murdering the woman of my dreams, and occasionally my nightmares. One thing was certain; and I would have wagered anything including the box of pearls back in my room, my lady was in no fit state to smuggle out our intended target or do anything at all for that matter as she knelt before Weishaupt passively swaying from side to side.

My mouth became dry and my trigger hand started to sweat round the handle of the bow. Weishaupt faced the top of the pyramid which was becoming increasingly shrouded in smoke from the priests' ceremonial urns. Indeed, I almost lost sight of the cushion as the fumes became so thick. He called out to the pinnacle of the

---

[20] Illuminati Kabbalist Priests. It is odd that S. Drechsler remembers seeing these priests during such a ceremony. Though the Kabbalah, a mystic form of Judaism, has many interpretations, some of them quite unsettling, this ceremony is unusual (as you may well imagine!). Traditionally, these men would have been clothed in long ornate robes and wearing necklaces decorated with twelve large precious stones representing the twelve tribes of Israel. The Kabbalah speaks of nine dimensions or 'spheres'. To travel from one to another a gate must be formed and legend has it the Kabbalist priests can achieve this phenomenon when performing certain mystic rituals. Much speculation, some of it terrifying, exists as to what is contained in these spheres.

edifice his voice clearly audible amidst the priests' droning chants which seemed to be coming to a climax

"Come to us, Oh Holiest of Ones. Come to dine with us and feast on those who have stood in our way. Oh glorious Horus, I exhort thee; create yourself for us now!"

Despite all this ludicrous mumbo jumbo to my astonishment the pyramid shuddered so violently that the first few rows of the congregation all took a step back.

"What is this energy?" I murmured, certain for one thing that a naked whore was not about to come out of the top and wish Weishaupt happy birthday. The vibrations were so pronounced that I found it impossible to concentrate on my target and, for just one second, I took my eye off the lens. As I did I witnessed a small mysterious point of light appear over the top of the pyramid. Trying to ignore it I focused back to the pillow relieved to see the knife still there. I watched it intently until, forced by the power of the growing brightness in the room, I had to look again and saw that the small point of light had become a swirling ball glowing vigorously under my line of sight. I heard the calls of Weishaupt straining from below, "Oh mystic night we hail thee. Come to us and show us thy glorious illumination!"

As this oath ended another intense rumble emanated from within the pyramid accompanied by an unearthly crackling noise whereupon the glowing ball magnified still further rapidly becoming too bright to ignore. Such was the power of the light I knew no one in the hall would have been able to look at anything else and then, as I stared in horror, in one awful moment the ball metamorphosed into a monstrous transparent eye. Unable to believe what I was seeing I froze as the dreadful apparition blinked revealing a huge iris which gazed down upon the startled crowd bathing them in a terrifying white light. The cultists gasped deeply at the sight which was hell itself right there in the room. I instantly envied Francesca who could not see it because you never forget that vision, that sight. For to witness it just once will mean that every minute of every hour of every day, for the rest of your life, you will see it again, and again, until it is burnt into your mind forever. My body shook, my teeth chattered and my hair truly stood on end at that dreadful moment when I saw the awfulness that is the eye of Horus.

So shocked was I that in my terror I had pushed myself against the wall at the back of the balcony with my crossbow in my lap and my hand over my face. Who would have behaved in any other way after seeing that? I don't know but if they claimed any different they would be a liar.

Weishaupt beseeched again, calling out amongst the blinding light and smoke, "You have come for the flesh that is your tribute Oh Mighty One. We are but moments away from that instant!"

There was a pause before the dastardly eye blinked its revolting lid again and then, Holy Mother of Christ, the thing actually spoke.

"Bring her to me!" It boomed. At least that's what I thought it said. It was strangely muffled and I wondered if there was a problem with the entity's voice. That's when I thought, as it hovered below me, 'You odious shit! Coming all this way for my beautiful Francesca then you get here and start shouting.' My dislike for the phantasm was growing. No doubt helped by the fact that it was not staring directly at me. For if it had been I would probably have run all the way home to my mother and jumped into her arms. Although I was nearly blinded by the rays I retrieved my status with the weapon and quickly found my target again as the cushion returned into my sights. Weishaupt must have been waiting for the moment the bombs were to go off at the Government Chancellery and I sensed that it was seconds away.

"Prepare the girl!" I heard him call and felt another rumble from inside the pyramid.

'Christ make these arrows fly true,' I prayed and nearly screamed as Francesca's head was pulled back revealing her long white neck. I knew it was time for action as I saw the man who was to complete the murder pick up the knife. Coolly I waited until he raised it above his head. That was close enough and I pulled the trigger. 'Click!' The arrow tore off and hit him in the face ending him right there and then. He was the first I ever killed.

Of course, he did not know what had hit him. Neither did anyone else. The room was very smoky down below and it must have been impossible to tell what was going on. The cultist flew backwards flailing into the audience and dropped the knife which I saw rattle across the floor.

"Find that you bastards!" I cursed as the idiots ran round constantly having to adjust their hoods to see where they were going. It would take them a while to work out what had happened let alone to find the blade. I focused back on Francesca. Out of the corner of my eye I saw a cultist who did not have the same problem as he had removed his hood and was standing right next to me. Good God! It was Jan Kohler insanely smiling down at me. He said in a chillingly conversational tone, "Sorry old chum," and stabbed me with his rapier. As the blade plunged down he pulled a face that I had only ever seen once before when he had beaten up a smaller kid at school with all too obvious pleasure. But in a million to one shot the blade deflected off one of the daggers in my pocket and hit the floor under my side. I kicked him in the balls for that. He wasn't pissing around so I wasn't going to either. "Aargh!" He screamed clutching his testicles and fell onto my chest knocking the wind out of me.

Somebody else who was not too pleased was the evil eye itself. I could feel its intense light burning the back of my head as it roared and the pyramid shuddered again. It seemed as though the spirit of Lucifer, or Horus, or whatever it was wasn't happy. Who was? It was a bad night all round. Lady Francesca was about to have her throat slit, Weishaupt was losing his control, the Devil wasn't getting his dinner and I was being strangled by my best friend. Jan's face lit by the glowing, crackling light pulled a fiendishly murderous expression and he shouted, "You're out of your depth college boy! You should have come with us when you had the chance. They will win in the end. They are too powerful to resist!"

His big hands tightened round my neck as though the power he spoke of was in his very fists. He was certainly still as strong and as heavy as an ox and I felt he was going to win as he had done when we were children. He had me pinned down with his knees on my arms and my position seemed hopeless. Surely I was going to die. Killed by my oldest friend I began to weep and prepared myself for death.

'Thud!' A silver arrow appeared in Jan's forehead forcing his eyes to bulge out with mortal shock and his blood to splatter down on my face. I pulled myself from under his writhing corpse then with the great power that a mother possesses when its child is in peril hoisted his shaking body onto his feet and leant him against the balustrade. I stood there on the balcony looking into his dying eyes and said, "Goodbye old friend," then shielding my own eyes from the radiating orb below us I released my grip. It was half instinct, half horror that made me let go and Jan tumbled over the rail. I had not meant to do it. It just happened that way. I watched as his body flail then hit the side of the fiendish floating eye and with an enormous explosion of ectoplasm and a mighty thunderclap the apparition disappeared.

Holy Christ! I took a deep breath but instantly coughed up the obnoxious smoke filling the air. Looking down into the crowd I could see bedlam all around but to my relief the gorgeous Lady Francesca was still intact and kneeling in the same position. I glanced across the hall to the shadows from where the arrow had come. Van Halestrom! It must have been him. I peered down but could not see Jan's body anywhere and shook my head in wonder. Though wondering was not the expedient thing to do at that moment and I knew it. It was time to act. I picked up the bow and, sticking one up at my fear of heights, spectacularly gate-vaulted the balustrade, sliding down the face of the pyramid and jumping up at the bottom ready for action.

Weishaupt was nowhere to be seen amongst the raving busy charging about in alarm after the explosion. But one of them, much cooler than the others, had somehow found the knife and was approaching Francesca from behind. He spotted me and thrust the blade out in front of him coming to attack. He didn't stand a chance. Now that I had killed once I was more than prepared to do it again. With a hail of bolts I almost cut the fool in half and the parts of him that were left fell to the floor. Three arrows in that one, 'must save ammunition,' I calculated and squatted down to reload. Glancing about it seemed that he was the only one who was putting up a fight and I pulled myself over to Francesca whispering softly, "It is me, my lady. Sebastian."

There was a vacant murmur from inside the bag which I hastily tried to remove. As I did I felt a tap on the shoulder and whipped my head round to see another robed devil standing over me. This bounder tried to punch me but I dodged the blow and sprang to my feet smacking him right between the slits. Feeling that somehow this evil blaggard considered Francesca to be his I went to hit him again. But before I could incredibly his hood was removed from behind. Seeing the unmasked man stagger backwards I got such a surprise my mouth fell wide open. Well I recognised *this* face for it was on half the statues in town! It was Joseph II Emperor of the entire Holy blasted Roman Empire with the Professor standing right behind him crying, "Not in the face! Not in the face! He's got to have his portrait painted next week."

I pulled back in disbelief as Van Halestrom, resplendent in full black attire with matching tricorn hat and neckerchief, supported the regent's fall. In a swift manoeuvre belying his years he swept the unconscious load onto his shoulders and proceeded to carry him like a butcher lifting a slaughtered pig, calling out, "Good work, Sebastian! Now take Francesca and lead the way out."

Obeying immediately I lifted up my lady and finished removing the bag revealing her beautiful face. My heart flew when she peered at me happily and slurred, "Jungkinda?" Clutching her round the waist I began guiding her through the surrounding pandemonium. The sentinel's tiny slits weren't helping matters and the panicking cultists kept running into each other in their haste to escape the smoky hall. It seemed that the sight of the Devil appearing and then blowing up in front of them was apparently enough to make even the most unrepentant Satanist run around screaming, "Aargh!"

What did they expect? Bloody idiots! Serves 'em blasted right! As we continued another one of the sentinels approached us looking suspiciously at our human cargoes. Unwisely, he went to stop us and I let him have it with a shot from my hip, 'Zut!' A bolt flew into his midriff and I cursed, "Happy All Hallow's Eve to you too! That'll teach you to go round raising Lucifer!" Then I shot him in his hood to prove a point. This one was silver and because the range was so short, it half-cleaved the bastard's head off flashing out the other side with a blast of crimson brain matter.

In the general panic everyone was making their way to the front of the temple but I knew there was a way out at the side. Making sure Van Halestrom was close behind I led us through a door into a large empty room which quietly reverberated with the sound of our hurrying footsteps. From this room we fell into the outer corridor and ran down it until reaching another door leading out onto the street. I tried to open it but this one was locked as I had suspected. I turned to the Professor not knowing what to do. He nodded and, still carrying the Emperor on his back, produced from under his cloak a stout blunderbuss that looked as though had been shortened. I threw the bow over my shoulder on its strap whereupon Van Halestrom tossed me the weapon. With one arm still around Francesca's naked waist I tried not to let her charms distract me and pointed the gun at the door. Shielding Francesca as best I could I fired. 'Boom!'

An explosion of splinters burst over us and I raised my head to see the destroyed hanging on its hinges. I finished it off with a kick and led us to the iron fence outside. Promisingly we were just short of the alley where I had left Petrova and I got ready to try a trick I had been practising myself. I gave a shrill whistle and within seconds my faithful beauty appeared round the corner and came to stand by the railings. This made the next part of our work much easier for it allowed Lady Francesca to be placed on top of the horse while I sat astride the fence. Then with the Emperor, of all people, we did the same. Until, finally I had the pair of them laid out over the saddle and covered with a blanket.

I had already heard the whistles of magistrates sounding from the front of the temple. Fortunately there was no one down our side of the building and I thanked my lucky stars for this as it sounded like a sizeable riot was beginning between the hordes of startled cultists and the arriving forces of the law. Turning Petrova in the other direction I nodded to Van Halestrom who had pulled himself up on the railing. He glanced towards the ensuing commotion and with the shouts and cries echoing round to us muttered, "I must see this. Go now and I shall see you in an hour at the meeting place."

After pulling up his neckerchief he leapt down from the fence calling out, "Stay in the shadows my friend." and heeding his own advice disappeared into the darkness. With the riot fading fast over my shoulder I did not look back but trotted off and found some secluded lanes to travel down to the pre-arranged destination. Keeping clear of anyone for a full hour I waited until the Professor reappeared along with Klaus in a small cart. We placed the bodies on board, tied Petrova behind, and made our way out of the city. Sticking to the back streets we saw not a soul and were soon rattling through the countryside.

Amazingly the two people we carried had not stirred at all despite being bundled about. Francesca was still in a trance wrapped in her blanket and playfully slurring every now and then, "No I don't want any more." Whatever that meant? I dreaded to think and hoped she might not remember. The Emperor, and I constantly had to keep reminding myself of that fact - the Emperor of Holy Rome was in the back of the cart! - was also still resolutely unconscious.

"I did not hit him that hard," I tutted considering that he was either a milksop or he'd had as much of the grog as the rambling Francesca. It had been convenient that they both slept before while we needed them to be quiet but now as we swept along I wished for her to wake up urgently so I could point out to her how truly heroic I had been. I asked Van Halestrom if he had any smelling salts which he said he hadn't with a wry smile knowing what I was about. He was right of course. I didn't give a fig about the pathetic Prince Joseph but that woman I wanted to wake up right there and then and so much it hurt.

"There will be time for that later," reassured the Professor before cleverly changing the subject. He regaled me with the tale of how, with Klaus's help, he had foiled the plot to blow up the chancellery catching the conspirators in the act and quickly enough to be able to come to my aid at the temple with the shot that saved my life - and ended Jan's. I had to fight back my tears when he asked me to forgive him for killing my oldest friend. Even though he had tried to kill me his death was a terrible blow. Along with the shock of the night's other events I soon found myself gabbling senselessly to the Professor and Klaus, "I can't believe it. Jan is gone and Lucifer! He is real. You saw him too, Professor. The evil eye appearing above the pyramid. God help us all."

But to my astonishment the Professor stoically replied, "Yes Jan is gone, Sebastian but as far as the Devil is concerned I believe that tonight we have been witness to 'Deus ex machina' as the Greek playwrights called it: The use of machinery to put the gods upon the stage. I suspect this performance was the work of a master illusionist employed to achieve much the same effect."

"Master illusionist!" I cried, confounded by his scepticism.

He raised a finger carrying on, "I believe the searing light and crackling noise was produced by a mixture of phosphorous and gunpowder. That is what you smelt after Jan's body fell into the eye." He nodded at my coat suggesting, "Smell your clothes. Is it not the same scent as when you've been hunting?"

I gave my sleeve a sniff. Though I did recognise the odour as that of gunpowder I recalled firing the blunderbuss at the door so I was still not convinced. But before I could argue he continued, "It is my belief that the eye itself was clockwork and the voice from inside the pyramid belonged to a human not the devil. Remember, Sebastian, mindless religion has done much of the hard work for Weishaupt; ruthlessly creating the superstition and ignorance in the minds of the populace to ensure their life-long credulity and manipulation. This is the fear that the master illusionist employs to achieve control, even over his own cult. After all, do you honestly think that Lucifer would be sent back to hell by a single body falling into his aura like that?"

Unable to control my peevish bluster any longer I finally managed to interject, "But, sir, tell me then, what about my dream? You said it yourself, you had the same one. Remember? We both saw the eye at the top of the pyramid. You told me it was Lucifer himself!"

"In the end, my lad, a dream is just a dream and originates from the same collective consciousness that produces all dreams. As far as the Devil goes, I'm sure the Illuminati believe he is real. I just don't share their opinion; that's all."

This was insufferable and again I went to argue my case, "But surely it was the blackest of magic, sir. Right there in front of us. You saw it yourself!"

"Ah, but what is magic, Sebastian? People expect magic to come in the form of a miracle such as a burning bush, a statue of Christ weeping blood, even a visit from an angel or a ghost while all the time they overlook the simple magic of the everyday world; the movement of a bat at night, the birth of a child, the earth-shattering power of nature," he smiled hopefully, "And even the strength of feelings we have for others."

I flashed a look behind me at Francesca knowing what he was insinuating then turned back to see him chuckle to himself. In my youthful ignorance and armed back then, as I was with a fertile imagination, I was still convinced that I had fought the very beast from hell and sent him back from whence he came. Thus I was thoroughly unprepared to have the wind taken out of my sails by theories of clockwork devils, blasted phosphorous and collective consciousness - whatever that was. Somehow though I knew that Van Halestrom's points were plausible because of my Christian upbringing I could not help but think I had seen the dark secrets of the world revealed. I prayed for Jan's soul and hoped that God would carry on protecting me from the evil forces which I had beheld.

After a five hour journey throughout which we carried on our vexing debate all the way we eventually reached Frau Hoffmeister's in the early morning. The stable lad was in his usual place sitting on a low branch of a tree watching as we rolled by and began following up the driveway. He haloed ahead between long stretching yawns and the welcoming old lady was there to meet us as we pulled up outside the farmhouse.

Despite all the night's extraordinary revelations the peck on the cheek I received from Francesca, who was pretty much herself by then, was the most magical of all. I grinned with pure delight as she waved and wished me goodnight with a saucy pout before Frau Hoffmeister escorted her and Klaus inside. The Professor followed them bundling the Emperor before him. I was still finding it hard to believe that it was our mighty Sovereign. Maybe because Van Halestrom had put a sack over his head which led poor old Joseph, who was obviously still slightly disorientated to bang his head going in through the front door. I laughed at this and sniffed the wet autumn air before letting out a sigh.

"That was a day and a half," I murmured and reflected that it actually had been. As this notion sank in I made my way inside and was soon enjoying a deep and restful sleep and happily having no bad dreams at all. *[21]

---

[21] Emperor Joseph II Holy Roman Empire 1784. Though I can find no official record of the plot to destroy the Bavarian Chancellery or a connection between the Illuminati and this famous European aristocrat there is every chance that they may both have existed. Joseph, historically known as one of the 'Enlightened Despots' and also the brother of Marie Antoinette, was definitely (though secretively) a Freemason, belonging to a lodge entitled ***Zur neugekronten Hoffnung*** (New Crowned Hope) and a member of 'many other' secret societies at that time. Interestingly, before this point, he had dealt favourably with Weishaupt's organisation but as S. Drechsler's account may explain, at the end of 1784 his treatment of the Illuminati definitely cooled. As the memoirs suggest any other stance may have posed insurmountable political problems for him. Historical examples of the destruction of buildings being used for political ends include, as the text mentions, Guy Fawke's failed attempt to destroy the House of Lords and also the successful torching of the Reichstag by the Nazis in 1933.

Chapter 22

Celebrations and Frustrations

Two days later all five of us stood at the end of the long table in the castle Landfried; myself, Van Halestrom, Lady Francesca, Bacon and Klaus. Happily bringing our glasses together in a toast we chanted as one, "To our great success!"

This salute was followed by a condescending cough from Bacon who held a bottle of French champagne before him.

"Will you be celebrating all night, sir or may I retire before tomorrow?"

The Professor excused him, "Yes, Bacon you may. We may be up for some time."

The butler slipped away leaving the bottle in its bucket and we eagerly took our places to enjoy the feast that lay before us. After finishing the dinner we relaxed around the fire in the adjacent room. Klaus and the Professor were discussing something called evolution while Francesca and I, after much steady flirtatiousness from us both, now came together for our first real intimate chat.

Her beautiful eyes twinkled in the candlelight as she spoke, "I am truly thankful to you, Sebastian Drechsler. You know that don't you? No jokes or tricks or fingers crossed behind my back."

She pulled out two crossed fingers from behind her back then laughed playfully and undid them to show that she was teasing.

It worked of course. But then everything she did worked in terms of increasing my romantic feelings for her. I smiled back happy to have this natural moment where we could talk like normal folk.

"This night you are truly more beautiful than I have ever seen you before," I sighed admiring her wonderfully fine yet haughty features and her flowing hair which trailed down seductively onto her pale shoulders.

"What? Even more beautiful than at the temple?" she joked, provoking me further with a seductive grin.

"Yes more, because tonight you are yourself. And that is the person I have always wanted to meet. That is enough to make you more attractive than my mind could ever invent."

Her demeanour changed to that of sincerity. "You really are charming, aren't you?" She smiled sentimentally as her lip quivered then in her eye appeared a tiny tear.

I read her mind and ventured, "I'm so sorry about your sister."

She resolutely stuck out her chin.

"It seems we have both suffered a loss recently. Though in my case, I had expected it for some time. It was a course Montarese had chosen for herself a long time ago. She had become very unhappy. We were separated as children when my mother ran away taking Montarese with her. I had only just met her again. Although sadly we were never close it made it worse to know her, if only a little, before she died."

She sniffed away her tear, perked up and asked, "But enough of these sadness's. How are your studies going? The Professor informs me you're an excellent student of everything you attempt and quick to gain an understanding of it. And from what I've come to know about you, and your bravery, it seems you have the ability to learn much and quickly: Which I like a lot."

And how I liked this? Of all the nights of good pleasure at the castle this was one of the best. The stunning Lady Francesca, for she *was* a real lady from Russian nobility as she explained, talked with me for a whole hour as we chatted happily between ourselves. Joking with each other and even touching sometimes like those who are courting do and in the most pleasing of ways. It was exactly what I had wished for since the first time we had met.

She explained to me that Jan had been seduced by Weishaupt's agents who met him through the money-changers where he worked. It was he who had followed me the night when I had sensed someone behind me returning on the road from Stuttgart. That's why she was sent to gain his confidences at the Chapel of Liebfrauenmünster. But she had lost him in the orgy and her sister, who was under the Illuminati's control, had lured him into performing the carnal act. On hearing this I felt sure that it was him who had left the note on my dresser to scare me away so we would not end up having to fight.

With these intricacies explained I felt as though a great weight had been lifted from me and after the pain of a friendship lost found great happiness in the thought of a new and perhaps much deeper one beginning.

Later on Klaus played the harpsichord and the two of us danced with such merriment that even the Professor joined us too. There was much joy and laughter as Francesca's and my own eyes constantly met happily exploring each other's real thoughts. These were obviously those of tenderness as we all joked and sang into the night.

After descending from our lonely rooms the next morning I was again immediately by her side. As we walked to breakfast she asked, "Are you always up this early, Herr Drechsler?"

"There was nothing else to do after dreaming of you all night but to be with you in the morning to see if my dream was real."

Feeling the moment was right I stopped and turned to her placing my arm around her waist. She smiled at me with perfect truth fully reflecting the care I felt for her and we kissed for the first time. And it was a kiss I shall never forget. Not too hard or too fast, her wet lips slid provocatively over mine as I heard her eagerly inhale. My heart beat like a savage's drum and I pulled her neck towards me as her bosom heaved against my own. Feeling my hand start to …

"That's quite enough of that you two," called the Professor, ruining the moment. He strode past with his regular grin and carried on, "Especially before breakfast. Come on. Bacon has a message for us."

We parted and laughed before sharing another moment of tender embrace. In the dining room we found Bacon who did indeed have a message for us delivered only half an hour before. He coughed loudly before opening it and began to read it out. Though the message contained was the best possible news such was Bacon's style of oratory this was a soliloquy of such utter tedium that its repetition now would greatly sully the pages of this fine manuscript. So for the sake of the story and the reader this is basically what it said: We had achieved our goals of exposing the Illuminati to the authorities who were preparing to exile the organisation along with the membership from Bavaria altogether.

We howled with approval congratulating one another deeply. It would not have happened without our work and the clever extrication then quick restoration to his throne of our pathetic Emperor Joseph, after a damn good telling off behind the scenes, leaving him in a position strong enough to let his more reasoned state officials clear out the nest of vipers altogether.

"Hurrah!" I cried at the top of my voice, only to have my hearty bonfire promptly flushed away with a huge bucket of horse's piss. For the snooty Bacon then announced that the Lady Francesca would have to leave that day for Russia to see her father, a Grand Duke, because there was business of great importance there.

Not now! Not now! Not when everything had been finally resolved. Surely this was the time for us to go walking in the forest kicking leaves over one another and spend long afternoons together in front of the fire like young lovers do. The business was of such insufferable importance that she could not delay the journey. And so to my utter blood-churning fury the woman was disappearing yet again. Before we could do what we both had obviously been thinking about so much the night before. I was not a virgin. I was a man and more aware of it at that moment than at any other time in my life as I watched Francesca waving goodbye from the carriage window. For she was the person to whom I wished to show all my manly bottled-up ambition. So to see her leaving through the castle gates that day was, for me, the epitome of frustration.

"She'll be back soon," the Professor persuaded me, putting his arm around my shoulder as we walked back to the castle keep.

I got over my lady's absence with a lengthy session of target practice on the quadre bow, thoroughly destroying several targets and leaving them in pieces. Two days later I was walking through the gates of the university with my head held high; a young man with a lot to look forward to. Oh and how right I was to think such a thing. How right indeed.

Things were easier at university then because after our incredible adventure at the Temple of Eleusis Weishaupt never taught me again. At the start of December I saw him arriving at the university in his coach. He had supposedly come for a dressing down by the curator of the faculty; Herr Vacchieri because of the ongoing investigation of the Illuminati. But this man had been given the job by Weishaupt's Godfather way back. So it came as no surprise that he received no more than a slap on the wrist from the university board. Though I was shocked to discover, at a later date, (Sweet

Jesus were they *all* at it?) Vacchieri was Illuminati too! *[22]

There were no other missions planned so, for once, I could focus properly on my education with only the thought of that gorgeous woman taking my mind off my studies every now and then. I still kept up with my training at the castle and received an excellent Christmas gift from the Professor, who told me that he had invented the thing himself.

I lugged the huge package all the way back to Tuffengarten where I was to spend the holiday with my folks. Van Halestrom had told me that I was only to unwrap the surprise the day of Christmas Eve itself as he was a stickler for this tradition. And some surprise it was. I could not work out what the gift was at first. My father and I stood there looking at it for half an hour before he suggested, "Are you meant to get aboard it?"

Whereupon he was, in fact, correct. The 'plank,' for that is what it was, was a vehicle. A 'board' to ride down a hillside covered with snow. It had a curved end at the front and straps with which to tie it to your feet.

The machine was incredible. At least it was when I finally mastered its control and the best way of directing it through the snow which lay in abundance that year in the Christmas of 1784. I could, after a while, attain great speed and also carve out great turns in the thick banks of snow, scattering the powered flakes in waves of shimmering iridescent particles. Even my father was impressed. Although he did not try it himself as he was worried he would cause himself great personal injury in the process. But he commented that, "This Professor of yours is a remarkable talent." Finding it easier to complement another who was miles away rather than a man who was standing there in front of him. He was right though. It was pure genius and such a simple craft in all its technologies. That's what

---

[22] The Illuminati & Ingolstadt University. Herr Vacchieri is mentioned in a book called '*Little Tools of Knowledge*' by P Becker and W. Clark 2001 (pages 104-134) and seemed to fulfil a role at the university similar to that of a modern school inspector though I can find no proof that he was involved with the Illuminati. S. Drechsler also mentions Adam Weishaupt's Godfather though not by name. Baron Johann Ickstatt was the Curator of Ingolstadt University up until 1778 and probably instrumental in getting Weishaupt his job. There also seems to be doubt about his membership of the Illuminati though it is hard to believe he did not know, somehow, about the intimate details of his godson's organisation.

real genius is, as Van Halestrom used to say; 'Genius is not complexity mused but intelligence which can be simply used.' My father proclaimed the board, "As revolutionary as Thomas Paine."

Like all revolutions it was conspicuous and I was spotted by some locals as I flew about the slopes. Once I slid by them with a happy nod as they toiled in the same direction making little headway themselves and eyeing the board with some suspicion. I heard at the local tavern that some of the more backward regulars who had heard of it proclaimed it, 'Black Magic!' and gossiped, 'it must be dark forces that make the thing work so well.' But the locals of Tuffengarten had burnt an old woman as a witch in the middle of the village square only seventy years ago for being able to cure someone from the sickness brought on by a bee sting so it was hardly surprising.

The New Year came and went and I waited for news of Francesca. Eventually it came and I burst into life when 'Lord' Bacon, as I jokingly referred to him, solemnly announced, "She will be here in February, sir. You have a mission of some urgency to conclude with her. I believe the Professor will tell you about it soon."

And so it was. My next meeting with the Professor was to mark the beginning of the next chapter of my incredible tale in which, like Persephone, I was to descend into a mysterious underworld where my life was to take on a series of bizarre and shadowy twists and become so much more dark and terrible than anything I could ever have imagined.

Chapter 23

The Eyes Have It

The snow piled up deeply on Van Halestrom's windowsill as I stared out from the comfort of his warm office over the icy roofs of Ingolstadt on a cold February morning of 1785. My heart was in a flight of fancy because of the up and coming rendezvous with my Lady Francesca. I gazed into the distant clouds and wondered where exactly in the world could she be? I was brought out of these longings by the Professor.

"Drink, Sebastian?" He asked, passing me a goblet of steaming mulled wine before encouraging the coals in the fireplace and making himself comfortable back in his chair.

"Well, my lad, looks like you're off to meet her. Let's hope you don't make as much of a mess of it as you did with your last game."

I glanced over at the chessboard where many white pieces surrounded a lonely black King and considered, with some annoyance, the way he had remarked, "I knew you were going to do that," after every move I had made.

"Yes, Herr Professor. As always after my visits with you I am inclined to consider working on my ability to conceal my thoughts."

"Good thinking, lad. Always an excellent technique to have mastered especially when it comes to matters concerning the fairer sex. I'm sure if women were able to conceive the central thoughts that men had about them they would be compelled to run away screaming and never come back again."

I wondered, as I had done on many occasions, about the Professor's relationships with women of which there seemed to be none. I felt that seeing as he had told me so much about so many other things if he had been disposed to mention this subject, which was of some significance, he would have done so. So I didn't pry and left those matters for another day. Anyway, I was on the edge of my seat as I waited to hear of my next meeting with Francesca. So my heart filled with glee when Van Halestrom announced, "You're going to meet her in a little place called Pettendorf over the border in Regensburg. There she will give you a set of papers which you will return to me. These documents explain the plot to overthrow the Russian empire and others too, toppling them one on another like dominoes so the Illuminati can control the outcome of the tumultuous epoch."

'Typical,' I thought. Nothing is ever small is it? Not with this bunch. Never want to rob the greengrocers or a bank. They certainly had a sense of grandeur. You couldn't take that away from them.

"How can this possibly be achieved?" I asked with some exasperation.

"There are many ways to achieve a revolution, Sebastian. We will have to wait and see. But this is my guess; remember how Weishaupt tried to put you off balance – to destabilise you? Well I believe that on a much larger scale a similar technique may be used to overthrow Russia."

I stared at him for a moment trying to grasp his point. What could he mean by this?

He saw my confusion and attempted to explain, "Try to realise, my lad; what is effective on a personal level can be just as powerful on the larger world. To attain the next level of understanding you must realise that, in many ways, the microcosm is not *like* the macrocosm – it *is* the macrocosm."

Expecting him to go on at this point I was rather frustrated when he sat shrewdly staring at me.

"Surely it couldn't be that simple?" I muttered to myself. As I wrestled with this concept his clerk burst in speaking so rapidly I could barely understand what he said.

"He's going. It happened just now. He's been given his marching orders by Herr Vacchieri, with all that, 'I don't want to but I have to,' rot. The viper has been told he must clear his things out immediately and leave. He is there now. We should hurry if you want to see him go."

Before I could ask what was happening Van Halestrom propelled himself out of his seat crying, "Come on, my lad. We must see this!"

I followed him out of his chambers and we ran down the corridors until reaching the corner before Weishaupt's rooms, whereupon we disguised our haste and returned to a stroll. Emerging round the corner as nonchalantly as possible we were at exactly the right time to see Weishaupt coming out of his door with an arm full of books accompanied by two attendant flunkies. He noticed us, returning our gaze with even more than his usual glare. Unsurprisingly he was angry to see that his tormentors had come to revel in his downfall but this was a look of such spitefulness that all the hairs on the back of my neck immediately stood to attention. Indeed, if the English phrase; 'stared daggers' could have been taken literally then we would have all been stabbed to death for sure.

After a moment he turned away and I watched as Adam Weishaupt finally left Ingolstadt University for the last time and strode off up the corridor with his toadying staff lugging his clobber behind him.

When he was out of sight I half-whispered, "Do you think that it is really over, sir?"

Van Halestrom shook his head replying ominously, "Oh no, my friend, somehow I don't think this will be the end." *[23]

Right! Right! Right! That's all he ever was, blasted right! I can't think why I never asked him what would happen at the end of my life because he would be bound to know exactly and therefore remove all subsequent mysteries from my mind. Because he *was* right; in no way was it the end. In many ways it was merely another beginning.

---

[23] Adam Weishaupt sacked from Ingolstadt University 1785. S. Drechsler's claim to have witnessed the Professor's departure concurs with official accounts. Weishaupt finally lost his seat at the University on the 11th February 1785 amidst continuing controversy surrounding the Illuminati. The Bavarian state's first decree against secret societies in June of the previous year had been quite mild but by this time favour for the Illuminati was definitely deteriorating making it impossible for a distinguished institution such as Ingolstadt University, who enjoyed the patronage of the state, to employ members from its ranks. Never mind the figurehead of its leadership.

Chapter 24

Incognito, No! 'Audacity, audacity!'

My heart was beating like a Frenchman's fist on the door of his local brothel on pay day as I played out the upcoming night's activities in my mind. I was scrubbed, shaved and dressed to the nines and speeding along in the smart, black carriage of the Professor's, or Bacon's, or the Castle's, or whoever it actually belonged to - I didn't care. At that particular moment I was more than happy reclining in the warmth of the back seat and brimming with youthful excitement to be on my next mission. Mercifully, Klaus and poor Bacon were riding on top amongst swirls of blustering sleet on a truly harsh winter's day.

To my resounding surprise and delight I was posing as notable dignitary Count Wolfgang Faber Castell and enjoying the deception greatly. Van Halestrom had devised the plan so as to obtain diplomatic immunity from the border guards at Regensburg which would aid the uninterrupted passage of the secret papers that I had been sent to collect. The Professor had said that our high profile would, "Counter-intuitively provide us with safety," boldly declaring, "Audacity, audacity, is the best way to proceed. No one will stop or bother you believing you are aristocracy."

It was certainly capital fun pretending to be. I wasn't sure if Van Halestrom had intended it but he must have known this would be a hoot for me. I wondered if in some way it was a reward for services rendered. Because for me being in charge, or at least apparently so, was excellent sport indeed. And so I endeavoured to make the most of it sticking my head out of the window and asking, "What's the weather like out there, boys?" when only a dead person would not have known.

"Cold, sir," chimed *Lord* Bacon's snotty reply.

I answered back encouragingly, "Never mind," and closed the window happily chuckling to myself. This was going to be a great night: Nay a marvellous night. Besides this wonderful opportunity to play the role of a man wielding great power and privilege with fine clothes, the carriage, servants, money and all the other accoutrements of that life, I was to meet the maddeningly beautiful Lady Francesca in the finest of inns. We were to enjoy a meal after which we were to retire together, into one room, with one bed, the both of us: It had been promised to me. I had seen the letter confirming the booking. What could possibly go wrong now? She knew I was coming and understood the sleeping arrangements as we were to appear as an esteemed dignitary and courtesan. She had not complained at this so I had absolutely no reason whatsoever to doubt that we would not be fully together on that very eve. My pulse began to pound once again like a busy blacksmith's hammer as I considered the details of her physical delights that would no doubt be in my hands in less than a few hours and my head almost came off at the thought.

As suspected our carriage was lazily waved through by the guards at border of Regensburg as soon as they saw our false flags and insignia. A couple of miles later we passed a sign for Pettendorf and soon reached the grand old inn; a fine building in the style of a traditional Bavarian hunting lodge pleasantly dusted with snow. Outside Bacon laboured with my heavy things as I confidently dismounted. As I did so I spotted a pair of pretty young women returning from a stroll and tried to impress them with my new air of authority. After all, shouldn't everyone believe we are who we say we are?

I shouted at poor Bacon, "Hurry up there Igor!" Taking the liberty of changing his name for my own comic effect.

But he replied, "Yes, sir," so slowly and objectionably that hearing his words was like listening to the fingers of a large armoured glove being dragged down the face of a blackboard. I smiled proudly in the women's direction but the titter it induced from them was not worth the agony of Bacon's aberrations and so I resolved not to do it again. Klaus stabled the horses and the carriage and met me at the front door saying, with a wink, "You're all set. She'll be here at seven, sharp. Enjoy yourself, sir."

With this he flicked the brim of his hat then turned round and strolled jauntily away to his quarters. I liked Klaus. He was a good stick. I liked them all. They were an excellent lot; Klaus the Professor even the maddeningly pompous but honourable Bacon and of course the delectable one herself. My spirits flew again at the thought of our now certain union and measuring all my other satisfactions about me I reckoned, 'What a night this will be,' and contemplated, whist looking around at the charming reception hall of the old inn, "How can this possibly go wrong?"

If I'd had a million years to work it out, I would have still needed a million more. For the sheer madness that was about to occur could only have been predicted by someone who lives in an insane asylum or of course Professor Van Halestrom himself. Although, surely not even he could have seen these things that were to come about, for they were of such utter and complete inconceivability in each and every way.

I bathed and Bacon helped me change into my evening wear which was of the highest quality. Regarding myself in the mirror I was impressed to say the least. Now I was indeed a man of bearing in such fine clothes and struck a pose that smacked of self-confidence.

"Not a bad looking chap at all," I remarked, as I revolved one last time in the mirror before leaving my room and descending the stairs. As I passed through the reception and entered the dining room I noticed the effect my new appearance was having on those around me. Several people who passed respectfully acknowledged me as I proudly took my place at my table. I ordered a bottle of wine from the attentive waiter and proceeded to have a glass.

I had barely started the second of these when, at last, Francesca arrived. In that moment I was so excited I nearly knocked over the table with my increased manly impulsions. For never was there another woman like her. Good God! What had I done to deserve this beauty? Well quite a lot actually and it was all certainly worth it now. For standing there before me was a Venus of pure delectation. Her fur cloak was effortlessly removed by the waiter whereupon she was entirely revealed to me in all her shinning beauty. Wearing a glittering gown that barely contained her heaving womanliness she floated towards me pouting fabulously and very much to my liking. My lady was sporting a seductive beauty spot and had put up her hair showing off her luscious bejewelled neck. I had forgotten just how attractive she really was and enjoyed the rapture of the déjà-vu as it all came gloriously flooding back. I met her in front of the table and kissed her hand.

"Good evening, my lady."

She purred like a cat that wants to be stroked, "I have missed such pleasantries, Count Wolfgang. The men in Russia are not as charming as your good self."

"I was hoping you had not the chance to find out about the men in Russia, my lady."

"Their company only made me realise how lucky I was to be coming back to you, dear sir."

What further guarantee could I need of my inevitable union with this beauty than exactly this type of flirtatiousness? I pulled out her seat for her and taking up my position at the table summoned the service to begin. This was the stuff of dreams. Maybe not everybody's but my dreams definitely. In the swankiest of inns at the most expensive table being waited on hand and foot by a team of obedient flunkies and dining with a woman so fabulously gorgeous that half the eyes in the room were focused upon her every single moment as waiters, and guests alike, walked into the furniture and each other as they gazed at this extraordinary darling sitting directly in front of me. Who, after this exceptional meal, was going to come with me upstairs into my ambassador's suite where I was going to get her out of that dress and those corsets fast and throw her in between the satin sheets of a scented bed and then bite and lick and fondle every single part of her naked gorgeous parts in the most carnal of ways. I shall then put my…

"What are you thinking, Wunderkinda?" Her eyes twinkled like diamonds and her jewellery tried to keep up but failed dismally.

"Oh … nothing," I replied, "… perhaps of how happy I am tonight."

"Go on," she prompted.

I attempted to elaborate, "Being here with you in all this splendour and opulence. The feeling of tenderness and … even love."

She smiled happily and squeezed my hand so I continued expanding my feelings in the same hopeful way.

"My thoughts are of the future, of peace and normality, of creating a safe place where I and another can live. A house maybe filled with children …"

"Slow down, Wunderkinda," she interrupted, "This world is a turbulent place, perhaps too turbulent for those thoughts to become true if they are to include me. The things I know to be happening are so extreme that to have a child, and leave them to face a future which will become a place of such inconsolable pain and corruption, would be impossible for me to bear."

"Surely things cannot be that bad, my lady."

"Of course they are and worse. You must understand the fate of the world by now has only one outcome and that is of civilisation's fall."

"What? By what process? How will this apocalypse come to pass?"

"Surely the Professor has told you of the Illuminati's plans. It is proved beyond doubt that the scheme is inescapable for it aligns itself with the fateful prophecy that predicts the fall of man. He must have kept it from you because he didn't want you to give up the struggle."

"Struggle? What … what are you talking about?"

"I speak of 'The End of Times'."

I shrugged in ignorance. She sighed forlornly and began to explain, "It is the belief that man's own immorality creates the destiny he shall inherit. For the majority of the masses are weak and only think of themselves. This denial of man's true value, in itself, has produced Weishaupt's Illuminati who in turn foster the decline. Finally, being so inherently corrupt, as predicted in the bible the descent of man is irreversible. Ultimately this sickness, harnessed by the dark forces that we fight, will create three huge wars covering the earth after which a single world dictatorship will be formed mirroring the antipathy of its spiritually broken people. The end will come in that moment and a social cataclysm born from which civilisation will not be able to return such as written in the book of Revelations." *[24]

"Right then," I sighed. She was never your average partner for dinner.

"Look around you; isn't everybody the same? Just soulless creatures constantly trying to make the best situations for themselves:"

---

[24] The 'End of Times Prophecy': The fateful prophecy predicting the Armageddon of civilisation mirroring the Bible's book of Revelations. Interestingly this particular ominous forecast recalled by S. Drechsler sounds strangely similar to extracts from a mysterious letter once rumoured to be kept at the British Museum which it is claimed was sent by Albert Pike, the then head of world Masonry, to an Italian revolutionary Giuseppe Mazzini in 1871. If S. Drechsler's account is to be believed it is incredible to think that such a frightening future for the world was even being talked about as early as 1785.

I followed her eyes. A waiter looked around slyly before pocketing a tip that was not for him.

She carried on, "The world over, you cannot stop it. The only thing man possesses is weakness and greed and fear and the lust for his own power. That is how he will be destroyed in the end. You're just a boy to think of it in any other way. I thought you looked to the future with too much happiness for it to be true."

I was hurt by these ridiculous sounding remarks and she noticed, squeezing my hand again. "I feel for you, Wunderkinda, but planning ahead knowing of this terrible future and in our business, even to next week, is an extravagance I can ill-afford."

"All of a sudden I fancy another glass of wine," I concluded, petulantly taking my hand away from hers. I grabbed a glass of Château Le - whatever it was - and downed it in one.

"Don't be like that Sebastian," she implored taking my hand back but I stood defiantly and announced I was going to the privy.

As I emptied myself in the water closet I cursed her over-seriousness. It was just one waiter scrounging a tip for pity's sake. It didn't mean that the rest of civilisation was about to explode into flames. I convinced myself I would be able to bring her round to my way of thinking after she had sampled the thirteen stone of purposeful manly vigour that I had been saving for her. I was even contemplating taking on the hordes of enemies that were contriving to make this ominous prophecy come true. Even calculating the amount of ammunition I would need to wipe them all out in order to persuade her to make a life with me. So it was with a renewed sense of determination and purpose that I returned to the dining room. That's when the nightmares I thought were behind us, started all over again.

As I smiled at her whilst approaching our table two of the waiters suddenly pulled her back from her chair dragging her out of the room. One of them produced a flintlock pistol from inside his coat and fired it at my face. The bang nearly deafened me and I felt the shot almost take my ear off before it smashed into something behind me made of glass. I ducked uselessly after the round was gone whilst the other waiters and guests shouted and screamed around the room.

"Not now! Not now!" I grunted, sprinting after her. "What is wrong with this blasted woman? Is there no one else that can be kidnapped but her?" As I ran out of the front door she was already being bundled into a carriage. "Get off that woman!" I screamed and was shot at again for my trouble. This round, launched by another shadowy henchman on top of the coach, tore through the cuff of my jacket. As I came up from my stoop affected to avoid the shot the carriage sped off and I desperately gave chase until eventually it pulled away. I stood panting in the frosted road before sprinting back to the inn where a group of concerned guests and staff had collected outside shocked to have seen such violence and mayhem. Once at the stables I found Klaus who, alerted by the shots, had already harnessed up our carriage and was almost ready to go after to our assailants. Acknowledging me with a, "Be with you in a trice, sir."

Moments later our coach burst out of the stable doors with me hanging out of the window, yelling, "Follow that blasted carriage!"

To which he happily replied, "That's my favourite sentence, sir," and stirred the horses into such action that I was fairly thrown back into my seat.

Good God! That man could drive a team of horses. He was a veritable ace at his trade. He slid the coach so widely on the snowy road that I thought we were surely bound to crash. But it seemed as though he was in full control of these wild manoeuvres, once even banging the rear wheel into a low wall over a bridge before rebounding and flying off down the icy lane.

I stuck my head back out of the window eager to see how we were faring and felt the whip of fresh snow sting my face. Staring out in front of us I could already make out the back of the abductor's vehicle which had covered lanterns mounted on its rear.

"Go on, by thunder!" I shouted as we caught up with our quarry at a prodigious rate. Feeling a rush of blood at the prospect of beating the living daylights out of the gang of thugs, and spurred on by the irresistible thoughts of getting that woman in my embrace once-and-for-blasted-all, I opened the door and attempted to get on to the front seat to aid the chase. Clutching the outside of the carriage I suddenly realised how impetuous this decision was as Klaus turned sharply into a tight corner covered in snow with a death-defying drop over its side. From my perilous position on the *wrong* side of the carriage I could see the snow-covered trees two hundred feet below me as the coach slid terrifyingly around a bend.

I gulped anxiously seeing the chasm looming past beneath us and tried to control my fear of heights. Taking my eyes off the drop I heaved myself up on the corner of the cabin and landed with a gasp on the front seat next to Klaus. He winked at me and whipped the reins shouting loud and clear, "C'mon then me beauties!" as the horses pulled us inexorably within range.

'Crack!' We were definitely in range. I ducked as the shot whistled over my head and I looked desperately around for our own firearms.

"One step ahead of you, sir," called Klaus thumping the board behind us which unfolded producing a tray containing a pair of shining muskets. My eyes widened with approval and needing no further encouragement I picked up the one and cocked it. After finding a target in the sights I released a shot, 'Crack!' causing the dark silhouette firing at us to cower down in fright.

"Take that pig dog!" I cried and immediately picked out the next musket bringing it to bear. This time I considered my next shot more carefully as it would possibly be our last and waited for the bastard to get up again. When he did I took my chance. 'Crack!' This time I got him and he screamed before falling from the coach and we promptly ran him over. As he went under the wheels I could have sworn he was wearing one of the Illuminati's red hooded robes and I yelled with a new found rage, "Damn that blaggard to Hell!"

"They must be heading for the Wolfsegg castle!' cried Klaus and ominously added, "I'm sure Weishaupt has connections with that place." *[25]

Him again! That would explain little-red-firing-hood. Right! That was it. I swore that if Weishaupt had anything to do with this I was going to kill him then resuscitate the bastard so I could do it again - twice! Now he was really starting to annoy me.

We carried on climbing up the mountain road although the pursuit did not slow down, if anything it just got faster and another shot rang out.

'Crack!'

---

[25]. Wolfsegg Castle. I cannot find any official connection between this ancient castle and the Illuminati though it has had many intriguing owners throughout its long history. Built in 1278 by Wolf von Schönleiten it has a legend of haunting and, owing to its prominent position, can be seen from miles around. It is still there to this day situated 15km North West of Regensburg and can be viewed on the internet, if you are interested.

How many kidnappers were there? It didn't matter as I knew that given the opportunity I would beat them all to a pulp being in possession of an all-consuming rage. Klaus, driving out of his skin, managed to pull alongside the abductors' coach and I saw Francesca's screaming face at the window. A hand appeared trying to pull her back but she bit it with fury before it was yanked away.

"Go on, Girl!" I yelled but as I did one of the hooded villains jumped onto the footboard of our carriage with his sword raised above his head. Astounded by this fellow's eagerness I had no time to stop him and his blade slashed down towards Klaus's face. Incredibly it didn't find its mark. For, somehow the heroic driver trapped the sword between his hands and held it inches from his face while blood trickled down his arms. I watched in silent awe as he calmly asked, "Could you, sir?"

He gestured at the reins which I took from him before he rammed the handle of the sword into his attacker's guts then stood up and powerfully head-butting the man off the carriage. But as the thug fell away he managed to pull Klaus with him and the trusty driver barely had time to say, "Excuse me, sir," before disappearing into the night. I glanced behind to see that Klaus had taken exception to this individual's treatment of him and was beating the unfortunate henchman in the road to within an inch of his life and perhaps more. I looked about me. Damnation! I was on my own. As I came to this stark conclusion the dark towers of Wolfsegg Castle loomed above the approaching trees.

"C'mon Seb! Do it before we get there," I urged myself, realising any amount of reinforcements could be waiting ready up ahead. I hollered at the horses, spurring them on again. As the carriages became level once more I decided what I must do.

I would have to jump for it. There was no other way. I stood up on the footboard lashing at the reins. The moment for my action came and I took a deep breath before hurling myself with all my might at the abductors' carriage. I made it but only just; landing with a crash beside the driver. Even from behind his slits I could see he was thoroughly startled by my verve.

"You weren't expecting that were you, you bastard!" I cursed. Then damn it if he didn't return the surprise by producing an enormous knife and start wheeling it about.

"That's a big one!" I moaned and dodged it twice. Before I knew it we passed through the castle's gates as the coach flew on regardless of our fight. He slashed at me again catching me on the wrist. Not a fatal wound but enough to send searing pain up my arm. I knew I couldn't take too many of those and tried to avoid the next one using my new fighting skills. We sped headlong into a snowy courtyard as I managed to punch the brute a couple of times hard in the face. Out of the corner of my eye I saw a running silhouette of a man slow the horses down and we came to a sudden halt. As I dodged another swipe of the knife the doors of the coach burst open and Francesca was dragged out by the two waiters. I realised they were far too big to be servants as they wrestled her towards the castle's keep. She glanced over her shoulder screaming, "Help me, Sebastian!"

"In a minute, my sweet!" I yelled sarcastically for it was obvious even for a man with his eyes in his arse I was having some troubles of my own. Although after another tasty feint then punch I felt my opponent's nose and a few other bones smash to pieces and he fell down to the icy cobbles. I jumped down to pursue my Lady's captors as three more thugs emerged from the shadows blocking my path. The first lashed out and I kicked him in the crotch but then the other two were on me in a rush and the blows started to rain in. One of these pole-axed me and I crashed into the wall behind. My head started to swim. I saw the man I had castrated pull himself together as his friends pinned me against the wall and he came over to finish me off.

"That's enough!" barked a voice and another silhouette appeared before me. Though I was half unconscious due to the barrage of blows I still recognised him. It was Weishaupt! The bastard came into the light and I struggled to break free from the henchmen but it was impossible. He enjoyed a conceited grin and laughed, "Two troublemakers for the price of one: Seems like a most agreeable bargain to me."

His arrogance enraged me even further and I tried once more in vain to throw off my captors but he smacked his lips in contempt and turned his back to go. I shouted after him, "I'm going to kill you some day, Weishaupt!"

"But that day is not today I wager," he crowed. That's when the thump came from behind and everything went black.

Chapter 25

The Pit of Despair

I've woken up in some bad places in my time; ditches, exams, tavern tables, churches, even in a brothel on my eighteenth birthday. And no I did not thank you very much. For they were all hideous dogs in that place: Anyway I was too drunk and had fallen asleep. But this was worse, much worse than the ditch, the exam, the tavern table, the church and the brothel all put together and multiplied a thousand times. I slowly came around in the darkness and started putting my memory back together.

'This is not my room at the inn,' I surmised, finding my cold rock-hard mattress most disagreeable. Feeling bonds on my wrists and ankles I wondered, 'Why would I be tied to the bed? And where was Francesca?' God knows why but finding myself tied up had immediately brought her to my mind. Then I remembered seeing her face pushed against the window of a strange carriage, biting the hell out of someone's hand. 'That's it!' I thought, 'She's been kidnapped! I have to rescue … Oh yes, that's right. Now I remember,' and it all came back in a flood of awful horror. I was in deep, deep trouble.

I prayed I was wrong and checked my bonds. I wasn't they were made from chains; big, heavy ones. I was lying on my back lashed to a wet, stone table in a cold dungeon in total darkness. I listened out for any sounds beyond the shadows but heard none. After a while my frustration got the better of me and I shouted, "Get me out here you dogs or I'll smash your blasted heads in!" My rage increased as I remembered how happy I was meant to be on this night and I yelled out desperately in the dark, "Let me go you slitty-eyed bastards or I'll kill the lot of you!"

At that very moment I heard the creak of a door and the approach of footsteps and the jangling of keys. I instantly began to regret my outburst realising it may have been a little rash if these people were coming to torture me. Lying in the dark chained to that table I felt very vulnerable indeed. With an inevitable clunk a door swung open and a group of hooded sentinels carrying flickering torches entered the room.

Weishaupt appeared from amongst them and came over to the table. Imperiously throwing his long cloak over his shoulder he stood over me mocking, "Well, well, Herr Drechsler. As I'm sure you can imagine we are quaking in our boots to have an Illuminati Hunter in our midst." There were sniggers from some of the guards at this as he carried on, "You, boy, have been a rather annoying thorn in my side for some time now. So I am looking forward to showing you the extent of my displeasure. My men were already following your indiscreet lady friend but finding you with her is most fortuitous."

"What …what are you going to do?" I bleated.

"It would seem, anything I want, sir,"

"You'll never get away with this, Weishaupt!"

"Oh, but, Herr Drechsler I believe I already have. Surely, even with your boyish imagination, you don't think you can escape from here. Within these walls I am free to do anything I please. It is even better than the university, is it not? At the faculty I wasn't allowed to torture the students. Though I'm sure their results would have improved as a consequence of the threat of pain."

Although terrified I wasn't able to contain my anger at his scornful boasts any longer and taunted him as Jan would have done.

"Well, I'm sure your mother would clean the kitchen better if you flogged her when she didn't do it properly. Maybe threatened to rape her too. I wouldn't put it past you, you perverted …."

"Silence!" he shouted.

I didn't blame him actually. I was quite proud of that one. 'Flogged your own mother and threatened to rape her too.' Yes! Stick that up your arse Weishaupt. If you're going to kill me you'll hear what I think of you first. I flew into my next tirade, "I bet you could train your servants to eat your excrement if you burnt a few of them on stakes …"

"That's enough!" He yelled and motioned to one of the guards who rammed a gag in my mouth.

But I was so crazed with fear I could not stop and carried on in my muffled voice, "Nuh, nuh, ne, nuh, nuh, nuh!"

He clicked his fingers signalling the guard to punch me in my gut which he did very hard.

That shut me up and I lay there in some agony. Weishaupt lent over me hissing, "How could you ever think you could stop us you arrogant fool? If you only truly understood what it is you are up against you would not have tried at all. No doubt that imbecile Van Halestrom has tried to convince you that you can stop something that has been taking place since the beginning of time. You have no idea. No idea at all. How could you, you meaningless idiot? You know nothing of this power. You don't even have the capacity to dream of it let alone what it will bring about." He moved closer menacingly breathing into my face, "Such is the nature of this force that eventually it will prevail not only the lesser or more important of the populace but over the best of men of all ranks, nations and religions until finally giving us absolute control over them all. The divine doctrine of almighty Lucifer is invincible. In the end all men will be forced to bow to the power of his eternal light."

By the time he had finished his face was nearly touching mine. With the flickering orange light of the torches licking across his intense features he finished, "You, Herr Drechsler are simply the next unfortunate flame who must be extinguished in order for his glorious light to shine."

"Aargh!" I wailed into the rag.

He whipped his head round calling to his men, "Take him down," then span back. "I was going to kill you here but now I have a much better idea. You can watch your lady be killed first. Yes that is what we shall do."

"Francesca!" I screamed though it sounded more like "Hununh!"

One of the guards came over to release my bonds and I was hauled up and dragged out of the dungeon along a maze of stone corridors. Eventually we reached a set of stairs and descended for several flights deep into the catacombs of the fort. The anger I had felt moments earlier quickly reverted to pitiful fear and with every flight of stairs my spirits fell a little further. Until, after the third or fourth of these, I was in the very pit of despair. 'Looks like this is the end, Seb. There's no way out of this.' Perhaps I could handle my own death at the hands of this murderous bunch especially if it was quick. But the thought of seeing Francesca hurt and then killed first would break me and I knew it. What was I thinking? These were the thoughts of an unrealistic hero from mythology not those of a pathetic student from the back of beyond. What had I done to deserve this? This was meant to be the best night of my life and now

I was in a freezing castle about to be killed by this mad man and his lunatic followers after witnessing the awful death of my lover who I had never even got to love. I worried for my parents too and imagined them hearing of my death and my eyes did moisten then and I prayed that God would save my soul.

Finally we came up to a door and I realised that this was to be the place of my doom. One of the hooded sentinels swung it open and I was pushed inside. The chamber was much brighter than the rest of the fort due to the presence of many torches on the walls. Unfortunately this allowed me to see, in exquisite detail, the numerous machines of death with which it was filled. It was as though every method of killing someone as painfully as possible had been assembled in this one place. There was a horrifying rack, a cage and a glowing hot basket full of coals and pokers lying next to an oubliette; its steep, conical sides disappearing into a dark man-sized hole at the bottom of which, were no doubt, heaped the bones of many long forgotten prisoners. Everywhere else I looked there were buckets of knives, swords, pincers and other terrifying tools of pain. I was gagging on the rag in my mouth by the time I saw an iron-maiden in the corner its open door covered in hellish spikes and a freakish skull motif on its top.

One of the guards bundled me over to a row of chairs set against the far wall which appeared to be the only pieces of furniture in the room that did not have a lethal purpose. Then I noticed they had. For each one was fitted with restraining clamps to keep their victims in their place while they suffered in awful agony. As I was pushed along the line my mind burst into a rampaging fit of fear as we reached one with a spike coming up through the seat. 'Not that one please, God!' I prayed and to my utter relief we stopped next to another on which I was forced to sit. The hooded thug placed pins through each of the clasps around my wrists but thankfully did not do so at my feet. Looking down I noticed deep gouges in the wooden arm rests of the chair torn by the finger nails of past victims during some unimaginably vicious fate.

The next thing I noticed was a large pentagram with Greek letters at its five points painted across the floor. I recognised this diabolic sign as a tool used by practitioners of the black arts. I had already seen enough evil magic in the last year to last ten lifetimes and now fully expected mine and Francesca's deathly fate was to have some extra demonic twist.

Where was she? If she was to suffer and I was to be forced to watch then surely she should be here too. Right on cue the door opened and then what happened next further unnerved me, if that were possible at this vilest of moments.

Francesca came in followed by a stranger dressed in a grand military uniform with a broad red sash over his shoulder and high white breeches. But then I had to look again. Was it her? There was a vacancy in her eyes that I had never seen before. Indeed, it was entirely out of character for this girl because her spirit was shown so much in her eyes and lively face. Both these were now plain and empty and devoid of all expression. I glanced at her companion the a large middle-aged solider whom I could tell was a fellow of some renown but possessed the same listless face. I noticed Francesca was not bound but that she did not struggle. I couldn't understand this as I knew she would have punched someone to blazes as soon as she was able. She did not even look at me but silently came into the centre of the room and stood next to the man in the uniform.

Weishaupt came between us chortling, "It seems as if she does not know you, lover boy. What do you think of her now?"

He motioned at my guard to remove the rag from my mouth and after gasping a few breaths of the foul air I wheezed, "What have you done to her you fiend?"

"Oh, Herr Drechsler, it must be love. I recognise it by the way you squeal. That will make this even sweeter. Love always heightens the pain. Seeing a stranger die one can watch, even get accustomed to. But one never forgets seeing a loved one perish before one's eyes."

He turned to Francesca slyly raising an eyebrow, his words sliding out of his mouth like a knife being brought out from its sheath, "And she is such a fine specimen. You have a good eye for the ladies, Herr Drechsler. Of course I knew her sister very well, in many different ways. Before her time finally came."

His hand appeared from inside his cloak grabbing at Francesca's chin and he flashed his cruel eyes at me. "She is indeed a beauty. I will enjoy this a great deal."

Damn it! if he didn't kiss her deeply on the mouth and fondle her breasts. I strained at my clasps enough to make my wrists burn with pain as the anger boiled inside me.

I screamed with fury, "If thought alone could be a weapon your head would be torn apart right now!"

He turned back to me as though inspired by the remark.

"Ah yes, my poor friend, if thought could be a weapon. Ha, ha, how little you know. Now, boy, prepare to see the real power of thought."

With this esotericism he brought Francesca into the centre of the pentangle and stood in front of her. He whispered something into her ear before staring deeply into her vacant eyes then abruptly clapped his hands.

Incredibly I saw in that instant her soul returned to her. Or that's how it seemed. I could not explain it in any other way. Her life force, for I'm sure that's what it was, was channelled back into her and the girl I knew and wanted so much returned in front of me with a startled gasp.

She glanced around the room in shock until her eyes met with mine whereupon she involuntarily stuck out her hand as if to move but appeared to be held by an invisible force fixing her to the spot. She gasped again with effort and cried, "Sebastian!"

I fought uselessly at my bonds shouting, "Francesca!"

Weishaupt laughed contemptuously, "Ah, young love is such a miracle, is it not?"

What the hell was going on? My mind seethed. What is this power he possesses?

He moved around Francesca while she wrestled to escape the unseen force. "As you well know, Herr Drechsler, there are many ways of controlling someone. Debt, illusion, fear, lies or even the power of their own minds."

He moved closer to her inhaling her scent and sniffed, "Many think that great power originates from gold. Some believe it springs from force. But this is the real wealth on this earth; the flesh of the young, their health, their vigour and their very thoughts. For therein lies true power."

"You're sick!" wailed Francesca but the louse clicked his fingers and incredibly her voice disappeared - just like that - causing her great distress. She tried again to speak and, although her mouth moved vigorously alas, nothing could be heard. Poor Francesca broke down at this her eyes filling with utter, needy, tearful despair while her expression pleaded for some relief from this dastardly curse.

Weishaupt heartlessly carried on, "Of course, I will make sure I release the spell in time for you to hear her scream."

He chuckled watching Francesca's helpless face contort with grief, "Heh, heh. But still she fights. Have you not heard the term resistance is useless, young lady?"

He tutted with disdain and moved over to the solider in the grand uniform.

"Now, this one I am particularly pleased with. It has taken many years of diligent work to produce a soul as reliable as his. Like a broken window pane I have smashed his original persona into a thousand pieces until, eventually producing this empty vessel into which I can place what I wish."

Facing the expressionless dignitary he asked, "Do you know this man, Herr Drechsler? He is a man of very great power indeed."

I did recognise the old character from amongst the crowd entering the Temple of Eleusis. Also I had a vague recollection of his features possibly from some old painting.

"He is General Frederick II Landgrave of Hasse Kassel. This nobleman has been in my employ for some time now," he grinned, "Although he has little knowledge of it at all. How many do you think there are like this around the world? Men of power who can unquestionably carry out our bidding:"

The old duffer didn't look like he was capable of completing anyone's bidding. If he had been a servant of mine I would have thought twice about getting him to brush my shoes such was the emptiness of his stare.

Weishaupt laughed, "Observe, boy the power of the mind when used as a weapon."

With this he clicked his fingers and the man briskly walked over to a table covered with torture tools. Without looking down he grabbed a ghastly looking spike and marched back to his original position then stood waiting with the vicious implement in his hand.

I started to sweat heavily fearing the torture was about to begin as Weishaupt sneered, "I like this part especially."

To my utter relief instead of using it on me the empty-eyed man raised the palm of his other hand and, without batting an eyelid, stabbed the spike right through it. To my further revulsion he twisted it around in the hole showing no pain at all upon his blank face. I was sure that I heard a bone snap and winced as blood began to pour from his hand making a small puddle on the floor. Weishaupt chuckled psychotically moving his forehead as if remotely controlling the intimate movements of the tool before, apparently becoming bored, he took his eye away from the grand looking solider who removed the spike and stood there as though nothing had happened.

"We will say that it was a hunting accident. People will believe anything these days. We shall start some rumours around the court explaining this and that, my friend, will be that."

Incredible! What can't he do with this blackest of magic? Then, remembering my place in this terrifying tragedy, I felt the fear erupt inside me because I knew it must be our turn next!

Chapter 26

The Chamber of Certain Death

So there I was; consumed with infinite, immeasurable, spine-snapping, eye-exploding terror in a torture chamber of certain death, four floors down in the bowels of a dark fortress, strapped to a chair, watching the cursed love of my life writhing in an invisible force field, in front of a vengeful Luciferian maniac who hated us both, surrounded by innumerable tools of vicious mutilation including a horrifying automaton which the fiend was no doubt about to use on us. I was just a history student for Christ's sake! I should have been tucked up in bed with a cup of hot chocolate studying my books.

My evil captor spoke with spiteful malevolence, relishing my abject terror, "I was going to have our friend the General abuse your woman first and have her here, right in front of you. That would have been interesting, before we really put her through some pain. Never mind. Sadly we do not have the time for that."

He nodded over his shoulder and two of the hooded sentinels pulled the iron-maiden into the centre of the room. They left it propped up behind the tearful Lady Francesca who still toiled against seemingly nothing. My heart was banging like a judge's hammer at a witch trial for I now believed that I was witnessing the beginning of the end for us both. I shook my head with rage.

"You'll pay for this Weishaupt! One way! One day! You'll pay! I know it in my bones. If not killed for your filthy evilness in this life then when your time comes God will punish your soul!"

The swine tried to make a joke of it. "I have noticed that when a man is about to die he reverts to the only thing he has left; hopeless faith in his maker to save him before he passes into the next life. But before that moment comes for you I have devised something to make your journey there a little more interesting."

With this he waved his hand and two of the sentinels dragged Francesca to the iron-maiden and pushed her inside.

"No! Francesca!" I shouted gritting my teeth with rage and fighting against the clasps at my wrists. I kicked out with my feet helplessly trying to put up some kind of struggle.

"Now, Herr Drechsler, my hapless student. We shall put you to a little test. This one is less academic than the exam at which you so cleverly cheated last year. This is a test of the physique."

A chain was produced by one of the sentinels and my mind raced trying to work out what Weishaupt had in store. Whatever it was I fully expected it to be cruel. I was right. It was.

"Now, young man because it is my wish you will be given the sad task of killing this good lady yourself. But first we shall test your strength and maybe the strength of your love for your dear, sweet mistress."

As he spoke a sentinel placed one end of the heavy chain in my hand whilst another unwound it over to the iron-maiden. Once the chain was taut he placed a link around the casket's handle then let the door down, finding the point where it took the weight. I began desperately trying to steady myself with my feet, feeling the cold chain pulling with great force out of my hand as the huge weight of the door hung in the balance.

The plan was obvious. The black spikes now hovered only a foot over Francesca's panting body as she stared round the door her with eyes as big as saucers. She shouted silently to me as the tears rolled down her cheeks and I strained with effort at the chain already tearing itself from my hand. I wondered how long I would have before I lost my grip, maybe a minute, maybe less.

The terror and the agony of it all was sending me mad. Was this to be my mad demise? I wondered if I would simply go crazy and lose my mind and then not be able to suffer but my senses only heightened as the hellish torture continued.

'Please God save me from this and I shall be in your service for evermore,' I beseeched, as Weishaupt and three of the hooded devils laughed at my calamity, eagerly enjoying something that they had obviously done before.

"You seem to love her a great deal, Herr Drechsler. But like all things the chain of love has its breaking point. Are you nearly there my friend?" Weishaupt laughed carrying on with revolting pleasure, "Not long to go now."

As he said this he chain slipped in my hand allowing the door to fall six inches but I caught the next link and just managed to hold onto it, grunting with the effort.

"No!"

I threw my head back summoning every ounce of strength I had into my fist.

"Oh! Nearly!" scoffed Weishaupt.

This was it! I was going to lose my grip. Weishaupt and his three men stood facing the wicked spectacle concentrating on its impending climax. Out of the corner of my eye I saw the fourth who had fixed me to my chair acting unusually and fumbling under his robes. He saw me watching him and I was stunned to see him put his finger to his lips outside his hood.

'What was this now?' I wondered, my mind in a blaze of pain and regret and fear of death. I focused back on the chain. I was coming close to letting go. Meanwhile, the odd hooded sentinel moved up behind the Weishaupt and the others surrounding the iron-maiden.

Weishaupt laughed, "As you may be able to see, Herr Drechsler, there is a window in the door. So you will be able to see the soul of the one you love leave this world forever."

"No!" I roared as the last remnants of my strength fell away.

I watched the quivering chain in front of me as the evil rogues laughed either side with glee. The fourth was now frantically fumbling inside his robes before suddenly producing a silver knife. Good God! It was Van Halestrom's! I knew it. I had seen him with it before. He turned to me raising a finger and moved a few paces closer to Weishaupt. What did this mean?

A minute? An hour? A blasted year! Could he not see how close I was to losing the chain? 'Do it now!' I screamed inside as he started to fumble underneath his confounded costume once more.

"C'mon you fool!" I shouted, knowing that no one would know I did not mean myself. But the clever old buzzard, for I knew it was him, still continued rummaging about. Now I recognised his familiar form underneath the robes. Of course! The finger to the lips, leaving the foot clasps undone, hoping for a chance to do something later no doubt. I did not care what miracle he had performed to get there I only cared that he would stop this insanity and before it was too late!

Groaning with the strain I felt the link about to burst from my hand. It was too much then and I knew I was going to let it go. I glanced up to see the Professor finally produce a small cutlass in the other hand. He held it up to me triumphantly as though impressed with his work.

"Just do it!" I cried in apoplexy and felt the link slip, watching the door drop down, screaming "No! Francesca!" I was stunned to see Van Halestrom throw the knife which, as if by utter magic, appeared in the latch of the iron maiden and stopped the door from slamming shut.

My eyes nearly popped out of their sockets upon seeing this. Before I knew it he skewered one of the sentinels with his cutlass pulling the blade out with such speed he was ready to smite the next with a powerful slash. This left one more and Weishaupt and old Fredrick who stood looking at the room as though he was considering painting it.

Three against the two, the odds were looking better although I was still in the chair but not for long. Van Halestrom bolted over to me athletically kicking out the pin from one of the clasps as Weishaupt finally registered what was going on.

"Yes!" I shouted removing the other clasp and immediately jumping up. The Professor threw me the cutlass which I caught and turned to meet the remaining sentinel who had found himself a javelin.

"Prepare to die!" I screamed consumed by an all-powerful of rage. I had enough fury in me to kill a squadron of pirates at that moment. The guard sensed it and took a step back. I flew at the blaggard crashing a storm of heavy, swiping blows against his iron javelin and driving him against the wall. I feinted one way with my blade then slashed it in the other taking the villain's head clean off in one swipe. It fell to the floor still in its hood and served the bastard right!

Meanwhile, Weishaupt had armed himself with a red hot poker from the basket using his cloak to stop his hand from burning. He held the rod out in front of him jeering, "Van Halestrom, you meddling fool! You have troubled me for the last time. Now prepare to meet thy doom," and provocatively beckoned the Professor with his finger.

"If it is my doom that I must meet then I go there with a fight!" yelled Van Halestrom taking down a spear from the wall and charging at his foe. Weishaupt dodged the lunge bringing his poker down with a hefty swipe and, though the Professor parried it, the smouldering spike broke the wooden spear clean in half.

"God's teeth!" cried the Professor taking two steps back.

Weishaupt laughed, "Ha, ha! Now let's see you fight," and clicked his fingers. Horridly the empty faced general returned to the table and lifted an axe above his head then marched towards me chopping it down like a terrifying figurine from the devil's own clock.

"You can do it, lad!" called Van Halestrom.

"Don't encourage him, Professor! You know that you are doomed to fail. Or have you lied to him about Man's true destiny?"

The general brought the axe down and I ducked out of the way. It smashed into the chair behind me and Weishaupt raged, "Ha, ha. Resistance is useless!"

In this moment of total despair I was amazed to hear, "The future is not written you piece of shit!"

Holy Mother of God it was Francesca! Freed from her spell of silence and escaped from the casket she dragged Weishaupt backwards by his cloak fastened round his neck. Grasping at his throat he dropped the poker pulling over the basket of coals and falling down himself.

"Yeeha!" I cried, narrowly avoided another deadly swipe from the general's axe. This blow crashed into the rack of spears behind me and while he sought to free it I noticed Weishaupt's cloak had caught fire, set alight by the burning coals scattered by the oubliette. He panicked, patting down the flames but it was no use as they had quickly taken hold. The Professor bravely picked up the sizzling poker off the flagstones and with his face seared with pain, thrust it at Weishaupt's face forcing the screaming fiend over the lip of pit. Shrieking a horrid squeal of death Weishaupt slid down the side in a plume of flames and smoke and plunged down the hole.

"That'll shut him up!" cried Van Halestrom throwing the poker after him and peering over the edge.

It was my turn to cry out next, "Now come here and help me!" The general had freed his weapon and was coming toward me again. I slashed my blade into his right arm almost cutting clean off but he didn't even blink and kept remorselessly chopping down his axe. To add to this torrent of action there was a stampede of footsteps from behind the door. Francesca tore over to it, slamming the locking bar into place seconds before the guards smashed into it with a crash of weaponry.

"What shall we do now?" cried Francesca.

"We shall help blasted Sebastian!" I yelled, frantically dodging another blow. The general chopped at me again crashing his axe into my cutlass. The Professor grabbed a sword and came over shouting, "If we can kill these others we can kill this one too!"

As he said this there was another huge smack on the door.

"We don't have much time," cried Francesca.

"Right, time to leave," declared Van Halestrom totally changing his blasted mind.

"Leave?" I shouted, simultaneously parrying another blow. "I don't know if you have noticed but there is only one door which currently has the castle's garrison behind it trying to get in!"

I flashed another swipe at the general half taking off his ear but it still did not slow him down.

"Nothing can stop this one!" I gasped.

But the Professor was at the other end of the room having miraculously opened an iron grill exposing a hole in the floor and yelled, "Come now!" as another massive crash nearly rammed the door off its hinges.

"Francesca, you first," he called.

"Sebastian!" yelled Francesca dutifully disappearing down the hole. Van Halestrom knelt next to the grill as I finally managed to force the general back with a flurry of cuts. One of these injured him terribly on his shoulder as much as would kill a normal man. I grabbed a burning torch from its bracket and stuffed it into his face slamming him against the wall. He fell down with his head half on fire and I threw the cutlass at him then dashed over to the Professor.

"Down you go, Lad!" ordered Van Halestrom and bursting with relief I jumped into the hole.

Chapter 27

No Light at the End of the Tunnel

I hit the cold floor on all fours with a slap and in total darkness. Although this was an improvement as the hole was not full of people trying to kill me - yet. Before I could get my bearings the Professor landed on top of me painfully pinning me to the ground.

"Ow!"

"Oh, sorry, Sebastian," he apologised and called into the blackness, "Francesca, are you there?"

"Exactly where else would I be, Professor?"

"You have a point," he conceded clambering off me and ordering, "Right, off we go."

I heard Francesca scramble away down what I could now make out was a narrow tunnel perhaps four feet in diameter. Van Halestrom followed after her with me bringing up the rear crawling as fast as possible.

After a moment I exclaimed, "Where are we going now?"

"Out," called Van Halestrom.

"I presumed that anyway," I panted, my mind beginning to clear as the shock of my freedom and potential safety started to sink in. Pulling myself along behind the Professor I called out, "In the name of God, sir, please tell me where we are?"

"I believe we are in the castle's sewer, Sebastian."

"Sewer!" I cried, astonished to discover the existence of such a fortuitous escape route. After pulling myself together I asked, "How long is it?" as there was no light at the end of the tunnel.

"I estimate, with the lie of the land and at our current trajectory; about twenty minutes."

"Well good news for once, sir, as that will allow me to ask several bloody important questions!"

"Fire away my lad," he replied with the calm of a man picking strawberries in the meadow. I collected my raging thoughts and began, "Why did you not tell me Weishaupt possessed such evil powers, sir?"

"It is not black magic he has mastered, Sebastian, but Doctor

Mesmer's hypnotism. I admit when I first saw Illuminati agents behave in a similar fashion I presumed they had lost their minds due to the heat of battle. It is an awesome power, my lad, but it is still only a trick of the mind."

"Trick of the blasted mind!" I wailed as my thoughts turned to the next point. "What in good God's name were you doing at the castle?"

"Ah yes, stroke of luck that really. I was following Weishaupt after he was refused an audience with The Elector Duke Karl Theodore effectively guaranteeing his expulsion from Bavaria. He fled Ingolstadt earlier today and so I tracked him here. Serendipitous wouldn't you say?" *[26]

"Serendipitous!" I yelled but before I could suggest he exchange this word for 'miraculous,' there was a loud clank in the dark behind us followed by a foreboding scraping noise. My blood froze solid in my veins for somehow I knew it was the sound of the axe still being carried by the grotesque general who it seemed did not want to die.

"How the hell is he still alive?" I moaned, "I've killed him twice already."

"Oh dear," muttered the Professor, "Better get a move on chaps."

We sped up as much as possible and although too scared to look behind and most unhappy to be the last in the shaft I continued chivvying Van Halestrom.

"Now, Professor, could you please tell me what took you so long to find your cutlass when I was about to drop the door?"

"Oh yes, blasted thing got stuck in my belt," he laughed. Although momentarily wanting to murder him for his breathtaking offhandedness, I murmured, "Thank you," for the shot that saved us all. Still there was more I needed to know. "Where did you get your

---

[26] Karl Theodore and the banishment of the Illuminati 1785. On March 2nd 1785 the second royal edict was passed banning membership in the Illuminati and making it an imprisonable offence to be part of the order. Weishaupt fled to the independent principality of Regensburg finally settling in the Thuringian State under the protection of the Duke of Sax Gotha. He is recorded to have hidden in many places whist fleeing from the authorities including amongst others in a chimney. Though S. Drechsler does not give a precise date for this evening we could have expected Weishaupt to have thought the decree inevitable and therefore may well have left his homeland some weeks before which would tie in exactly with these recollections.

robes from?"

"I found a dead sentinel in the road leading to the castle."

"Well, it was me or Klaus who put him there," I told him with some pride. Next, I suddenly recalled the most important point of all. "One more thing, Professor; this 'End of Times' prophecy that we are all doomed?"

"Ah yes, what about it, lad?"

"Well, damn it! Would it not have been a good idea to tell *me* about it too?"

"Oh that old story: Look, Sebastian some people will always be hell bent on fulfilling biblical prophecies. Of course, being Luciferians the Illuminati would like to believe what is written in the book of Revelations where Satan's armies successfully conquer the world. But the idea that this was inevitable was a rumour started by that idiot the Comte De Viriue after he realised that the Illuminati had aligned themselves with the biblical prediction of the future. This trick is known as a cosmic trigger. *[27] There is no doubt that Weishaupt's agents will do their best to spread this insidious idea so that eventually man thinks it is his destiny to finally succumb to evil - with all that 'six, six, six' mumbo jumbo and 'no man shall be able to buy and sell without the mark of the beast.' You see, this dogma has always been the inherent problem with organised religion …"

He was straying from the point and I reminded him, butting in, "Professor, does the prophecy exist? Yes or no?"

"Of course it exists, Sebastian. But so do many other prophecies. Think of it this way: Surely the fact we are here at all, and choose to fight is proof that God, whatever God is, has not forsaken us. Moreover, we are the evidence of the existence of man's freewill which, in turn, means logically there is every chance we will succeed in the end."

As you may imagine this was a difficult philosophical conversation

---

[27] The Illuminati & the Compte De Viriue. This French aristocrat was made famous by his statements about the Illuminati after attending the order's grand congress in Wilhelmsbad 1782. He said, "*The conspiracy that is being woven is so well thought out that it will be, so to speak, impossible for the Monarchy and the Church to escape from it.*" He could thereafter only speak of Freemasonry with 'horror'. The 'cosmic trigger' has been termed a 'thought tunnel' by Robert A. Wilson, Illuminatus (1977). Also known in certain traditions as the 'Chapel Perilous' it broadly refers to an induced public state of mind.

to have when crawling down a pitch black tunnel listening to the scraping axe of a seemingly unstoppable zombie shuffling along behind you. But it was so critical to everything that was going on and, if it was true wouldn't YOU want to know? We were still arguing about it ten minutes later when we emerged from the tunnel into the bottom of a steep, rocky gulley the sides of which were dotted with patches of snow brightly lit by the moonlight.

"But, if it is possible that we might prevail then why did you tell Francesca that this prophecy is inescapable?"

"It is only a prophecy, Sebastian. Like all prophecies it is not carved in stone or any such like. Perhaps one shouldn't believe everything I say."

"Would it not be wise, Professor for you to indicate when we should or shouldn't believe what you say?"

A moment of awkward silence passed between us which Francesca broke by imploring, "Can we…?" before casting a worried glance at the dark mouth of the tunnel. We nodded at one another and moved off in a hurry.

It was true that the Professor was my guardian angel, looking over me and coming to my aid in times of need. But should an angel let me get into these situations in the first place? "Audacity, audacity," he had boldly declared, "You'll be fine pretending to be the Count." Well, that had blown up in our faces like Francesca's exploding jewellery box. As we ran down the hill between the snow-covered trees I remember thinking that, though he was not perfect, life had certainly become a lot more interesting since making his acquaintance. At that moment I felt we might actually survive the petrifying night and live to tell the tale. But it wasn't over yet. Not by a long chalk, as Van Halestrom would have said.

We heard the roar of rapidly moving water and soon came to a river. Daunted by its high banks and fierce current we hurried on down the hill trying to find somewhere else to cross. A little further on, we discovered a fallen tree spanning the gorge. Francesca got on it first followed by Van Halestrom then myself and the three of us proceeded to shimmy along. Snap! I flung my head around hearing something crashing through the undergrowth behind. Through the trees I saw the blood-stained white breeches of the general marching towards us.

"We should be quick," I suggested.

The gruesome general appeared at the riverbank and, in one awful moment, clambered onto the tree using his axe to drag himself along. Half his face and his right arm up to the shoulder were horribly wounded. I couldn't believe he was still alive let alone able to keep up with us. Now there were four bodies traversing the rotten trunk and one of these was belting it with an axe. Perhaps unsurprisingly, it started to creak beneath us. As the four of us edged across it could bear the weight no longer and creaked once more, before snapping in half and plummeting towards the crashing water.

Mother of God! It had already been a bad night but it was about to get even worse. With a huge splash the pieces of the log hit the ice-cold water but incredibly we all managed to hang on. Even the mad general, who to my maddening despair clung to my half with extraordinary resolve. We were quickly gathered by the current and swept along in the turbulent water.

"Sebastian!" cried Francesca, her voice barley audible above the noise of the roaring brook. The piece of the log she was sharing with the Professor was not travelling quite as fast as mine as I was closer to the centre of the river and so, unfortunately I surged on downstream without them.

"Curse it! I'm losing her again!" I wailed and watched as the Professor caught the branch of a tree sticking out from the bank and manage to pull them to the shore. I stared into the darkness as they faded from view and heard Van Halestrom call out, "Audacity, audacity, Sebastian. Don't worry we will find you," before finally losing them from sight.

"Francesca!" I yelled, but my voice was lost in the crashing of the water. The log tossed violently in the powerful current nearly throwing me off and I had to brace myself with both hands to stay on. I glanced up the writhing trunk to see the general balance himself barely six feet away and horridly continue to pull himself closer, still on his mission to kill. No! How is he capable of this? I blabbered a flurry of blue curses as the log passed into some rapids, briefly submerging before bobbing up again. Even though the log was thrashing about like a wild horse the general still managed to move another foot towards me. Good God! If there were ten men like this surely they would be invincible. How could I get away from him? I frantically tried to work out what do to.

The log sloshed on, all the time picking up speed. We slammed into a rock and I grabbed at it but the slippery stone was inches too far away and I couldn't get a grip. Onwards down the stream we tumbled, the noise of the water increasing to a deafening roar and that was the terrible moment when - I saw the waterfall.

I screamed, "I don't believe it!" with such force that it blocked out the fury of the crashing water around us. I could see the top of a distant range of mountains looming up beyond the lip. It was obviously a long drop down because of the lay of the land and also because of the ever increasing volume of the water pouring over the edge: The edge that I was remorselessly being swept towards.

Now I panicked seriously – again and started jabbering, "God I know I've asked you once already to save me and I haven't yet had time to keep my promise but if you're still listening please save me again tonight!"

I screamed with dread as the general came up closer now seconds from being in range. Why was God keeping me alive only to throw me back into another maelstrom of endless peril?

Suddenly I saw a fragment of hope. Speeding towards us in our course was one more glistening rock before the fall. I leant as far as I dared off the side of the trunk to pull myself up to the boulder when it came by and tensed as we rushed towards the black shining lump knowing that I would have but one chance. The current was impossible to swim in. Any man would have perished in the icy deluge or been swept over to his death. I had to make this work or I would die. The log dipped and rose once more in the rush and roar of the powerful current and I reached my arms out in readiness then let out an immense shriek as the general came within range and pulled his axe up to kill me for sure.

Chapter 28

The Hounds of Hell

The mad general's emotionless face stared at me as he swept the axe above his head and the water crashed around us. I lunged at the rock desperately clinging on to it while the other end of log swung over the edge of the falls. I'm sure the balance of the axe managed to tip it in my favour. The trunk hung for a second before I kicked it away and finally the mad general dressed in full ceremonial uniform and still with his axe raised over his head tipped over the side.

"Thank Jesus Christ for that!" I gasped, staring into the space where he had been. "I was beginning to think that he would never leave."

I held onto the rock for a second longer before pulling myself up to get away from the water splashing up my legs. I was only two yards from the lip of the waterfall and I carefully stood up gazing over the edge. The view was so stunning it took my breath away - even further: Such beauty in such a mad, mad world. The snow-covered Bavarian mountains all around with their jagged ridges lit by a sky full of stars and a huge glowing moon. Yes, it was indeed a beautifully clear night and that's when I realised, I was wet and I must get warm or I would perish. It took me a while to leap from one stone to the next to get to the river's bank. The stones, to my good fortune, were just close enough together. If I had had to go fully into the water I would have died from cold or been dragged over the side such was the strength of the current.

I clambered onto the bank and ran off through the trees, more than aware that the best way to get warm was to keep moving fast. I wasn't totally soaked. Indeed, the upper half of me was surprisingly dry. So maybe I would be able to survive. That's when I heard shouting and saw lanterns coming down the hill. A search party: Damn it! I wasn't out of this yet. Now I couldn't go back upstream to find the others. I prayed they were safe and bolted down the hill. Tearing through the snowy undergrowth my heart jumped again on hearing the awful sound of barking dogs. I pushed on even harder for I knew they had released the hounds.

Flying down the steep hill I barged between the trees and bushes once or twice taking a tumble but then running on again. The dogs were faster than their masters and, such was my progress, after a while the glow of the lanterns and the shouts began to fade. But I could hear, sometimes very well, the snarling of a dog.

For maybe fifty paces behind me I could hear the movements and growling of what I estimated to be a very large creature indeed. It had obviously picked up my scent and was moving in for the kill. I flung myself on ever faster, my lungs burning with the effort. Making a long jump downwards I landed on some shale and slid down to the rocks at the base of the waterfall, descending thirty feet in a matter of seconds. I didn't stop but vaulted over the rocks and sprinted on down the river bank thinking, 'Let's see you do that as fast you stupid animal.' And as I did, of course, I tripped and took a fall.

It was like a tumble that a damsel would make in a poor play when the writer can't think of other way of letting her be caught by her pursuer. I would have kicked myself for doing it had I not ended up on my arse. In some pain I pushed myself up on my haunches only to see the mad general marching towards me still holding his axe above his head.

"Nooo!" was all I could shout as I pathetically put my hand up in front of my face. Somehow he had survived his fall and was but five yards away striding over the rocks while I was stuck helpless on the ground in front of him unable to think of anything else but, 'He's going to get me after all!'

I heard the snarl of the dog first and gasped as the huge beast flew out of the shadows clamping its jaws round the general's throat. They crashed into a sprawling heap behind a boulder as the animal tore away at its prey. I didn't stay to watch what happened next but sprang up and bolted off in utter disbelief at the attack that had saved me from certain death.

"Christ that dog is big!" I panted, dashing into the night. But when I had only got twenty yards I heard a stunted whimper. What's this? Has he killed the thing? I couldn't believe it! Sweet Jesus! Could nothing stop this one-man army? The dog was as big as a blasted bear for God's sake. After a moment more running I was sure that I could hear the creature behind me yet again. Or was it another? There was definitely something chasing me though whatever it was it wasn't catching me up. Eventually I guessed it must be the same animal but now wounded by the general's axe it had been slowed. Did this mean the giant beast had actually got the better of him? I prayed to God it had and that the mad General Frederick had, at last been killed. It wasn't surprising after the barrage of deadly blows that he had received. *[28]

Now at least it was only the wounded hound pursuing me. But by the sounds of the growling, it seemed even more determined to catch me than before. Though I was determined too. The land at the base of the valley opened out into a flat narrow plain with near vertical flanks. Due to my terror I was going at a fair pelt. I was twenty two years old and fit in those days - really fit. After a few minutes I found my natural running pace and looked up far above me. I must have lay unconscious in the castle for some time because I could see the first glow of sunrise over the mountains to the east. I carried on going. Now I was getting warm.

"Come on dog. Let's see who can win this now," I muttered and pushed on through the night.

And so the chase went on. For a time I thought I had lost the thing but it seemed that it could keep up whilst we ran on level ground. So, as soon as the terrain allowed it, I started to climb. Making good use of my new-found mountaineering skills I ascended the side of the valley but was shocked when I looked behind to see the huge black animal already halfway up and staring back at me.

"Christ! They certainly feed that dog well," I puffed, "or maybe not well enough."

At the top I ran on once more, determined to lose the animal. Sprinting as fast as I could for a whole mile at least I was confident it would give up the chase. However, an hour later I saw the creature again. Though it was a whole rise behind it was still doggedly pursuing. At that moment I even considered confronting it but I

---

[28] General Frederick II of Hesse Kassel. This well-documented aristocrat, who made his fortune renting Hessian troops to the Americans in the War of Independence, definitely had connections with the Illuminati, although his death is recorded as being on 31st October (All Hallow's Eve)1785 some seven months later. If the author's description is to be believed the General would have had to cling on to his life for some time with an amazing set of injuries before finally dying. Although S. Drechsler never actually sees him die and this may explain this intriguing anomaly in the story.

thought better of it fearing the hound's powerful jaws and its extraordinary energy.

"Every time you let me think I've got away, Lord, I find it to be an illusion." I cursed the never-ending chase. It felt like a test had been sent down to me by a misanthropic Greek god. Well, if it was a test then, like Hercules, I was determined to survive it and I sped up my pace again. By this time Francesca and I should have pleasured each other extensively and I sighed as I imagined the sweet smelling scent of the warm sheets of the inn and my sweet lady herself who was now somewhere so far away.

And where the hell was I? The lie of the land had forced me to travel the opposite direction to Pettendorf but after another mile noticed that up ahead for the first time there were now actually two different paths I could take. I could go west back down into the valley or turn east and carry on up the snowy ridge where I could see some steep bluffs that would favour my own abilities over the dog's. I glanced behind me. Though the brute was nowhere to be seen I knew it was still be stubbornly following after me.

I pushed on up the ridge finding another sheer wall of rock and spent several minutes climbing the escarpment, certain the animal would be unable to get a purchase on the tiny finger holds. Once at the top I looked down and was amazed to see the persistent beast arrive below. It glared up at me, barking viciously and limping round in circles obviously unable to get up the sheer face. I could see that its front leg was badly wounded. Why didn't the blasted thing just go home? I wondered if Weishaupt's soul had somehow entered the creature instead of going to hell or that maybe it was possessed like the mad general.

Well it would be a possessed hound that they sent after me, Cerberus himself no doubt. Not any usual mutt - not me - of course not. That would be too easy. At the top of the escarpment I stuck a finger up at the beast before making myself scarce. Sure that was the last I would see of it I still kept up a trot just in case. It had been a night of such incredible occurrences that every yard away from the dog and the castle made me feel a little better.

Hours later with the winter's sun at its highest point I marched on through the heavy snow at the top of another peak in the fresh morning air of the mountains. I relaxed then, about the chase anyway, certain that the beast and everyone else had given up. Now the most important thing was to get shelter because I was getting tired. The countryside was a white wilderness in every direction and I had no idea which way to go to find someone to help me. It was still a freezing cold February day in the mountains and I held myself to keep warm as I forged on through the snow.

As I came to the top of the rise my spirits toppled like a felled tree when I saw the dog's black head appear over the lip of ahead of me. Somehow it was back, a full six hours since I had seen it last. Dragging its front leg but growling ferociously the terrifying creature stared at me with death in its eyes from thirty yards away and moved in for the kill.

I tried to run off but the snow was too deep and it was impossible to get away. There was no cover around and no tree to run up like a frightened cat. Shit! Shit! Shit! What was I to do? When the beast got within ten yards I turned around with my hands out ready for its attack as it lowered itself to spring.

It leapt at me and I desperately tried to catch hold of its mouth. "Damn you!" I screamed but lost my grip as its massive head thrashed about trying to catch me in its jaws. It nearly got the better of me but I smacked it on the nose and it pulled away. God it was huge: Nearly as big as me. I tried to get my breath back but before I could it leapt at me again. This time I caught it by its face and using all my might to hold its teeth, somehow I managed to wrestle it to the ground. It really was the size of a small bear but its front leg was virtually useless and it was also bleeding heavily from its neck. I'm sure it was these injury that allowed me to get it on its back and force its jaws apart. Had it not been hurt I fear it would have easily won.

This was a fight till the death and I knew it. It was me or him. One of us was going to die. I had been told that the only way to kill a dog with your bare hands was by ripping its mouth apart and although the thought disgusted me I had to make it stop. It put up such a fight trying to remove me with its back legs and find the power in its jaw I feared it would not give up. But after ten truly horrifying minutes I eventually overcame its strength and, with a terrible whimper and an almighty crack, its jaw bones snapped and the dog from Hell itself was dead and I knew the chase was finally at an end.

I burst out crying with the relief and fatigue and pain and

sympathy for the poor animal. I no longer believed it was possessed but that it was simply determined to do what came naturally. Unlike a man obeying cruel orders the dog somehow had more dignity. It had no idea of morality. I was simply its prey. There was no wrong and right to its savagery. It was just its way.

I pushed the dead carcass off me and got up, wiping my face with the back of my hand. The animal had bitten me after all. I had not realised in the fight but I was actually bleeding badly from my ear and saw droplets of blood stain the snow. Turning around I moved off again, keeping to my course. Now I was exhausted, freezing *and* injured. I knew I had to find some people or a road soon or I would be in real trouble.

Three hours later with the sun already going down I started to panic as I had still not seen anyone or a house or a road or even tracks in the snow. There seemed to be no sign of life anywhere. By then I must have walked and run twenty five miles over extremely rough terrain. I was lost, tired, scared and getting colder by the minute and too exhausted to move about quickly to keep warm. I stopped for a minute trying to get my bearings shivering in the biting wind.

My mind was awash with self-pity and regret. I couldn't be killed now. Not by the cold. Not after I had fought off such odds and come through. I stumbled on feeling angry with myself. If I died it would be my fault for getting lost. I dreamed of Francesca and the warmth of the Professor's room at the university and the comforts of my family's house and my mother's cosy kitchen with sweet smells coming from the oven. My mind started to wander as I staggered and I looked above me. The weather was worsening and a blizzard was beginning to gather. I knew I must find shelter soon or perish.

An hour later with only a few minutes of life-preserving twilight left I blundered on amongst a swirl of snowflakes that travelled so fast they were like flying nails striking against my skin. I staggered on blindly with my arm out in front of me as the last of my strength finally ebbed away thinking, 'It's all over Seb. You're going to die.' I had exerted myself so heavily over the past day that I had nothing left and eventually I went down on my knees in the snow unable to go any further. I began to pray, 'At least I tried, Lord. But in the end I have failed to stay alive and keep my promise to you. So prepare to receive me into your arms.' With the storm raging about me I was about to curl up right there and die because I knew there was simply no point to go on.

For some reason I lifted my head up once more and stared into the gathering dark. I don't know why. It was just instinct. As I squinted through the blustering flakes I thought I saw a light twinkle in the distant gloom. Was it a mirage or my imagination? I couldn't tell due to my deluded state and the blizzard swirling around me. Then I saw the light twinkling again and I knew that it was real. My heart leapt at the sight and I stood up sensing it must be a house. Joy of joys! I was to be saved - again. I pulled myself together for the final part of my awesome journey, pushing myself on and gasping, 'You're going to make it Seb! You're going to blasted make it!'

I sped up feeling a new found vigour flowing through my aching, freezing limbs, inspired by the hope of warmth and safety. For a moment I worried that the house might be full of thugs or even worse monsters like the ones I had already fought. But I was so cold didn't even care. I just wanted to be warm and wouldn't have given a fig if the Devil himself was sitting in front of a fire pouring himself a cup of tea. As I came up to the tiny cottage I was certain that it was safe when I saw two lines of horseshoes on the door to ward off evil spirits – the Devil doesn't usually have good luck charms hanging on his house.

Seconds later I was pounding on the door which was opened by a family eager to help a needy traveller and give him shelter from the storm. They took me in and I was saved as the warmth of their fire flowed into me. I was given broth and a blanket and I knew the chase was finally over and that the terrible ordeal had, at last, come to an end. After all the horror that had befallen me on my astonishing adventure and all the heinous evil I had seen it was the humblest things that had been my saviour. A fire, a roof, some food and care from those decent people. I realised in that moment that however much death and terrible horror exists in the world there is always love somewhere. Sometimes, thankfully, in the places you least expect to find it. And thank God for that.

Chapter 29

Odysseus Returns

My odyssey wasn't fully over and perhaps I was beginning to understand that nothing ever was. We were snowed in for two days by the blizzard that surely would have killed me if I had not found refuge when I did. The master of the house told me I was only a few miles from the main road leading to the border and that I had been unlucky not to find any other track the way I had come. He promised to take me to Regensburg as soon as the snow had cleared where I could make arrangements for my journey home. I lied, of course, about the exact circumstances that had brought me to their door. I'm sure they had no wish to hear the real version of events. So I kept my mouth shut about my adventures not wanting to risk being thrown out for scaring the children. Fortunately my clothes, although quite damaged, convinced them I was a man of some distinction so they treated me well whilst we waited for the snow to clear and I prayed that my friends were safe.

Two days later the master of the house brought me into Regensburg aboard his old cart. I thanked him kindly for his family's hospitality and paid him for his help then booked myself onto a stagecoach with the money I had remaining. Twelve hours after that I was finally back in Ingolstadt and walking through the door of my humble lodgings.

"Sweet Lord it's good to be home!" I cried. My little place seemed so wonderful at that moment and I finally felt completely safe. Somehow instinct told me my friends had also escaped and, with the whole business at an end, we could finally relax about the future with our work thoroughly completed. I hurriedly changed into my normal clothes and, after finding the box of pearls under my bed which had been much on my mind, ran to the university to find Van Halestrom and hopefully Francesca to tell them I was alive and of my incredible adventures.

Sure enough, the Professor was there and thrilled to see me safe and sound in his chambers and we exchanged our amazing stories of escape. But on hearing his final piece of news I shouted out in misery, "What do you mean she's gone again?"

For it was true. The blasted woman had gone again. This time to Paris of all places.

"Paris!" I cried, as if to confirm it, considering that this woman and I were like a pair of opposing magnets constantly repelling each other whenever brought together.

"But why in Heaven's name?" I wailed.

The Professor opened a drawer in his desk pulling out his pipe. "There is much social upheaval in the land of France, my lad. Threats of bloody revolution sweep the streets. Brave Francesca travels there because we believe the Illuminati wishes to control this force, which may be natural, or maybe not. Though I believe it is the latter and has been created in order to bring about their plans: Starting the fall of an entire nation by stealth." *[29]

I shook my head. "Is this possible?"

"Oh yes, my lad, believe it." He sucked on his pipe and sparked his ingenious lighter into life. "A few men sitting in a room hundreds of miles away can most certainly induce such massive change. Francesca has gone to find out who these men are and she will return when she has done so and not before." Lighting his pipe he blew out two large rings of smoke before settling back into his chair. "Just be patient, Sebastian. The best things come to those who wait."

As I had hoped desperately to find her there after coming through so much and so far and with nothing else on my mind but to make that woman mine I quipped, "Patient, sir! I have been patient for a blasted year," and pushed myself out of my chair impetuously going and find her.

"Calm yourself, lad. If it is truly love then I'm sure it will survive

---

[29] The Illuminati & the French Revolution. Many historians have long contested that the Illuminati were involved in the fermenting of revolutionary forces that led to the overthrow of decadent King Louis XVI's '*regime ancien*' which ruled France until 1789. Notable works such as Nesta H. Webster's 1924 '***Ritual and illustrations of Freemasonry***' and John Robison's '***Proof of a conspiracy***' 1798 document detailed plans of how the Bavarian Illuminati along with the French Freemasons conspired to bring about a popular nationwide uprising which included at it head, amongst others, The Duke of Orleans (Freemason), The Marquis de Lafayette (Freemason) and the Jacobin Club radical nucleus of the revolt formed by other prominent Freemasons.

the test of time." He chuckled to himself and blew out another ring of smoke.

His patronising attitude was insufferable and I snapped, "But what do you know of love, sir? I see no woman in your life."

As soon as I said these churlish words I realised that I may have crossed a line. He looked me in the eye and said, "Perhaps it would be best if you sat down, Sebastian. I feel there is something that I must tell you."

I eased myself back into my seat as the Professor rose from his and faced out of the window. After a moment to collect his thoughts he spoke earnestly over his shoulder, "I can understand your longings for Francesca, Sebastian because, like you, I was once very much in love myself. I have not told you of this before as I felt it was unnecessary but now I feel that I must explain." He paused and stared into the distance then began, "I was married a long time ago to a wonderful woman called Theresa. Much like you my feelings for her were such that I did not care about the ramifications that our union would have upon our lives. At that time I was a member of an organisation which barred its membership from matrimony and although I tried to keep our union a secret, eventually it was discovered and I was asked to leave. This may not seem important but it had huge consequences for those around me especially poor Bacon. For, he was the one who had mentored me during my indoctrination into the order and because of my indiscretion he was also made to go. I believe he has already told you of the system to which we adhere. This was a legacy of the order to which we once belonged. It was the most laudable order of the Rosicrusians. *[30] This esteemed group of men originated to oppose the dogma of established religion and to support ideas of science, empiricism and

---

[30] The Order of the Rosicrusians. The Rosicrucian order was a mysterious secret society founded in late medieval Germany by Christian Rosenkreuz though the real origins of the order may predate this. The sect is believed to have influenced many notable historical figures over time including; John Dee, Queen Elizabeth I head of security, and also Dee's pupil Francis Bacon. As S. Drechsler describes the mandate of the order was one of scientific empiricism over religious dogma especially that of Roman Catholicism though its teachings contained much deep spirituality. The Order seems to have an interesting intertwined relationship with the Illuminati some historians even connecting the two in purpose and manifesto. It is worth noting that S. Drechsler's recalls being told that the Rosicrusians had been 'infiltrated' by the Illuminati.

the true understanding of nature. Presiding over the society were eight members who took oaths to heal the sick without payment, to maintain a secret membership, to find a replacement for themselves before they died and to remain a sworn bachelor. When I was found to have broken this last oath unfortunately both my and Bacon's involvement was at an end. Though we had both realised that in the future it would not be the church that posed a threat to civilisation but the Illuminati, it was still humbling to be excluded from the society in which we had invested so much of our lives and it came as a terrible blow."

'More secrets,' I thought but he had still not told me everything and so I probed, "But then, what happened to your wife, sir?"

He sighed before turning back to me. "That is the worst part of all, Sebastian. Theresa paid the ultimate price for my membership. She is dead,"

"Good Lord. I'm so … sorry, sir. How …?"

"I killed her."

"Holy Mother!"

"When the Illuminati infiltrated the Rosicrusians they found out that we knew of their plans and we became marked men. Thus those around us also became targets. The Illuminati kidnapped Theresa's parents and threatened to kill them if she did not kill me. She had no choice in the end. Of course, I did not know it was her when she came for me but thought that the robed figure was one of their agents and sadly I took her life."

I could not believe this earth-shattering news. It was as though a millstone had been dropped on me from a great height. What could I say? What could I do? At least *now* I fully understood his obsessive will for the Illuminati's destruction. My mind struggled to think of a way to console the man but it was impossible. In the end I considered revenge and ventured, "But, sir, why did you not do away with Weishaupt? You have had so many opportunities."

"This happened before Weishaupt was enlisted into the order. He was merely a Jesuit scholar back then. It is those that are behind him whom I seek to destroy and Herr Weishaupt was useful in leading us to them."

A rare silence fell between us and after a while I pushed the box of pearls onto the desk. I did not know how I could console him and felt ashamed for the way I had brought up the harrowing subject.

With these revelations weighing heavily on my mind, and obviously his own, I decided I should take my leave.

"I should go, Professor. I'm sure there is much that requires your attention."

Humbled, I got up and made my way to the door. As I opened it he asked, "I trust you took one of the pearls for your old age, Sebastian."

I hung my head. "Yes, Professor."

"Then I fear I have more bad news for you. It seems that you have been labouring under more than one misconception. I'm afraid the pearls are fake. Weishaupt has used a similar trick before. He was always the illusionist - even until the end."

He was so confident that he did not even turn around to check. I was devastated to hear this. My mind shot back to the pearl hidden at my house. It would have been worth a fortune. Now, along with my dreams of a pension, it had been taken away in the blink of an eye.

"Though it will not be equal to the amount you have lost, Sebastian, I will of course pay you for your recent work. I will have my clerk make up the sum and deliver it to your lodgings."

"Thank you, sir" I answered humbly.

He remained staring out of the window and I left, gently closing the door behind me. Walking back to my lodgings I was suddenly possessed with an overwhelming sense of grief. Good Lord. I had been so happy moments before. Glad to be alive and overjoyed that those close to me were also safe from danger. But the Professor's recent revelations had changed everything. Not only was I crestfallen about the pearl but his terrible story forced me to worry anew.

My walk took me past Jan's old rooms. It was a path I had been reluctant to take only a few months ago as I feared accidentally bumping into him. Now the pain of his loss was made raw again by the awful tale I had heard. I had already lost my oldest friend. How many others in my life might die if I carried on my battle with the Illuminati? Van Halestrom had lost his wife, Francesca her sister. Who might be taken away next? Francesca? My parents? Let alone me. It seemed that my new self was merely the old one but with a hundred terrible ordeals polluting my memories. Whatever it was that I had discovered in my new life it had not given me the courage to go and beg my best friend to change his ways. The money that I had earned had made me feel as though I was a gentleman with the things it allowed me to buy, the fine clothes, the saddle for Petrova but was it really worth it if I was dead along with everybody else?

There was another uncomfortable aspect that occurred to me. Was I being used by Van Halestrom as an instrument of revenge? This may seem cynical but I worried that, in his eagerness to smash the order that had wounded him so terribly, he would overlook the safety of others. I could not be sure. At that moment all I wanted was to find Francesca and convince her to move away with me to the country to a place that was unknown to anyone. A place where we could be together and be safe from the seething forces of darkness that conspired against us. I also thought then, for the first time since beginning work for the Professor, if I really wanted to carry on in his employ. Even picking up a letter for this man could have potentially lethal consequences and doing anything more than that was surely always going to be a matter of life and death.

I sighed deeply as I let myself back into my house. Van Halestrom had told me to be patient. 'The best things come to those who wait,' he had said. And as I considered this I realised that there was no other option. All I could do was wait and hope.

Chapter 30

The Waiting Game

And so I waited, and waited, and waited and, even as the spring came and burst all around me, I waited but still she did not return. It was three whole months later in May when, at last, I received a letter sent by her from France. Though it had been a long time her tender words instantly brought my fondness flooding back in waves. She thanked me for saving her in the dungeon and told me how she would come to me instantly if she was not so far away.

This was a great relief to me as during the past months I had begun a friendship with a pretty young woman from town of whom I had grown fond. Though I had not attempted to consummate this relationship, having not given up the hope of seeing beautiful Francesca again, I had found that this lady's company eased my mind and I was proud to court such a beauty. I worried that, in the end, I was only a man and I could not wait forever. Simultaneously, I realised that Francesca was just a woman, a woman with so much on her plate, so to speak, that I could not reasonably expect her to be faithful forever too. However hard it was for me I tried to put these pangs of doubt to one side.

You must understand that, though I truly believed I loved Francesca, it had been three long months since I had seen her last and that had been for less than ten minutes at the inn where she had called me a foolish boy. It had been another four months before that when we had shared a single kiss at the Professor's castle. I wasn't a priest. I was a just a normal young man. So don't go thinking good-old-Seb was disloyal to his romantic feelings and go calling me a heartless cad or worse, thank you very much. I was just a human being, that's all, and a lonely one at that.

There was still much gossip around the campus about Weishaupt's disappearance along with the banishment of the Illuminati and, though my meetings with the Professor continued, there was noticeably less urgency in his plans. Although he still maintained there was, 'much to do' and that 'the fight was not over by a long chalk' I found this hard to understand. Surely if Weishaupt was dead, sent back to the rancid hell from whence he came, and the order had been banished what were we fighting against? But the Professor assured me that 'the forces of evil still lingered in many places' and, though I was growing evermore reluctant to envisage myself as part of the army that would defeat them, I remembered the cast of despicable villains already supplied to the fray and it wasn't so hard to believe. But then nothing happened for a month and, by the beginning of June, I began to think that nothing would. Van Halestrom went away on business and the days turned into weeks.

Meanwhile, my strangely fractured social life still refused to die and, as such, I had been both pleased and honoured to receive an invitation to a wedding. I say friend when actually he was more of an acquaintance: Aristocratic Otto Goring from the university shooting club. It was the society wedding of an English aristocrat's daughter marrying into Prussian nobility. The ceremony was to take place in Vienna, a city which I had never visited before but which I had always wanted to see. It was later that month and, although I received the invitation by post and did not know the bride or groom and would not see Otto until the wedding itself as he had already finished his studies, I decided that I would go.

Along with the invitation I was surprised to find in the envelope a banker's draft for one hundred thalers. Otto informed me this was to pay for my journey and to buy some new clothes 'befitting a ceremony of such distinction.' The amount of money was much greater than the sum required, even if I had gone to the emperor's tailor. This was more than convenient as I had not worked for the Professor for a while, and of course I had lost my pearl, so I was once more finding myself severely out of pocket. Whilst considering Otto must have been slightly eccentric to be giving away his money like this, in my vanity, I decided that although we were not the closest of friends he had done well to select me as his honourable companion at such a refined gathering and I hastily went out and bought a fine new outfit.

In the days leading up to the wedding I began to look forward to the prospect of the lavish ceremony and the fine food and drink with which we were no doubt to be indulged. I was also secretly interested to see for myself the envious lives of the aristocracy and hoped that, if I was lucky, I may also be able to seduce one of the elegant bridesmaids that would, no doubt, be in abundance. I had recently parted from my new young lady friend from town as no love had been forthcoming on my behalf, probably because I was pining for you-know-who. But after receiving no other communications from distant Francesca I wanted to try again to forget her. And so, for the want of some free food, some casual romance and the chance to sample the grand life of a gentleman, I had sealed my fate as the next part of my tale was now determined. For, as you have probably guessed being no village idiot yourself, my tale is far from over. And you would be right. It is far, far from over.

Chapter 31

The Wedding

The two hundred and twenty mile journey to Vienna on board a packed stagecoach was exhausting but because of Austrian efficiency achieved in less than thirty six hours. Unfortunately, due to the hard Prussian seats, my poor backside was as sore as a blind cobbler's thumb by the time we finally reached our destination; The Imperial Hotel De Place in the heart of the old city and my spirits lifted upon seeing its gracious towers as we rattled painfully up the cobbled driveway. I enjoyed an evening in the serenity of the hotel and rose at seven the next morning to make the most of the day. The service itself was at ten which allowed me two hours to have breakfast then take my morning constitutional and show off my splendid new clothes.

As I strolled past the plush suites on the ground floor, to my surprise, a door flew open in front of me and the figure of a priest came out and pulled me inside the room. I say he was a priest because he was wearing a cassock with a dog collar and a huge silver crucifix that dangled down to his knees. But if he hadn't been so attired I would have know him to be Professor Van Halestrom. Not of course that that was possible as it would have been sheer madness. And then it all started to happen again.

"Hello there, my lad. Good to see you," Van Halestrom embraced me but I was too shocked to hug him back.

"What are you doing here?" I asked soberly, as he smiled and adjusted his cassock.

"I'm to carry out the service at the wedding."

I hadn't seen him for several weeks and was out of practice with the way my mind started to fly about when he spoke.

"What do you mean? You are not a priest."

"Exactly!" He spun round admiring himself in the mirror, "That is the plan."

"But you will be recognised. There will be people here from the university."

"We don't think that will be the case."

"We?"

Klaus appeared from the door of the adjoining room carrying a tray.

"Hello, sir."

"What are you doing here?" I hissed, trying to conceal my growing consternation.

"Part of the operation, sir."

I noticed that on his tray there was a wig and a huge false moustache. The Professor sat in a chair in front of the bureau and puckered up as Klaus passed the unusually long piece of facial hair to him with a pair of tweezers and Van Halestrom stuck it on his lip.

"You can't wear that," I cried, "Priests don't have moustaches."

"This is Austria, Herr Drechsler. Everyone has a moustache. Even the babies are born with them."

He turned to me and grinned with the preposterous thing hanging over the sides of his face. Klaus placed the wig upon his head, completing the disguise, and the Professor put on some blue tinted glasses. Although I knew it was him I had to admit he now looked totally different and he began speaking with a hammy Russian accent, "Anyway, I am Bishop Uzbek Natzirkov and as a Russian, thoroughly expected to have a fine display of facial hair."

I shook my head as he groomed himself in the mirror.

"Why is this deception to be performed?"

"This is an Illuminati wedding, Sebastian, a sham marriage that is, in fact, a political arrangement to unite the families of Schweizer and Oglethorpe. Two eminent European houses of huge influence, privilege, and great wealth coming together in the interests of dynastic tyranny, not love and we, through a certain degree of serendipity, find ourselves in the position to ruin the deal. If the priest is found to be an impostor the union will be annulled and thus we will have spoiled their plans."

He raised his eyebrows which were the only thing on his face that were not fake, apart from his eyes which were deadly serious.

"So let me understand. You are going to perform the ceremony then pronounce it null and void. Won't they just marry again?"

"It is all about timing, my lad. This is the plan; I marry them. They believe they are so. Then, as we have discovered, the unfaithful groom intends to reveal his countless infidelities to the bride to spite her and she will become trapped in this unhappy union. The Lady Philippine is not as joyous as her groom about the marriage brokered by their clans but is prepared to submit to appease the families because she does not yet know the extent of his debauchery. After his affairs are made clear I will write a letter to the church explaining that I was a fraud and that my claim to this is sealed in the envelope containing the marriage certificate. Once the ceremony is proved to be a hoax an avenue of freedom will become available to the bride. She will thus be able to have the marriage declared null and void and the deal will be broken. This will, in turn, destabilise the conglomeration of their political power and put the Illuminati's plans back several years."

I glanced at Karl then back at Van Halestrom who raised his eyebrows knowingly and I ventured, "Such complexity, enough to make the mind boggle."

"Ah. But your job is clear."

"My job? What is that? I am merely a guest."

"And as a guest you will kill the father of the bride."

"What! Kill the father of what?"

Infuriatingly he began to repeat himself, as was his way.

"Kill the father …"

"I heard you! I heard you! All the Saints! That's why I'm shouting, because I heard you!"

Klaus interjected, "Best not to, sir, especially the word, 'kill.' Although they look it the walls here are not that thick."

He was right. I had shouted it loud enough to be heard on the other side of the city. But it was because of the shock you understand. Of all the things the mad Professor could have said apart from kill the bride herself what could be worse? What was this darkness that had come into my cursed life again?

"He is an English gentleman; Brigadier James Oglethorpe, member of parliament, banker, murderer and one of the secretive Kabbalist priests you saw at the Temple of Eleusis. He has achieved much authority in the Illuminati since Adam Weishaupt's departure and is the order's top agent in the Americas. As the founder of the state of Georgia he provides them a foothold from which they inject their evil into the new colonies.

"So I must ... kill him. Why me?"

"I am the priest. I cannot."

"But you are not a priest."

"And you are not a proper guest. We elicited your invitation ourselves."

Klaus nodded affirming this deception. Apart from everything else I was now insulted that I was not a genuine guest.

"So you got me here to complete this task using trickery?"

The Professor conceded, after a fashion, "Yes. In a way, I suppose it was. We sent you the invitation as we believed you might not come if you knew what we wished you to do."

Before I could complain Klaus handed me an impressive breach-loading pistol and half a dozen cartridges.

Van Halestrom carried on, "That's it. Remember, in the head."

"What!"

"Yes, after the speeches. You will find Oglethorpe in the drawing room of the hotel. He will be waiting for a courier to collect his letter informing his Illuminati masters that the wedding has taken place as planned. Then, when the deed is done, you will leave in the dumb-waiter situated at the back of the room finding Klaus in the basement to provide you with your alibi. When the murder is discovered the party will be broken up whereupon you will make your getaway."

"But …"

So that was apparently that, or so the old bird thought. I walked through the hotel reception nervously glancing over my shoulder and feeling the gun bulging inside my coat thinking, 'He must be truly mad if he thinks I'm going to carry out this barbaric act. What on God's sweet earth does he think I'm capable of?'

I left the gates of the hotel and hurried round the corner to find a café and have myself a drink. Two large glasses of beer were necessary before I finally started to calm down. Of all the lunatic suicidal violence: To shoot a man dead at his daughter's wedding. Could anything be so cruel? There must be a word for this act? To inflict such terror on those around you; terrify, terrorise, 'terrorist.' Yes, if a man made it his life's work that would be his name.

I could not go through with it. It was as simple as that. It was sheer madness. Weishaupt was dead. The Illuminati, as far as I was concerned, or could tell, or care, were dead too. Killing this man who posed no obvious threat to me, apart from telling me off for seducing a bridesmaid, was utterly pointless. I finished my beer and checked the time by the church clock in the square. I was going to be late if I did not get a move on so I hurried off across the city and got there just in time.

A queue had formed in front of the elegant medieval church, a beautiful example of early Gothic masonry. Its flying buttresses were so outstanding I did not see what was coming. And it was the sight that changed my life. For when I reached the church steps I had to look once, then twice and then again until glaring in disbelief. As there, within the line of dignitaries, I saw him; the human devil Adam Weishaupt, shaking hands with the guests.

Horrified, I edged round the back of the line desperately trying to hide my face whilst chattering to myself, "But he's dead. He's dead. He's blasted dead. I saw him die at least twice; set on fire then shoved down the awful pit and falling to his death in the ghastly dungeon. Surely that should have been enough?"

I wondered if God would have to take him apart piece by piece, getting down to the individual tiny fragments smaller than grains of sand and obliterate every single one of them until he was finally gone. I looked again to make sure. It was definitely Weishaupt and no mistake. There was never another like that and I felt my brain start to burn with fear. I sneaked behind a cluster of bridesmaids standing at the foot of the steps and chewed at my nails. What should I do? Shoot him with the gun I had? What would be the point? He'd just keep coming back again and again. I remembered what the Professor had said about 'the lingering forces of evil' and the awful feeling of wickedness returned. I bowed my head and ran up the steps seeking the sanctity of the church.

I crossed myself going through the doors and found a pew in the shadows at the back amongst some old ladies. Presently, Weishaupt came in with the heads of the families and they took up their positions at the front below the altar. Why did he not burst into flames inside the sacred house? Couldn't God smash him for us? Or was the prophecy true? Had God indeed forsaken us and left us to our fate? The remainder of the guests came in, the huge church organ started to play and, without further ado, the ceremony began. The bride entered escorted by my elderly target, James Oglethorpe. I wondered if he was indestructible too. Although I knew I could not complete the deadly act anyway. So what did it matter if he was gunpowder-proof?

The bridal procession made their way to the front and joined the husband-to-be. Although there were two attending clergymen, I noticed that Van Halestrom had not joined the service yet. I wondered if things were not going exactly according to plan and sure enough, when he finally appeared even under his disguise, I could tell he was flustered. Yet his timing was expedient for the moment he walked out and took his place before the altar the music ended and congregation sat down as one.

He collected himself and began in his overzealous Russian accent, "Dearly beloved, we are gathered here today in the sight of our Lord to join these two children of Almighty God in holy wedlock."

He paused for a breath, gazing at the congregation. As he did his eyes fell on Weishaupt in the front row and the sight stopped him in his tracks.

"It is … it is … it is…," he spoke as if his tongue were nailed to a spinning top. I realised he must be going through the same shock as I had on seeing Weishaupt. In my own state of mental imbalance I had not considered how it would affect his performance. He stumbled once more and uncharacteristically crossed his chest staring in horror at our nemesis.

"Come on, Van Halestrom." I muttered to myself, fearful that he would ruin the service in thoroughly embarrassing fashion in front of a hundred guests and dignitaries. It may seem strange but I was so sensitive to acts of a publicly humiliating nature such as these that I considered my exposure, and all its consequences; incarceration, violence and even death, a mere inconvenience in comparison. There was a lonely cough in the silence of the church.

"Please God. Let him do it." I murmured from the very edge of my pew. Then to mine and every other person's relief, at that moment, he pulled himself together – 'just.'

Glancing back and forth between Weishaupt and the congregation and with his hammy Russian accent coming and going he stumbled on, "Marriage is the most important of human bonds …"

I listened to his every word during the rest of the service praying for its safe and punctual delivery so desperate was I for it to be made without error. Until, thankfully we finally reached the end.

"If there is any man who knows of a good reason why this happy union should not be brought into fruition then say so now or forever hold thy peace."

Well if everybody was to have a go we'd be here until Christmas I reckoned. With all the affairs, infidelities, deals, and other immoralities going on behind the scenes we would have a line consisting of half the down-trodden of Europe and the World beyond running out of the church and halfway round the city ready to disclose their own particular list of sordid unpleasantries preventing this 'happy union.' Although somehow there were none forthcoming and so Van Halestrom carried on.

The pair exchanged vows and, after dropping the ring twice, the Professor finally ground the ceremony to a conclusion but only maintaining his deceit by the very skin of his teeth. There had been gasps of surprise when he had mistakenly asked the groom if he would, "Take this *man* to be your lawful wedded husband." Although he laughed it off and corrected himself, repeating the question the right way round, there were a few angry murmurs from the guests around me. One old fossil in a military uniform blustered, "This priest is a fool. He should be sent back to the steppes aboard the donkey on which he came."

At last the Professor's improbable Russian accent boomed out, "So with the power vested in me by the Holy Church of Rome I declare these two children of our Lord bound together in eternal matrimony."

With this the ceremony finished, the congregation stood, the organ played and this part of the awful day ended. The crowd spilled outside and milled around on the steps. I spotted the Professor greeting some of guests and made my way over.

"That is an ecumenical matter, my child," blabbed Van Halestrom. I winced as a man ten years his senior walked away with a confused look on his face.

"Well, I think that went well," whispered the Professor under his moustache and feigned greeting me.

"That is a use of the word 'well' which I have been previously unaware." I grumbled under my breath, "It was excruciating."

"But as far as they are concerned legally binding and that is the point." He glanced about slyly from behind his beard and glasses.

I recalled the more pressing matter at hand, "Weishaupt! Did you see?" I glimpsed over my shoulder at our arch enemy who was in discussion with a group of men at the bottom of the steps.

"Of course I saw him. Did you not see me see him?" coughed Van

Halestrom, "He must have been saved by the water in the dungeon's oubliette dousing the flames."

My mind flashed back to the dungeon. Could it be true? I stuttered, "But ... what are we to do?"

"Carry on, my lad. You know what you must do. With Oglethorpe gone and the dissolution of the marriage, and therefore the merger, the Illuminati's plans will be greatly undermined, saving many thousands of lives in the future and the stifling of their rancid movement. Remember, my lad? Moral calculus. I have sealed the marriage certificate with my letter in an envelope and secreted them in the church. That part of the mission is complete. Now we must finish the rest. "

He looked over my shoulder and smiled, "And now how can we fail because help is indeed at hand."

I spun round and was stunned to see Lady Francesca, of all things, a bridesmaid. She stood amongst a gaggle of other women as the bouquet was thrown by the bride. To my great frustration she watched with complete disinterest as the flying bunch of flowers was eagerly grabbed by a tall woman with horsey features then raised an eyebrow in contempt as the giggling woman excitedly showed the bouquet to her jealous friends.

"Francesca? Here?" I murmured.

"Oh, did I not tell you she was coming?"

"No you did not tell me she was coming." I griped, secretly thinking that I had actually planned to seduce a bridesmaid.

He put a hand on my shoulder. "Klaus will take you to the hotel in a carriage whilst I cause a diversion to keep Weishaupt here until the speeches are over." He looked me in the eyes. "Remember, Sebastian - in the head," and pointed to his own before finishing, "I will see you later, my friend. Good luck."

"In the head! In the head! Yes." I peevishly repeated. He squeezed my arm and shuffled over to Klaus. Turning my attention to Francesca my heart leapt as she sailed up the steps regarding me happily.

All I could do was sigh, "You're here." Before, remembering our perilous situation, I pulled her behind a group of men.

"I see your mind is as sharp as ever, Sebastian," she teased, looking around, surprised by my seriousness. She was wearing a beautiful gown of satin and lace and would have made Aphrodite look like an old prostitute who worked at the docks but my pleasure was curtailed by our most urgent problem.

"Have you seen?" I threw a glance down the steps. She followed my eyes until gasping, "Weishaupt!" Whipping her face back she covered it with her shawl and hissed, "He's alive!"

Her eyes turned to stern resolve as she compelled me, "Then we cannot afford to fail. You know what you must do?"

"Yes, yes, I know what I must do. All but the Pope himself keep reminding me. I must approach the man who has me as a guest at his daughter's wedding and I must shoot him."

"Remember, in the head."

"Yes! Yes! In the head! I would like to take this chance to point out, that it's the part most hard to forget."

"Good: God's speed. I must retire with the other bridesmaids back to the hotel."

She kissed me on the cheek before replacing her shawl and gliding down the steps to find her carriage leaving me in a wild fit of apoplexy. I watched her pull away with my mind a torrent of stress and morbid confusion and reeled once more when I noticed Weishaupt glancing in my direction turning my bowels inside out. Hiding my own face I slipped away to find the carriage and found Klaus sitting behind the reins. He went to speak but I interrupted, "If you also attempt to remind me what 'I have to do,' I'll shoot you in the head myself." He nodded in his own understated way as I boarded the carriage and we set off back to the hotel.

Rattling through the streets I was gripped by an ever-intensifying sense of delirium. Though the reappearance of Weishaupt back from the dead was hard in itself to get over it was the impending act of the murder I was expected to perform that now raised my pulse to a frenzied blur. Assassination was something that I had never even contemplated. Yes, I had killed and rightly, or so I thought. For those I had slain would have done the same to me, or my friends. But this man was not trying to kill me. In fact he was not, as far as I could perceive, trying to do me any obvious harm at all. How could I take his life in cold blood?

I wasn't any better by the time I entered the banqueting hall of the hotel and felt the hot prickle of sweat clinging the shirt to my back. The reception was already underway and was full to the brim with a hundred of the most pretentiously dressed individuals I had ever seen. Keeping my head as low as possible I navigated my way through the crowded room and went to find my prescribed table. It struck me that there was some fine music coming from a somewhere amongst the crowd and I saw a rather frail looking man behind a harpsichord in the corner. I recalled being told that the famous composer Mozart had been hired to play at the wedding. His music was the only pleasant thing in the room as the entire place was a forest of obnoxiously high, white powdered wigs on top of pallid pompous snobs with self-important expressions and supercilious smiles. *[31]

I did enjoy the better things in life, it was true, but this lot were beyond the pale. Though I had thought my fine new clothes a trifle immodest before in comparison they now seemed plain and I felt thoroughly under-dressed. Looking around I recognised no one. Fortunately Weishaupt was nowhere to be seen but my heart sank as I scanned the room and could not find Francesca anywhere. Joining the party at my table I did not like the look of the characters who were already seated. After pulling up a chair my suspicions were confirmed when one of the philistines proclaimed, "Mozart bores me so these days. He is too complicated. I fear his music has too many notes."

I had heard the same meaningless complaint from an idiot student who had no doubt heard it from another idiot who did not understand what he said. Mozart was obviously a genius. Any man who was not a fool could hear it; especially as he played but thirty feet away.

Angry anyway, due to my dreadful state of mind, on hearing this ridiculous remark I could not help but spit, "He is over there right now. Why do you not go over to him and tell him which notes you would like him to remove so you could enjoy it more?"

Suffice to say the next ten 'minuets' went by uncomfortably. I

---

[31] Mozart & the Illuminati. There is no doubt that Mozart was in Vienna at this time. The young composer was also a friend of Adam Weishaupt and a member of the local Masonic Lodge 'Zur Wohltatigkeit' ('Beneficence ').His most famous opera, The Magic Flute uses an array of Masonic rituals and symbolism and his presence at the wedding shows the influence the Masons had on the cultural life of the day as he would have been at his peak then and very much sought after. Much speculation exists suggesting that he was actually killed by the Bavarian Illuminati but this topic is so contested that it would require a book of its own.

cowered in my seat petrified that Weishaupt would appear and spot me while the snobs took it in turns to show me their contempt. And they were snobs of the worst sort. Most of them had their servants in attendance who they abused and humiliated with great pleasure. Van Halestrom's lessons had transformed my ideas on matters such as these and now this type of treatment thoroughly sickened me to the core. After the speeches had finished I left the table to relieve myself of both my company and the contents of my bladder considering that they were pretty much the same.

I found the hallway and crept to the men's room in a state of feverish apprehension as the moment of my heinous task fast approached. I slumped down on the fine porcelain toilet in my cubicle with my head in my hands in a flush of sweating fear. The fact that I was on the finest lavatory in the whole of Europe could not ease my raging mind or my shuddering bowels.

I was a student for God's sake. Not a trained assassin. I shut my eye and sighed deeply. What would my parents think? Maybe I could tell them one day and they would understand. I only had to consider this briefly before realising the impossibility of it. In a fit of desperation I explored any possible alternatives. That was it: I would gather my friends together and we could shoot Oglethorpe with cannon from half a mile away. Yes. That was the way. A great distance was the best range from which to kill a foe in cold blood. None of this close-up stuff.

Then, as you sometimes do when sitting on the water closet, I overheard something which, even in my unhinged state, was of great interest. Outside two men were talking. The first a vain, old Englishman, boasted, "As you know I have much profitable business in the Americas representing a financial interest lending money to the government for their wars with the British. And, therein lies the trick, old boy. You see, my associates and I are also funding the British but not to the extent that either side can become the ultimate victor. Then, as the length of the conflict and the interest of its debt can be controlled, the adversaries become like the slaves on my plantation and will never be free. Haw, haw."

The voice of the other man, an Italian, chipped in, "I hear there were terrible casualties in this war, Brigadier Oglethorpe"

"This is of little consequence to me, my dear Salieri. After all, sir, I am a banker not a doctor. Haw, haw. Maybe one of you composer fellows could write an opera about me? I'm a ♪ banker ♪ not a doctor ♫: Dah de ♪ dah, dah ♫. Dah de ♪ dah, dah ♫. Haw, haw."

They both laughed and washed their hands before leaving and I peeped out of the closet to see James Oglethorpe and his acquaintance, who I guessed must be Antonio Salieri, Mozart's rival, and the man thought to have eventually brought about the great composer's downfall.

I came out of the cubicle and faced the mirror. The young black servant in attendance looked up at me with a doleful expression. I considered the thousands of men dying in the war that had been spoken of so callously and recalled the wickedness I had already seen in my battles with the Illuminati; the scheming, the killings, the sacrifices, the horror and thought of the same devilishness taking hold in another country far, far away. I felt the bulge of the pistol under my coat and looked at my reflection once more thinking, 'Well, this is it Sebastian. This is when you find out whether you are man or mouse.' My decision was made then.

It was 'mouse!' and I scurried off like a little brown one who is being chased by a big hungry cat; out from the privy, into the hallway past the doors of the banqueting suite and away. I could not do it. I was no killer. I was an ill-disciplined student who was going to go home right away and read his books. Someone else could do this; Van Halestrom or Francesca or Klaus or even Bacon or the courts or anyone but not me. My father would spank me for ten years, disinherit me, sell me into slavery then buy me back so he could do it all over again. And I wouldn't have blamed him. Not one bit. What had I been thinking? Some killer me; Francesca, Jan, Weishaupt; they were right. I was just a boy, a boy who was way, way out of his depth.

Hurrying along the corridor towards the entrance I cursed my luck when Van Halestrom suddenly appeared out of a door in front of me still wearing his audacious disguise. Even with his back to me I could tell that he was vexed and no doubt looking for me to remind me of what I 'had to do.' Realising that he would see me if he turned round I dived through a door at my side and hastily crept through a room then out into another corridor. When I heard loud voices coming from somewhere behind me, in a moment of extraordinary fate, I burst through yet another door and nearly screamed as I did.

I froze in the doorway paralysed with fear for ten paces away the elderly Brigadier Oglethorpe hovered over a petrified servant boy with a cane raised in his hand. Without looking up he whipped the boy yelling out, "When I want you to clean the piss off my boots, boy then that is what you shall do!"

He struck the youth in the face with an appalling blow, spilling blood from his mouth and driving the blubbering child to the floor. I took a step closer but Oglethorpe shot me a stare and wheezed, "What the blazes do you want, man? Can't you see I'm conditioning my servant?"

I spun around biting my lip and murmured to myself, "Just walk out of the door Seb." But I could not help and glance back when the boy shrieked out in pain as Oglethorpe unleashed another storm of vicious blows. Again and again he whipped the cane down, his mean old voice panting with exertion, "If-I-want-you-to-clean-the-piss-off-my-boots-boy-then-that-is-what-you-shall-do!"

I stood before the door clenching my fists feeling an intense wave of anger fill me as the boy's harrowing screams rang in my ears, "Please, sir, no more! No more! Please ... please!"

At that moment I was so consumed with an inseparable mixture of fear and rage that I could no longer tell them apart and, in a haze of bewilderment and fury, I turned round pushing my hand inside my coat and pulled out the gun. Taking a handful of uncertain steps towards the Brigadier I awkwardly cocked the hammer and held out the pistol in my trembling hand. Seeing me over his shoulder he contemptuously laughed, "Ha! You don't have the guts, boy," and struck the servant even harder grunting with effort, "Haw! – Haw! When I've finished this one I'll teach you some manners too! Like one of the niggers on my plantation."

He brought down his cane with such sickening force that I thought he would kill the youth and I took another step closer holding out the pistol. Feeling my sweating hand gripping the handle and with my heart in my mouth - God have mercy on my soul - I pointed the pistol at his head and pulled the trigger.

'Click!'

Saints alive! The gun was empty! Empty! In my delirium I had forgotten to load it. The Brigadier glared at me, clearly shocked that I had tried to shoot him and also that he was still alive. After a handful of confusing seconds his eyes narrowed and, realising he was too frail to beat me with his cane, he dashed to a table and pulled out a flintlock from a drawer. Moving with trained military precision he quickly primed the weapon. I watched him in a daze unable to believe what was happening. What should I do now? I didn't want to have to beat the old man to death in the drawing room. If I had to kill him I wanted to shoot him. And apparently I did as he was already ramming his powder home.

I fumbled open the breech of the pistol before digging a cartridge out of my pocket and pushing it in the barrel. I glimpsed anxiously at Oglethorpe. For an older man his hands moved at an astonishing rate and I could see he was about to finish.

"Come on, Sebastian," I muttered as my sweaty fingers slipped about cocking the hammer as I heard the click of his. I raised my gun to find myself staring directly down the barrel of his. I fired into his shocked face as his gun flashed at mine.

'Bang!'

He missed. I didn't and a dark red blast of blood spat out over the portrait behind him as he fell to the floor. Amidst the powder smoke hanging in the room I gasped, "That could not have been closer," and turned around to see a smoking hole in the wall behind me.

My very next and overriding thought was, 'Flee!' Stealing a glance down at Oglethorpe's lifeless body and, seeing that the servant boy was at least groaning so still alive, I ran across the room and up to the dumb-waiter throwing open the hatch. But to my unforgettable horror I found that it was as empty. Empty! Like the blasted pistol. Shit! I span around exploding with panic. "Why did I do that? Why did I do that? What on earth have I done?"

My mind raced, 'I will be definitely caught for this murder and that will be the end of me. But it was self-defence,' I reasoned, 'I was trying to save the boy and myself. Everyone would understand wouldn't they?' I frantically recalculated, 'Of course not you fool!'

This was the end for me and I knew it. But then as I was trying to remember if they had the death penalty in Austria, I saw the rope hanging in the shaft.

Two seconds later, after slamming the hatch behind me, I was sliding down the rope with my hands almost catching fire from the friction. Shrieking with pain and the fear of death I landed on the dumb-waiter in the basement with a mighty smack.

The hatch opened and Klaus muttered, "Well done, sir," offering me his hand he urged, "Walk with me."

I got out rubbing my arse with my burning hand and relentlessly complaining under my breath about the abject failure of his part of the plan; i.e. to have the dumb-waiter ready so I didn't nearly have to kill myself. He explained that it had jammed when the waiter took it down and swore it was the only eventuality that he could not control but he had been confident I could use the rope. We hurried up the stairs and into the courtyard where he handed me a cheroot as all hell broke loose around us.

The shots had, of course, caused a serious commotion at this; one of the most respectable marriages of the year. In no time at all, the whole place was heaving with hotel staff, authorities and members of both families and their servants dashing round in the confusion. My alibi was confirmed as I was now with Klaus strolling from the courtyard. Also I was sure the servant boy had not seen my face and would probably not be conscious for a week. Incredibly, it seemed that I had got away with killing the vicious old bastard but my hand still shook as I smoked the cheroot. I have never have been a man of tobacco believing it to be poison but at that moment I pulled the smoke right in. Coughing loudly I collected myself as we strode around to the front of the hotel where all hell was indeed breaking loose - literally. Because it was then that I saw Weishaupt leaving in his carriage escorted by two riders. As his coach flew out of the gates I nervously smirked, "Get your friends at court to say '*that* was just a hunting accident' you evil gloating smartarse."

Klaus murmured next to me, "I should find the Professor," and slipped away into the throng of people pouring out into the driveway. The women in their gowns crying and screaming, the men pompously advising each other what to do now that the deed was done, and the abused servants from time to time, sharing secretive grins. In the middle of all this was the poor bride who was crying and screaming more than anyone else. Her day, if not for love but much earnest preparation and care, was now ruined. How could it be worse?

It was Lady Francesca who showed her exactly how. Leaving no doubt in her mind that being married to a greasy, cheating, pox-ridden liar and having a dead scheming Illuminati father were not the only indignities she would suffer on this, the most important day of her life, *My Lady* roared into view standing on the footboard of the bridal coach, cracking the reins with fury and calling out, "Get on, Sebastian! The bastard has the marriage certificate!"

I have suffered some ungracious moments in my life but jumping aboard a stolen bridal coach driven by an obviously uninvited impostor after the father of the bride had been assassinated within earshot of said bride and her family friends by me was one of the worst. Maybe if no one had been watching but in front of the crowd outside the hotel and the bride herself, for whom this really was the last straw, marked for me a new social low.

"Sorry." I called, attempting a pathetic and thoroughly useless apology. Perhaps unsurprisingly, it didn't help much and she fainted into the arms of her bridesmaids with the shock and despair of it all. Our speeding coach sped out of the hotel's gates and so, along with my first foray into high society, the ruination of the wedding from hell was over. Although come to think of it because of Van Halestrom's deception, in reality, it had never taken place at all. *[32]

---

[32] Brigadier James Oglethorpe & the Illuminati. There is some interesting information on the internet suggesting that this venerable English politician and Freemason was actually an important Illuminati agent responsible for founding the 13th state of Georgia in the U.S.A (on the 33rd parallel). It is also intriguing to note that James Oglethorpe is recorded to have died on 30th June 1785 in London which would have given time for his body to be returned to England. Unsurprisingly, no details of this wedding exist, though if S. Drechsler's version of events is to be believed, this could have been for any number of extraordinary reasons.

Chapter 32

Secrets of the Ancients

"Well that's the last wedding of theirs I get invited to," I muttered to myself as the bridal carriage tore along and Francesca bellowed at the galloping horses, "Get a move on you buggers or I'll take you to the glue factory myself! Come on there! Yah!"

She shot me a stare and shouted, "Did you do it, Sebastian?"

"Do what?" I wailed, still in a daze. I searched her eyes before remembering, "Yes! Yes! In the head! In the blasted head!"

She smiled and gazed up ahead cracking the reins and bellowing even louder, "C'mon you buggers! Yah!"

Vienna is a beautiful city and I had been looking forward to viewing the wonderful buildings that lined the pleasant streets. But now these buildings flashed by so fast that I could not have seen them even if we had hit one, which we nearly did on several occasions. I gulped and stared forward bawling, "What are we going to do now?"

"You jumped on board, Wunderkinda, so I assumed you knew! We need the marriage certificate and Weishaupt is on his own apart from the driver and the two horsemen."

I knew how much trouble just *one* of that son-of-a-bitch's friends could be and thought I might need several pairs of fine white breeches if I was going to go a few rounds with another bunch of terrifying bastards like that.

"Right then!" I shouted, "That makes four when we are two."

"I'm so glad you're here, college boy. I had not brought along my abacus for my corset would not allow it. Now instead of impressing me with your arithmetic why don't you shoot one of them?"

I scowled at her and took out the pistol. The reloading was made easy by the cartridges and I soon brought the gun to bear.

"Steady, make it count," I murmured, trying to find the range of the closest horseman. The moment he bounced into the gun sight I let him have it. Boom! Sweet Mother of Christ, I got him and he fell away from his horse. Glancing down as we passed the body I tried to look as nonchalant as possible though I was probably ready for the first pair of new breeches right then.

The other rider spotted us and, seeing his dead friend gone, turned to meet us steadying his horse in the middle of the road as Weishaupt's carriage flew on up ahead. This rider, forewarned of our presence, was a different kettle of fish entirely. He looked mean as mustard and as pissed off a Spartan warrior who had just seen his boyfriend killed in front of him. By me! Curses! I frantically pulled out another cartridge as we clattered on towards him and barely managed to reload in time. As we reached the horseman he swiped his sword at me and I shot him in the chest. 'Boom!' But he was wearing a breast plate under his tunic which I had not seen. Though he was knocked back by the shot, and made only a faltering sweep with his blade, he quickly pulled himself together and came after us at a gallop.

The coach was no match for the rider and he soon caught up, flinging himself into a storm of flashes with his sword and smashing away several large pieces of the carriage roof. Feverishly trying to locate another cartridge I worried that the horseman was an automaton like the general but knew he was not when I heard his manly grunts and curses. I ducked to avoid another powerful sweep when damn it! I dropped the gun and watched it bounced off the footplate.

"How is it going there?" yelled Francesca glancing over.

"It is going well," I cried, "I calculate there are now three of them left and two of us. Tell me fair maiden am I right? Maybe you could get your abacus out of your blasted underwear and check for me!"

I prepared myself as the horseman came in again and made another lunge. This blow was so fierce that his sword became stuck in the carriage. Now I took my chance.

"Take that!" I yelled and I smacked him in the face as he rode next to us. He flew clean off his horse and fell away, tumbling painfully along the cobbled street. 'That was a good punch.' I reckoned rubbing my fist and watching the horseman come to rest in a twisted heap. His steed stayed with us for a while then faded as Francesca cracked the whip pushing the horses on with another stream of blue curses. I wrested the sword free from the carriage's roof and brandishing the weapon took the chance to draw attention to my heroic deeds, "Did you not see that? Superb!"

I said this with such swagger that something bad was bound to happen, as so often after a little cockiness comes a fall. Right on cue we shuddered to a halt behind Weishaupt's carriage which had suddenly pulled up causing me to fall headlong into the arse of the horse in front of me. As I came up, after freeing myself from the backside of the confused animal, Francesca remarked, with her crooked eyebrow aloft, "I think that may serve you quite right."

What did not serve me right was the next painful indignity as a dagger shot into my expensive new coat fixing it to the seat with a whack.

"Where the devil did that come from?" I cried, glancing up to see that it had indeed come straight from a devil. For Weishaupt's driver was facing us over his shoulder. With his eyes hidden in the shadow cast by the brim of his black hat and with a black neckerchief wrapped round his features it appeared that he had no face at all. The ghoul lashed his horses and pulled off with the obstruction now cleared. We followed on after them through the pigs, chickens and townsfolk strewn across the road.

"There is definitely something of the night about that one!" I declared, as we chased after them once again. But the deathly driver had little care for anyone else on the road and so increased the distance between us by several lengths. After series of countless swerves and near accidents we tore round a corner just in time to see them drive through a pair of open gates leading to a fine white house.

'What this?' I thought, 'Where are we now that Weishaupt feels safe? This does not feel like a good place for us to be.' And it wasn't. And I knew it as soon as our carriage came round on the gravel driveway.

We came to a halt with a "Whoa you bastards!" from Francesca who looked about smartly. I shared her surprise. Where *had* they gone? The carriage had clearly come that way but there was no sign of them anywhere and nowhere for them to hide.

The windows of the grand three-storey villa were shuttered up and there were no signs of life at all. We dismounted and ran up the front steps, Francesca somewhat hastier than myself for I expected no one to answer. But when she beat on the door it opened with an ominous creak.

'Oh no! Not again.' I groaned to myself, remembering the torture chamber and the all-consuming terror of the other run-ins with this murderous crew. I had been secretly relieved not to see Weishaupt as we came round the corner as it meant not having to fight the devil and his sinister driver. Though he had run away from us? Was he indestructible or not? I peered into the shadowy hallway.

Uneasy, to say the least, about what lay in wait I whispered, "Look. They think that they are married. Oglethorpe is dead and we have got away with it. We have been lucky to get this far. Maybe we should leave?"

She threw me a disdainful stare.

"It's all for nothing without the papers. We must get them for the fight."

"For the fight? You've changed the tune you play on your harpsichord. What about, 'There is no point you stupid boy?'" I said this in a faux French accent trying to provoke her and it worked.

"You are still a stupid boy!" She taunted. "My views have changed wildly since I have been away."

Most women's views, or so I had been in the habit of noticing, had the tendency to change wildly even in the short time it takes them to go to the privy. So having not seen this one for a period much greater than that I resolved to put this down to experience and simply stirred an eyebrow. Though it occurred to me that if her present plans could be considered which involved entering an ominous house, through a mysteriously open door, to chase an unkillable devil then why not marriage to me and children too?

"C'mon," she whispered and I followed her inside holding the sword out in front of me. Inching down the corridor I worried that this single weapon might not be enough to defeat whatever lay behind the double doors ahead. So when Francesca flung them open with a confident, "Ha!" I was relieved to see an empty chamber surrounded with purple curtains bathed in the dappling light of several flaming torches and, at the far end, the wedding documents on an altar.

"What were you worried about, Wunderkinda?" called Francesca, running over to the altar. "Here are the documents."

And there they were, remarkably right in front of us. How easy was that? Too easy by half: Something was wrong.

"Wait!" I yelled and put my hand out but too late. As she reached the middle of the room horrifyingly a coffin-sized slab fell away beneath her and she disappeared into the bowels of the earth.

"Sebastian!"

"No!" I yelled and ran towards the hole that had appeared from nowhere frantically throwing myself on the floor. I reached over the edge but she was already six feet below my clutching hand.

My heart froze as I heard Weishaupt jeer, "Oh, it is a cruel, cruel world that keeps the things we desire tantalizingly out of our reach."

I glanced up to see him appear from the shadows behind the altar picking up the documents and flashing me a sadistic leer.

"Curse you!" I roared, vainly trying to grab Francesca's outstretched hand and endure the pitiful look of despair on her face. But damn it! The distance was too great. My mind raced. How was it possible to move stone with such speed?

Weishaupt read my mind, "Yes, boy. Witness the secrets of the ancients. These are the methods with which the Pharaohs protected their treasure long ago. But you have not seen the half of it yet."

Frightened enough already I couldn't imagine what he meant. Bewilderingly there was a thunderous shudder and the walls of the underground chamber began to move towards each other like a vice.

"Holy Mother of God!"

Francesca desperately tried to climb out but there was no foothold on the smooth walls and she slid helplessly back down.

"Ha, ha! The process is irreversible so this time I promise you *will* see her die."

"Pig dog!" I shouted and in my frustration threw my sword at him but it clattered harmlessly across the floor.

"Temper, temper," he scoffed, revelling in our predicament and producing a knife from his side. Clutching the papers in his other hand he circled behind us coming between the door and the pit. "You were never the brightest of students, Herr Drechsler. Have you still learnt nothing?"

"I ... I ..." I desperately stammered, unable to accept what was happening.

"Look at you. Dressed up like a peacock in your elegant new clothes. Is that all it took to entice you here; a bit of dainty lace and linen? Vanity is a powerful vice. Is it not? Or was it your lust for this woman which made you come? And look at her crying like a baby; when it is her pride that has got her in this mess. You, your greedy friend, her, everyone; you are all so weak. It will be your undoing in the end. Don't you see, boy? That is why man will always fail."

I glanced at my stained lace cuff as it stretched towards Francesca's terrified face. Damn it! He was right. I was just a pathetic chump tempted to this wedding by my weaknesses and lured into this trap by my blasted foolishness. There had been so many chances to get away and stay away but I had squandered them all. Now Weishaupt had won and we were certainly done for.

He jeered on, "Imagine the prostitutes, the pimps, the thugs, the lawyers, the priests, the merchants, the generals and even the Kings we have at our beck and call: The money, the bribes, the traps, and, like you, the poor pathetic fools we have in our clutches. No one can escape us. We will control everything in the end!"

Francesca screamed again and I tried to reassure her crying out, "Fear not my lady."

Weishaupt threw his head back laughing, "Yes, fear, you pathetic fool. Because now fear is all you have!"

"Don't fill the lad's head with that filth, you pervert!" rang out a defiant cry. Saints alive! It was Van Halestrom. I had wished so deeply for him to appear at that moment that when the silver bolt flew through the doorway it was as though I was in a dream. But when the arrow ripped the documents from Weishaupt's hand and propelled them to my side, even I could not have dreamt that. Amazing! I picked up the papers and stuffed them inside my jacket.

Weishaupt dropped the knife clutching at his wrist. "Curse you Van Halestrom! I will hunt you down one day."

"It is I who will do the hunting," called the Professor striding through the doorway with his bow at the ready still dressed in his cassock and crucifix like an avenging priest of old. Trusty Klaus came to his shoulder giving me a valiant nod.

Miracle of miracles! I was to be saved by my loyal friends in the nick of time. But before I could even blink Weishaupt's ghoulish driver suddenly materialised behind Klaus and fell on him like an evil shadow.

"Look out!" I cried but it was too late and the fiend ran Klaus through with a vicious spike. With blood splattering from his mouth the driver crumpled to the floor in horrible agony his face a terrible picture of hopelessness.

Van Halestrom turned on the man in black unleashing a hail of arrows into him. The ghoul toppled backwards pulling down one of the blazing torches spreading the fuel across the floor and igniting the bottom of the curtains. Van Halestrom spun on his heel going to find Weishaupt in his sights but the coward had already run for cover into the shadows behind the altar.

"Leave him Professor! Come and help us!"

Van Halestrom was next to me in a flash while Francesca squealed, "Hurry!" as the walls rumbled together and the fire started to blaze in the corner.

I had the plan. "Professor you will hold my arm and let me down the hole so I can pull her out."

With a swift nod Van Halestrom stuck out his hand which I clasped tightly before edging off the lip. Grunting with the weight he steadied himself and lowered me down as the walls inexorably came together the fire took hold around the room.

"Come on, Francesca," I implored. Feeling the ends of our fingers touch I strained with all my might to span the vital extra inches as the rumbling mechanism churned away beneath me. The pressure on my arm was excruciating and I felt it would tear off but finally I felt Francesca's palm in mine. Clutching her hand with every ounce of my strength I turned to the Professor to tell him to pull us up but as I did I gasped as Weishaupt's maniacal face appeared behind him.

"No!"

With a fiendish grin the Doctor kicked the Professor off the lip and we came crashing down into the chamber with Van Halestrom painfully crushing down on me.

Weishaupt taunted us from above, "You have the papers but they will do you no good if you are all dead." He glanced around at the fire that was now lighting up the ceiling before turning back and goading, "Though I am sorely tempted to stay and watch your painful deaths unfortunately I fear I must leave. But what sweet joy it is that you will all be perishing together. Remember my face when you die won't you?" His menacing eyes glinted down on us, "What is the phrase to use at a time such as this? Oh yes. That's it, heh, heh - vengeance is mine."

My rage boiled over and I screamed, "Damn it! We cannot win against this phantom."

'Bang!' A deafening explosion rang out next to my ear.

Incredibly, Van Halestrom managed to shoot him with a tiny pistol hidden up his sleeve and our tormentor yelped in pain clutching at his chest.

The Professor muttered, "He is no phantom, Sebastian. He bleeds like all men."

With dread pain etched across his face Weishaupt fell away behind the lip. I prayed he was dead but cursed him anyway because surely he had won and we were all going to die in the dastardly pit. We struggled to our feet standing three abreast with me in the middle as the dusty walls relentlessly closed in inches from our faces. I could not believe what was happening, and now panicking terribly, the awful realisation exploded inside my mind like a bomb. What a wretched way to go; all three of us squashed to death in this wicked mausoleum. I reached out for Francesca's hand feeling it trembling next to mine and squeezed it tight.

It was no good. There was no way out. I was sure the slabs rumbling towards us even faster. This was surely the end and I knew it. We were all going to die. With all hope gone and our fates sealed instinctively I began to pray as I'd seen my mother do so many times, begging, "God of mercy and power, you have made death a gateway to eternal life ..."

Through the din and the dust the Professor yelled out, "Why do you continue to pray to him, lad?"

"Because he is our saviour!"

Van Halestrom tried to educate me even during our last moments on earth with the walls bearing in on us he cried out, "What are the chances of one group of believers being right over another? If you had been born in India you would be a Hindu, or in Persia a Muslim or even a Buddhist. You just have the propensity for faith that's all. It is much more likely that you are all partly correct and that God, whatever that really means, is a unifying energy that binds us all together ..."

"Is there not a better time for this conversation?" howled Francesca. I managed to glance at her longingly for the last time knowing now that I would never get to do things with her that would probably enrage all the Gods because they would have been so jealous. Damn it!

As I thought this and with the walls squeezing in on my chest, I forced my head around and saw the Professor's silver crucifix glinting in the dark. With an inkling of hope I grasped over and tore it from around his neck.

"What are you doing?" he called but there was no time to explain.

I held the cross up as high as I could and just in time for the walls to push down on its ends, trapping it tightly in their grip. 'Please God let this work!' I prayed and amazingly, with a huge shudder and a crunch, the walls came to a stop.

"Now move!" I called pulling myself up on the crucifix I was able to get on top of it and to reach the lip then heave myself out. I rolled onto the floor gasping, "Quickly! We don't have much time!"

Weishaupt was nowhere to be seen but the inside of the room was now ablaze. Huge flames bellowed up onto the ceiling and the heat from the fire was extraordinary. Francesca came up next and I pulled her out of the hole as a huge burning joist crashed to the floor only ten paces away.

"Hurry!" called Francesca passing her hand down into the hole. The Professor pulled himself up and we both grabbed his shoulders lifting him from the pit with an almighty jerk. As we did there was another hefty rumble as the crucifix bent before with a creak it finally snapped and the walls smashed together with a colossal thump.

"Everything has its breaking point," assessed Van Halestrom and cried, "Come on!"

With Francesca's hand in mine and ducking for protection the three of us ran to the door. Agonisingly we had to jump over Klaus's crumpled body for we would have burnt to death for certain if we had stayed one second longer. Sprinting for our very lives we ran through the thick, black smoke filling the corridor and burst out of the door gasping for air. Without pause myself and Francesca jumped aboard the bridal coach as Van Halestrom mounted his. With the cracking of whips and much encouragement of the horses we launched out into the street and flew off down the road.

Holy mother of God! Somehow we had escaped from the evil pit and the house of death. I felt my heart rate subsiding though it still galloped along like our horses at ten to the dozen. Still panting and wiping the sweat from my brow I glanced back over my shoulder in the direction of the house to see huge flames and a plume of thick black smoke billowing into the sky.

We geed the horses on and hurtled out of Vienna leaving the city walls behind us. After a couple of miles our two carriages pulled up at a crossroads and the three of us dismounted. I pulled the all important marriage certificate from inside my coat and handed it to

Van Halestrom.

"Well done, my lad." He stared at me forlornly, "Sadly I do not have time to either celebrate our victory or to share the sorrowful words for poor Klaus that we will, no doubt, exchange in the future. That is for another day. But be sure of this: He died fighting for what he believed in. Now there is much urgent work to which I must attend."

He hugged Francesca warmly. "Thank you my dear. You are as courageous as you are beautiful." He took her hand and kissed it adding, "And you are very courageous."

Francesca appreciated these sentiments greatly and with a tear in her eye show it by performed a theatrical curtsy whilst smiling from ear to ear. Next Van Halestrom turned to me placing his hand on my shoulder.

"And thank you, Sebastian."

"For what, Professor?" I asked, "You must have saved my life ten times at least."

"On the contrary Sebastian, I think it was you who saved us back there. Remember, my lad, education is a two way thing. I believe I've learnt a great deal from you along the way. One day we might even make a teacher of you. Eh?"

He smiled with earnest sincerity and I knew he meant the inheritance of his work. The enormity of this possibility overwhelmed me and I flapped, "But, sir what should we do now? If Weishaupt is still alive how can it be over?"

"Alas, I fear that it may never be over, Sebastian. But think of it like this; he is certainly injured and maybe even dead, he has lost his job and been banished from Bavaria along with his evil Illuminati. Hundreds of his accomplices have been incarcerated, several despicable ceremonies, not least this illicit wedding, have been ruined, a barrel full of his viperous friends have been dispatched to the void and we have lived to tell the tale and fight another day. Suffice to say, for now anyway, I believe we can all breathe a sigh of well-earned relief." He smiled glancing between us and heartily shook my hand carrying on, "Well done both of you. It is always a pleasure and an honour to fight with such brave and decent people at your side. You should be very proud of yourselves: Very proud indeed." *[33]

As he turned to walk away I hesitantly went to ask, "Herr Professor. Please tell me ... at what level am I now, sir?"

He shook his head before turning back, "Of course, though I knew you were going to ask that, Sebastian. I had still hoped you would not. I believe we have been through this before. When you are at the right level you will no longer need to ask."

He smiled again. "But that day is not today, my lad. You've come a long way already. Let's see how much further you can go."

With this he leapt onto his carriage calling out, "I will be back soon to continue that interesting theological conversation, Herr Drechsler."

He waved and called out, "Until then good luck. And always remember my friends - stay in the shadows!"

With a crack and a cry he stirred his horses and rumbled away without his trusty driver. We waved once more as he disappeared down the road then glanced at each other before leaving ourselves.

---

[33] The banishment of the Illuminati 1785. S. Drechsler's recollections are quite accurate here as a wide section of historians agreed with Van Halestrom's appraisal of events. This is a quote from H. W. Coil: **Coil's Masonic Encyclopedia.** Speaking of this period (summer 1785) he wrote '*Not only Illuminism, but Freemasonry was exterminated in Bavaria and neither ever recovered their former position. The Illuminati seem to have completely disappeared from everywhere by the end of the 18th century.*' Though, the last point would seem a more contentious topic which, if a reliable answer is sought, demands much lengthy research. Good luck. {After researching the background of this story I am mindful that if one looks hard enough then it is possible to find the whiff of a conspiracy anywhere. This point could not be better illustrated than by the fact that upon finishing the notes it has come to my attention that there are 33 chapters in the book and also, although it was never my intention, 33 footnotes as well. But I would like to assure you the reader that this is no conspiracy but simply strange coincidence.}

Chapter 33

Homeward Bound

The Professor had told us to go to Frau Hoffmeister's for, although it was over two hundred miles away, it was the closest place that was definitely safe. So we set course and travelled day and night, receiving many strange looks in our shabby but expensive clothing and battered bridal carriage. It was five o'clock in the afternoon two days later when we finally arrived at the farmhouse and a lad sucking a piece of straw in the low branch of a tree waved happily then ran before our carriage shouting up ahead. As we approached the cosy homestead Frau Hoffmeister came to greet us.

We dismounted and the stable lad dutifully led the coach and horses away. I stopped to watch him for a second then, feeling a mite impetuous, called out after the boy, "You can have one of the horses if you like." He spun around with his face a picture of happy astonishment and the Frau asked if I was sure. Whereupon I said that I was certain and that we didn't need a whole team of horses to make the rest of the journey home. Surely it was greedy to have so many when others who wanted only one had none. Sweet Lady Francesca was delighted with my gift and held me round the neck grinning, "I hope you will be as generous to me, sir."

And so, at last, a few hours later in the humble farmhouse bedroom I was, and we were, over and over again. And all the riches in the world were finally mine and I cared for nothing else. The delectable Francesca was everything I had hoped for and so, so much more. I found out just how truly ignorant I had been about a great many things that night and morning too. For our exertions were seemingly without end such was the desire we both felt for each other; a desire that had been building for such a long period of time. Indeed, a whole year had passed since we had first met which I felt made it quite respectable. Although I had wished every time I saw her during that time that it had been sooner. Suffice to say a whole other manuscript could have been penned on our exploits describing just that night alone but my honour and all known licensing laws prevent such carnal publications.

When we woke that next morning and sat outside on the garden bench watching the sunrise the day seemed so beautiful it was as though we were in a dream. I squeezed Francesca round the shoulders and watched her beautiful face catch the first rays of the new day's sun. I thought we could have been in heaven then or maybe the Garden of Eden, as Adam and Eve before us so very long ago. Maybe, if I tried hard to be a good man, perhaps God would not forsake the two of us. I watched Frau Hoffmeister pick a rotten apple from the tree and throw it to her chickens while she chatted away to them.

Was it really all over or would I wake up to find myself back in the torture chamber with the evil Weishaupt leaning over me? I considered that I did not know for certain if anything was real or a dream any more. Happily, I concluded that if this day was a dream then I didn't wish to wake up but to carry on sleeping forever.

I smiled deeply and gathered my thoughts. So much had happened in the last year that I could never have believed possible only twelve short months ago. What had I learnt from it all? Never mind university: The adventures, the battles, the fear, the love, the losses and the victory. As the Professor had said it seemed as though we had actually beaten the Illuminati and, of course, along with all these other incredible experiences this triumph had a profound effect on my thoughts.

Even if Van Halestrom was right and some of the terrifying foes we had fought were products of my own wilful imagination, I had still witnessed so much that was truly unbelievable that I found it impossible not to think that God had somehow been helping me through the adventure: For what reason I do not know. Maybe to use me as a weapon against those who had opposed him? I could not explain the extraordinary feeling of merciful fate any other way. To say nothing of lightning strikes, crazed dogs and sheer incredible luck coming to my rescue again and again.

Paradoxically, it was the sceptical Van Halestrom who was the most miraculous of all these. A saving angel capable of such extraordinary feats of wonder, so miraculous in themselves, that any priest would think twice before trying to explain them to his own doting congregation let alone men of science. As a student of reason

I knew that without the aid of empirical proof one simply has to make up one's own mind. In the end I was ready to do just that. For thankfully I had seen good overcome evil and so this is what I believed.

At that moment I was sure that God was good and that this same goodness existed in man but to achieve it man must prevail over his weaknesses. For if he does not he might find a dark lord presiding over him. The Professor had once taught me that all energy in the universe was benign and therefore, as we are made of the same energy, life's duty was to be benign as well. To illustrate his point he recited a little poem;

> Because the sun is warm not cold
> And trees not black and dead
> The World's a ball of wonderment
> And light my friend.
> So then wouldn't it be a shame
> If we did not try with all
> Our energy and might to be the very same:

Touching words I felt, and fine sentiments to boot…

Well I had done my best to be and in the end that's all anyone can do. So I relaxed content that I had fulfilled my promise to God to stay alive and be in his service. Whatever darkness or light fate held in store I was sure that I could meet these challenges with a clean conscience and an open heart. For I was certain, beyond my deepest depths, that I had done what I believed was right and happily, in doing so, I had found the new self which I had set out to discover in the beginning. I had also overcome great adversities and lived to tell a tale. And, oh what an incredible tale I had to tell. What an incredible tale indeed.

Appendix of Footnotes & Hypertext Addresses

1. There is no record of a Professor Van Halestrom working at the University of Ingolstadt at this time but staff records are sketchy at the best so this is no surprise. Although no solid information exists to back up this theory, for which you will have to forgive me, because it is one of the most speculative in the footnotes, it is my honest belief that the Professor's part in local history was such that in some way it has led to it being the inspiration for Bram Stoker's famous character Professor Abraham von Helsing in his 1897 novel ***Dracula***. This point is given credence by the fact that Stoker had spent several years studying European folklore which I believe may have recorded some of Van Halestrom's exploits. If this seems unlikely then I merely suggest you read on.

http://en.wikipedia.org/wiki/Abraham_Van_Helsing

2. Adam Johann Weishaupt. This immensely intriguing character was certainly lecturing at the University of Ingolstadt in 1784. Although S. Drechsler refers to him as 'The Doctor' he was, in fact, Professor of Canon Law and the first non Jesuit to hold this position at the faculty in over 90 years. It is one view that the young academic's education by the Jesuit priesthood, which would have probably been extremely harsh, was the reason he adopted his revolutionary anti-Christian philosophy. At the time the story is written he is known to have denounced his Catholicism and adopted the doctrines of the Hermetics, Manicheans and those that revolved around astrology, medicine, magic and the mysteries of ancient Egypt taking special interest in the pyramids at Giza.

http://en.wikipedia.org/wiki/Adam_Weishaupt

3. Katzenstein Castle. This impressive castle, originally constructed in the middle-ages, is situated thirty five miles west of Ingolstadt on the road to Stuttgart and is shown on the map at the beginning of the book. It probably still looks much the same as when S. Drechsler saw it and can be viewed on the internet if you wish to verify the

authenticity of the author's account. Bavaria is home to hundreds of similar castles.

http://en.wikipedia.org/wiki/Katzenstein_Castle

4. The Bavarian Illuminati. This infamous secret society was founded by Adam Weishaupt on May 1st 1776. From a modest beginning of five members, after much administrative, financial and organisational help from other 'free thinking' collaborators, its ranks had swollen to as many as two thousand by 1784. Membership included many well-connected and influential figures such as; Johann Wolfgang von Goethe, Johann Gotfried Herdér and the Dukes of Gotha and Weimar. So much has been written about the order by hundreds of notable historians and their less reliable counterparts that it is hard to deny any other quasi-political organisation, apart from the Freemasons, has been responsible for such speculative hysteria, intriguing legends and conspiratorial myths that still continue to this day.

http://en.wikipedia.org/wiki/Illuminati

5. The Owl of Minerva. These meetings facilitated an academy in which young initiates to the Illuminati could be selected and groomed for higher positions within the organisation. The class of Minerva was a relatively low rank in the scheme of things. However, it was the soul of the Order and functioned as a sort of assembly line for recruits. Candidates advanced from *Novice* to the *Minerval degree* where they were properly vetted, scrutinised and indoctrinated. Another layer of the owl symbolism was to remind its initiates that the Illuminati does its bidding at night.

http://www.conspiracyarchive.com/Articles/Owl_of_Minerva.htm

6. The Cremation of Care Ceremony. Interestingly Drechsler's recollections bear much in common with similar ceremonies filmed at Bohemian Grove in California available on the internet and the owl, in this case, is sometimes referred to as Molech. Though, in antiquity Moloch, the Canaanite deity, is represented as a legless bull with arms. This pagan god would be worshipped by the

Israelites during times of apostasy (without religion) and is associated with the sacrifice of children. Lev.18:21 'Neither shall you give any of your offspring to offer them to Molech.'

http://www.conspiracyarchive.com/Blog/?tag=cremation-of-care

7. The Illuminati & the Founding Fathers of America. The extent to which the Illuminati had penetrated revolutionary American politics via the Freemasons, of which all the founding fathers were members, is unknowable. However, Thomas Jefferson, as Ambassador to France from 1785-1789; knew Weishaupt and wrote sympathetically about his professed basic aim of '*making men wise and virtuous*' and contended that, unlike the new American republic, '*secretive methods were a necessity under the religious and aristocratic tyranny of Europe*'. Hundreds of conspiracy theories persist to this day concerning the Order's involvement with revolutionary America as many have noted the Masonic symbolism stamped into the Great Seal of the United States and even upon the street layout of Washington DC.

http://thefoundationforum.com/2008/11/real-story-of-founding-fathers-and-2/

8. Khazaria: Birth of the Illuminati. As S. Drechsler describes the thirteenth tribe originated from Khazaria and King Bulan oversaw the country's conversion to Judaism in 740 AD. Much speculation exists about the 'secret hand' of the Khazarians and these conspiracy theories also include more radical claims; for example that ancestors of the tribe have a controlling influence over modern history and contemporary geopolitical events. There is also a wealth of information concerning Illuminati and Luciferian interpretations of the Kabbalah.

http://wesdancin.wordpress.com/2011/11/14/history-of-the-khazar-empire-and-the-illuminati-jack-otto-top-expert-last-conference/

9. Weishaupt's codename Spartacus. S. Drechsler's recollections are accurate here. Adam Weishaupt's codename in the Illuminati was Spartacus, after the revolutionary Thracian gladiator who led a slave

uprising against the Roman Empire. Other leading lights in the order also took their secret titles from antiquity: Baron Von Knigge; Philo. Baron Barrusus; Cato: etc. Ancient pseudonyms were also used for cities and states. For instance Munich was known as Athens, Frankfurt as Thebes and, as the author points out, Bavaria was Achaia.

http://www.bibliotecapleyades.net/sociopolitica/sociopol_proofsconspiracy.htm

10. Weishaupt & the Lodge of the Golden Dawn. It is interesting that S. Drechsler recalls hearing this. It is hard to trace the exact origins of this sect. While mainstream historians record its inception as being in England in 1887 under the auspices of William Wyan Wescott there also exists speculation that Weishaupt was responsible for its invention and that the order was a satanic cult which provided a meeting place for those with designs of spreading the Luciferian doctrine throughout the world.

http://www.ordeniluminati.net/english/ordeniluminati.html

11. The spear the axe and the arrow. I can find no record of this particular combination of symbols being attributed to the Illuminati though the individual insignias go back to antiquity. The spear mounted with the Phrygian cap has had revolutionary symbolism for centuries. Since ancient Roman the cap has represented those who seek liberty and was made infamous during the French revolution of 1789 with the red of the cap also being linked to Bolshevik and other communist insignia. The axe surrounded with the bundle of birch rods or fasces also has its roots in ancient Rome and was the symbol for strength and authority: Through many; strength. In the context of the story it is interesting as these insignia were to be used by opposing political ideologies; Communism; the red cap: Fascism: the fasces and the basis for the word 'Fascists'.

http://en.wikipedia.org/wiki/Phrygian_cap

http://en.wikipedia.org/wiki/Fasces

12. Illuminati & the Goyium. It is odd that Drechsler recalls Weishaupt using this term which originates in the Talmud and is not part of Bavarian (Austro-Prussian) dialect. Though, it is believed that Weishaupt was originally from Hebraic stock which might explain the usage of language here. There are many translations of this word. These range from 'nations', 'people', 'gentiles' and perhaps most unfortunately a derogatory slang usage of the word which is rumoured to translate as 'cattle,' though tellingly it is not mentioned on the Wikipedia site.

http://en.wikipedia.org/wiki/Goy

13. Abbot Jacob Lanz & The Lightning Strike. Incredibly, though there seems to be some conjecture about the precise timing of this amazing event, according to one of the most notable sources *Pawns in The Game* by W. Carr published 1958 this top ranking Illuminati official was actually struck by lightning and killed on 10th July 1784 near Regensburg Bavaria. When the authorities discovered his body they mistakenly decided that he was carrying the incriminating documents. Now it has become widespread belief that the abbot was, in fact, on a mission to deliver the papers to Paris where they would be used to aid the French revolution and that the papers were sewn into his robes. If we are to believe S. Drechsler's version of events it is fascinating to uncover the real truth behind what is already an incredible, but little-known, historical event. Either this is the event chronicled by so many historians and conspiracy theorists or we are party to an absolutely astonishing coincidence.

http://www.nwodb.com/main?e=03583

http://en.wikipedia.org/wiki/William_Guy_Carr

14. Franz Lange Councillor of Eichstatt & the Illuminati. S. Drechsler's recollection of this character's gruesome death would seem to explain an anomaly from the official stories. This member of the Illuminati is often confused with the Abbott Jakob Lanz (very similar to 'Lange') who it would appear, after being struck by lightning, also perished on the same night. Interestingly I can find no official date for the obituary of F. Lange so it is certainly possible

that the author's version of events is true. Also the similarities in the names and histories go a long way to account for conflicting reports of the men's deaths.

http://www.bavarian-illuminati.info/2008/11/lang-or-lanz-myths-about-the-myths/

15. The original writings of the Illuminati. The original documents found with Abbot Lanz's body after the lightning strike have not survived so there is no record of the text to back up S. Drechsler's account. Although other papers seized from Illuminati agents on later dates bear strong similarity to those the author describes. These documents were printed and released by the Bavarian authorities in 1786 to warn foreign countries about the Illuminati and their political intentions. Interestingly, the text also bears a strong resemblance to the Protocols of the Elders of Zion. This, the mother of all conspiracy documents, is widely understood to be a hoax produced for political ends. Though it is a strange coincidence that the document S. Drechsler recalls bears such a close resemblance to this text released over a hundred years later forged or not.

http://www.conspiracyarchive.com/Blog/?tag=original-writings-of-the-illuminati

http://en.wikipedia.org/wiki/The_Protocols_of_the_Elders_of_Zion

16. The Bavarian Illuminati High Court Case. In June 1784 the first edict banning membership of all Bavarian secret societies was passed though these measures were only seen as half-hearted. Tellingly, the authority's suspicion of the Illuminati continued to mount after this date which may well be explained by the author's exploits. Charles Theodore, the Prince Elector presided over these hearings. Obviously those who were in charge took a dim view of an organisation which sought to bring about the overthrow of governments. Baron Adolph Knigge was a highly influential aristocrat who notably fell out with Weishaupt halfway through 1784. Despite other explanations being given in the official accounts for the Baron's defection it was definitely true that Weishaupt had suddenly become unpopular at this time.

http://www.stjoachimorder.org/enlighten.htm

http://en.wikipedia.org/wiki/Adolph_Freiherr_Knigge

17. The Illuminati & Frankenstein. This must be S. Drechsler's little joke though possibly an insightful one. Being a scholar he would have been familiar with Mary Shelley's novel ***Frankenstein*** of 1818 set in Ingolstadt University three years later in 1787 so maybe it was a nickname given retrospectively to one of his more morbid fellow students. He also may have been trying to be cryptic given the context of the story as there is much speculation about the symbolic connection of the Illuminati and Frankenstein. It is rumoured that Percy Shelley, Mary's husband, may have been a member of the Illuminati and that there are many fascinating metaphorical connections between the novel and Weishaupt's order.

http://en.wikipedia.org/wiki/Frankenstein

18. Illuminati & the All Seeing Eye of Providence. This symbol, with its intriguing Latin inscriptions, remains perhaps one of the most famous conspiracies of all time though the engraving S. Drechsler describes would be slightly different to the one we are familiar with today. Interestingly an early version of the symbol had already been accepted by the founding fathers in 1782 as the Great Seal of America. Perhaps its most celebrated expression is on the reverse of the US one dollar bill, first printed on the notes in 1933 under the auspices of President F.D. Roosevelt. Speculation about this esoteric symbol and its usage, meaning and history would appear to be almost endless and a great deal of time would have to be set aside to research this one topic alone such is the volume of literature written about it. Good luck!

http://en.wikipedia.org/wiki/Eye_of_Providence

19. Freemasons & the Illuminati. The commonly held belief that the tradition of Freemasonry has provided the Illuminati with a host body in which to conceal itself has existed for hundreds of years and been speculated about endlessly. This claim is given weight by the

official ratification of the two organisations at the Congress of Wilhelmsbad in 1782. It is said that the leaderships' true goals are only revealed to adepts at the higher degrees while the lower members are unaware of these plans and naturally defend the integrity of the institution. It is interesting that S. Drechsler recalls his mentor describing its influence like a 'hidden hand,' a term which has now become commonplace.

http://en.wikipedia.org/wiki/Masonic_conspiracy_theories

http://en.metapedia.org/wiki/Congress_of_Wilhelmsbad

20. Illuminati Kabbalist Priests. It is odd that S. Drechsler remembers seeing these priests during such a ceremony. Though the Kabbalah, a mystic form of Judaism, has many interpretations, some of them quite unsettling, this ceremony is unusual (as you may well imagine!). Traditionally, these men would have been clothed in long ornate robes and wearing necklaces decorated with twelve large precious stones representing the twelve tribes of Israel. The Kabbalah speaks of nine dimensions or 'spheres'. To travel from one to another a gate must be formed and legend has it the Kabbalist priests can achieve this phenomenon when performing certain mystic rituals. Much speculation, some of it terrifying, exists as to what is contained in these spheres.

http://en.wikipedia.org/wiki/Priestly_breastplate

21. Emperor Joseph II Holy Roman Empire 1784. Though I can find no record of a connection between the Illuminati and this famous European aristocrat, historically known as one of the 'Enlightened Despots' and also the brother of Marie Antoinette, there is every chance that there may well have been one. He was definitely (though secretively) a Freemason, belonging to a lodge entitled *Zur neugekronten Hoffnung* (New Crowned Hope) and a member of 'many other' secret societies at that time. Interestingly, before this point, he had dealt favourably with Weishaupt's organisation but as S. Drechsler's account may explain, at the end of 1784 his treatment of the Illuminati definitely cooled. As the memoirs suggest anything else may have posed several insurmountable political problems for

him.

http://en.wikipedia.org/wiki/Joseph_II,_Holy_Roman_Emperor

22. The Illuminati & Ingolstadt University. Herr Vacchieri is mentioned in a book called '*Little Tools of Knowledge*' by P Becker and W. Clark 2001(pages 104-134) and seemed to fulfil a role at the university similar to that of a modern school inspector though I can find no proof that he was involved with the Illuminati. S. Drechsler also mentions Adam Weishaupt's Godfather though not by name. Baron Johann Ickstatt was the Curator of Ingolstadt University up until 1778 and probably instrumental in getting Weishaupt his job. There also seems to be doubt about his membership of the Illuminati though it is hard to believe he did not know, somehow, about the intimate details of his godson's organisation.

books.google.co.uk/**books**?isbn=0472111086

http://en.wikipedia.org/wiki/Johann_Adam_von_Ickstatt

23. Adam Weishaupt sacked from Ingolstadt University 1785. S. Drechsler's claims to have witnessed the Professor's departure are accurate here as Weishaupt finally lost his seat at the University on the 11th February 1785 amidst continuing controversy surrounding the Illuminati. The first decree in June of the previous year had been quite mild but favour for the Illuminati was definitely deteriorating by this time making it impossible for any distinguished institutions such as Ingolstadt University, who enjoyed the patronage of the state, to employ members from its ranks. Never mind the figurehead of its leadership.

http://one-evil.org/content/people_18c_weishaupt.html

24. The 'End of Times Prophecy': The fateful prophecy predicting the Armageddon of civilisation mirroring the Bible's book of Revelations. This ominous forecast recalled by S. Drechsler sounds strangely similar to extracts from a mysterious letter once rumoured to be kept at the British Museum which it is claimed was sent by Albert Pike, the then head of world Masonry, to Giuseppe Mazzini

in 1871. If S. Drechsler's account is to be believed it is incredible to think that such a frightening prediction for the world was even being talked about as early as 1785.

http://en.wikipedia.org/wiki/End_time

http://en.wikipedia.org/wiki/Albert_Pike

http://en.wikipedia.org/wiki/Giuseppe_Mazzini

25. Wolfsegg Castle. I cannot find any connection between this ancient castle and the Illuminati though it has had many owners throughout its long and interesting seven hundred year history. Originally built in 1278 by Wolf von Schönleiten it has a legend of haunting and, owing to its prominent position, can be seen from several miles away. It is still there to this day situated 15km North West of Regensburg near the village of Pettendorf and can be viewed on the internet, if you are interested.

http://ebookbrowse.com/wolfsegg-castle-pdf-d270447357

26. Karl Theodore and the Banishment of the Illuminati 1785. On March 2nd 1785 the second royal edict was passed banning membership in the Illuminati and making it an imprisonable offence to be part of the order. Weishaupt fled to the independent principality of Regensburg finally settling in the Thuringian state under the protection of the Duke of Sax Gotha. He is recorded to have hidden in many places whist fleeing from the authorities including, amongst others, in a chimney. Though S. Drechsler does not give a precise date for this evening we could have expected Weishaupt to have thought the decree inevitable and therefore may well have left his homeland some weeks before which would tie in exactly with these recollections.

http://modernhistoryproject.org/mhp?Article=FinalWarning&C=1.2#Exposed

27. The Illuminati & the Compte De Viriue. This French aristocrat was made famous by his statements about the Illuminati after

attending the order's grand congress in Wilhelmsbad 1782. He said, "*The conspiracy that is being woven is so well thought out that it will be, so to speak, impossible for the Monarchy and the Church to escape from it*." He could thereafter only speak of Freemasonry with 'horror.' The 'cosmic trigger' has been termed a 'thought tunnel' by Robert A. Wilson, ***Illuminatus*** (1977). Also known in certain traditions as 'The Chapel Perilous,' it broadly refers to an induced public state of mind.

http://www.biblebelievers.org.au/wilhelms.htm

http://en.wikipedia.org/wiki/The_Illuminatus!_Trilogy

28. General Frederick II of Hesse Kassel. This character who made his fortune renting Hessian troops to the Americans in the War of Independence had definite connections with the Illuminati and must be who S. Drechsler is talking of although his death is recorded as being on 31st October (All Hallow's Eve)1785 some seven months later. If the author's description is to be believed the General would have had to cling on to his life for some time with an amazing set of injuries before finally dying. Although S. Drechsler never actually sees him die and this may explain this intriguing anomaly in the story.

http://en.wikipedia.org/wiki/Frederick_II,_Landgrave_of_Hesse-Kassel

29. The Illuminati & the French Revolution. Many historians have long contested that the Illuminati were involved in the fermenting of revolutionary forces that led to the overthrow of decadent King Louis XVI's '*regime ancien*' which ruled France until 1789. Notable works such as Nesta H. Webster's 1924 '***Ritual and Illustrations of Freemasonry***' and John Robison's '***Proof of a Conspiracy***' 1798 document detailed plans of how the Bavarian Illuminati along with the French Freemasons conspired to bring about a popular nationwide uprising which included at it head, amongst others, The Duke of Orleans (Freemason), The Marquis de Lafayette (Freemason) and the Jacobin Club radical nucleus of the revolt formed by other prominent Freemasons.

http://www.sacred-texts.com/sro/pc/index.htm

http://en.wikipedia.org/wiki/Nesta_Helen_Webster

http://en.wikipedia.org/wiki/John_Robison_(physicist)

30. The Order of the Rosicrusians. The Rosicrucian order was a secret society founded in late medieval Germany by Christian Rosenkreuz. The sect's manifesto was heavily influenced by Alchemist astrologer and occultist John Dee, Queen Elizabeth 1st of England's head of security, and also Dee's pupil Francis Bacon. As S. Drechsler describes the mandate of the order was one of scientific empiricism over religious dogma especially that of Roman Catholicism which might explain Van Halestrom's philosophical approach though the Brotherhood certainly did not shy away from mysterious theology themselves. The history of the Rosicrusians and the Illuminati is interestingly intertwined, some historians even connecting the two in purpose and manifesto though if S. Drechsler's comments are to be believed this seems less likely.

http://en.wikipedia.org/wiki/Rosicrucianism

31. Mozart & the Illuminati. There is no doubt that Mozart was in Vienna at this time. The young composer was also a friend of Adam Weishaupt and a member of the local Masonic Lodge 'Zur Wohltatigkeit' ('Beneficence'). His most famous opera, The Magic Flute uses an array of Masonic rituals and symbolism and his presence at the wedding shows the influence the Masons had on the cultural life of the day as he would have been at his peak then and very much sought after. Much speculation exists suggesting that he was actually killed by the Bavarian Illuminati but this topic is so contested that it would require a book of its own.

http://en.wikipedia.org/wiki/Mozart_and_Freemasonry

http://en.wikipedia.org/wiki/The_Magic_Flute

32. Brigadier James Oglethorpe & the Illuminati. Although I had to

dig for it there is some interesting information on the internet suggesting that this English politician and Freemason was an important Illuminati agent who was responsible for founding the 13th state of Georgia in the U.S.A. It is also extremely intriguing to note that James Oglethorpe is recorded to have died on 30th June 1785 in London which would have given time for his body to be returned to England. Several conspiracy theories exist, not least the ones posted at the web address I have given, surround the setting up of the state of Georgia, the majority of which seem to have a numeric significance centred around the numbers 33 and 13 both important in Freemasonry; founded in 1733 coincidentally on the 33rd parallel making the U.S.A 13 parallels wide etc. Perhaps unsurprisingly no details of this wedding are recorded though both the Schewiser and Oglethorpe family names do have connections, if certain websites are to be believed, with the Illuminati so the account in the book is at least plausible. If S. Drechsler's version of events is to be true then this lack of an official record of a planned union could have been for any number of extraordinary reasons.

http://www.davidicke.com/forum/showthread.php?t=134513

http://www.davidicke.com/forum/showthread.php?t=134513

33. The Banishment of the Illuminati 1785. S. Drechsler's recollections are quite accurate here as a wide section of historians agreed with Van Halestrom's appraisal of events. This is a quote from H. W. Coil: ***Coil's Masonic Encyclopaedia.*** Speaking of this period (summer 1785) he wrote '*Not only Illuminism, but Freemasonry was exterminated in Bavaria and neither ever recovered their former position. The Illuminati seem to have completely disappeared from everywhere by the end of the 18th century.*' Though, the last point would seem a more contentious topic which, if a reliable answer is sought, demands much lengthy research. Good luck!

http://www.overlordsofchaos.com/html/illuminati.html

Special Thanks.

I would like to take this opportunity to thank my tireless research team Robin and Carol for their dedication, late nights and general perseverance. I'm sure that they realise I could not have done it without them but on this particular occasion, and I'm sure they will agree, it's better to see the words in black and white than to hear them so - Thank you. Also to everyone else who has been so patient with me whilst this book was being made ready for release. Especially Abigail, Felix, Yvette, Jonah and all the other kind people that had to listen to me endlessly talk about this incredible book that I found, not so long ago, in a junk shop in London - Thanks again.

Request:

We are always interested to hear the views of readers. With this in mind we humbly request that, upon finishing the book, the reader would please send an email expressing your opinions good or bad with name, occupation, town, and a mark out of ten to; illuminati-hunter.views@hotmail.co.uk

More information about the book, reviews, news and the background to this fascinating story can be found @Illuminati Hunter.com

Lightning Source UK Ltd.
Milton Keynes UK
UKOW07f0827061214

242753UK00001B/2/P